Excuse Me For Living

A Novel By
RIC KLASS

Arcade Publishing • New York

Arcade Publishing books may be purchased in bulk at special discounts for sales promotion, corporate gifts, fund-raising, or educational purposes. Special editions can also be created to specifications. For details, contact the Special Sales Department, Arcade Publishing, 307 West 36th Street, 11th Floor, New York, NY 10018 or arcade@skyhorsepublishing.com.

Arcade Publishing® is a registered trademark of Skyhorse Publishing, Inc.®, a Delaware corporation.

Visit our website at www.arcadepub.com

10 9 8 7 6 5 4 3 2 1

Library of Congress Cataloging-in-Publication Data is available on file.

ISBN: 978-1-61608-780-7

Printed in the United States of America

This novel is dedicated to my late brother Jim who inspired me since my childhood with his love of the written word.

I would like to thank the members of the Sound Shore Writers Group for their helpful comments on the novel during the writing, including: Maureen Amaturo, Alan Beechey, Kim Berns, Bonnie Council, Ed Keller, and Suki Van Dijk. In particular, Kent Oswald made a great contribution with his keen observations and ongoing support. I would also like to thank my editor Jeannie Reed for her excellent suggestions.

Not Blue Waters

flow beneath the men.

"Let the fuck go of me," Daniel says, tugging at his sport coat.

"Can't do that, sonny boy."

"I'm not your boy, and you can and <u>will</u> let go, Goddamn it."

Daniel gazes up at the gray clouds blanketing the evening rush hour traffic next to him. The color matches his own dull-colored eyes and pallor. He then peers down into the strangely inviting muddy Hudson River and takes a deep breath of the sweet and foul sewer gas wafting from the wastewater holding tanks not far downstream. Dan ceases to struggle. He smiles at the obese NYC cop practically strangling him with one beefy hand and clutching him around the waist with his other tree limb of an arm. The changeling Giaconda beam now startles this New York's Finest and he lets go for a second. That's all Daniel needs. Even in his inebriated state, he's still experienced with the grin-and-leap maneuver. He jumps off the ledge, but his jacket tangles on the Martha Washington Bridge (the lower level, beneath George), giving Officer Franklin another chance to snatch this stupid young bastard – temporarily at least – from the yawning mysteries of eternity. Franklin rips the coat, pulls it over Daniel's head, and drags him back from the just-dying to the just-looking side of the M-W barrier.

"Watch what you're doing, for Christ's sake! This is a real Armani. My father will sue your ass."

"I don't care if Mary, Mother of God, weaved it herself. You're not killing yourself on my beat. And tell your daddy he shoulda done a better job of teachin' you some respeck."

One last thought occurs to Daniel, and it's not all that helpful. He tries the happy-flashing-teeth gambit again and takes a telegraphed swing at the man in blue. Like his last, not one of his best ideas.

Tranquilized

and dizzy from various concoctions including two white lines, nearly a lid of maryjane, and a very solid right jab to his jaw, but not deadhead unconscious either, the wan, emaciated 6'1" twenty-four-year-old in $250 jeans gamely pleads in own defense.

A hurt puppydog guise while rubbing his sore jaw, "I was simply taking a leisurely stroll to visit my poetry professor in Hoboken, your honor, when this very large policeman accosts me from nowhere, applies a no-doubt steroids-induced thrashing, and conjures what's probably a $150 tailoring repair job on my Bill Blass jacket."

"He claimed it was Armani," pipes up Officer Franklin.

"Screw the couture," interjects Judge Leominster Karmel.

"Koo who?" inquires the cop.

"Bless you, Officer Franklin," wises off Daniel, tottering somewhat. "And overall, I might say, Judge Camel. . . ."

"Karmel." The judge's jaw tightens. He isn't in a mood today for more shenanigans from the familiar druggie in front of him.

"Yes, Caramel. This large gentlemen and supposed protector of the court proved himself to be, in effect, extremely inhospitable to say the least. Broken appointments with distinguished poets, terrorized upstanding citizens, and brutalized fabric creations are nothing to joke about. Nevertheless, in the spirit of the Christmas season I'm willing to drop all charges against him if you'll just kindly. . . ."

"Remove the handcuffs? And May 16th is not typically thought of as a winter religious holiday. You're getting to be quite a regular here, Daniel Topler. It's unusual to see even young drug addicts like you here three times in a month."

Karmel's laser gaze burns a tiny – yet visible to the defendant's mind-expanded vision – hole through the left eyeball and out the back of Daniel's noggin. He slowly turns his head to see if there's also damage to the wall behind him. Seeing that the picture of New York's first governor apparently remains ship-shape eases his natural concern for government property. In fact, he never before realized he had concern for any property whatsoever and feels uplifted by this new realization of public-spiritedness. Dandy, as he's called by his prep school friends, plainly sees, i.e., with his right un-nuked eye, it's not going well. The small, drab, white fluorescent-lit courtroom stinking of the sweat of the accused seems familiar somehow. "Yellow walls do nothing for the décor. Why are the lights so dim?" he muses to himself aloud.

"Mr. Topler, are you feeling OK?"

Despite Karmel's irritation at seeing this punk again in his courtroom, a troubling thought seeps in. *He's just a kid, and his father's got a hell of a powerful law firm. They can make trouble if this clown gets ill under my supervision.*

The last of a trinity of misconceptions and poor execution floods Dan-Dandy-Daniel's addled brain. He gets as far as one finger on the handle of soon-to-retire and ex-Green Beret Franklin's 45-caliber pistol when it's. . . .

Lights Out,
Then Fit To Be Tied.

The air smells delicious. If one were standing at the window, the vision of sparkling blue salt water waves gently licking the edges of freshly swept dunes of the East Hampton beaches in the spring sunshine would fill that someone's heart with joy and tranquility. Unless that someone were Daniel Topler. And, in any event, he isn't standing in that upscale and well-appointed room of walls washed with muted earth tones and carefully highlighted with soothing white linen cushions and soft blue taffeta chairs.

He is tied to the bed.

Paradise Found

Daniel Topler and not the other way around. In the courtroom the day before, Judge Karmel considered that the young coke-crazed joker had tried killing himself before. *Put him out of harm's way – including mine – for awhile*, the soon-up-for reelection magistrate decided.

The good Judge Leo then gladly turned over all responsibility for the silver spoon-up-his-butt man-child to deserving shrinks. In light of Danny's bravura repeat performance, Karmel needed no oral history to put the dazed young lunatic lying unconscious on the floor in front of him into the custody of Live Free or Die, a somewhat inappropriately named health spa (rehab clinic) nowhere near New Hampshire but directly on a chichi Long Island shoreline with exclusive beach rights.

"Get someone to mop up his drool, Franklin," signified the hearing's amen, and let's break for lunch concluded the disposition of the unwelcome case.

In fact, the lushly vegetated ten-acre paradise complete with mud (imported from Italy) baths, six tennis courts, heated indoor and Olympic-sized outdoor pools, individually monogrammed ultra-absorbent bath towels, bamboo-ed gazebo vitamin shake bar, free cranio-sacral therapy massages (an amenity not truly imagined as free by its partakers at the $12,000 per week establishment), four volleyball courts, shuffleboard (only one), bowling alley, super-sized surround-sound HDTV screening room complete with movie theater-like seats, mahogany green-felt-laden poker tables (gambling for money technically not permitted by the posted rules), and for every guest a souvenir two-thirds life-sized fleece "Nipper" (the original, late LFOD piebald St. Bernard mascot now stuffed and on display in the lobby) could well be thought of as a second home to various members of the Topler family.

Albert Topler, the patriarch of his clan, founded – along with his brother, Hyman – the Universal Recycling empire. Al commands what has operated *in toto* as a cosmically profitable junkyard since WWII and provided jobs and income for every Topler nephew, niece, in-law, and distant relative for the past 50 years. He often visits LFOD when his mental constitution doesn't require it. Offers by Albert to personally pay for installation of his favorite outdoor sport, horseshoes, had been rebuffed by the LFOD administration due to an unfortunate incident some years prior when a guest (inmate) threw a metal tray at his CA (*chez ami* – euphemism for personal warden), nearly de-nutting him. Airborne metal now carries a *persona non grata* status. Albert likes to walk the shore in early a.m., hoping to catch a glimpse of nearby Hollywood celebrity neighbors, so far without success. Furthermore, according to Mrs. Harriet Topler's P.I., rumors that Albert has a "thing going on" with Ms. Bushkin, the *zaftig* activities director, have never been confirmed by an eyewitness.

The Left Eye Opens

and surveys the domain before the other eyelid dares to lift. A housefly buzzes on the nose, creating an intense desire to scratch the nostril. For some reason Dan-Dan, as his sister Coco calls him, can't seem to get his arms free. His longish dirty-blonde hair partly covers his eyes, too. The lad panics, tentatively opens the right lid to gain full parallax vision and espies the probable perpetrator of his current dilemma.

"Dr. Frankenstein, I presume."

Visiting psychiatrist, Dr. Jacob Q. Bernstein, clad in the white tunic of his profession, leans over Daniel and smiles.

"Bonhomie won't disarm me. Forgive the rhyme and untie me, you quack." Viewing now also the marine blue designer strait jacket encumbering him as well as the attractive red-and-purple tie-dye lanyards (LFOD uses nautical terms at the spa) tethering him to the antique Indonesian four-poster bed Daniel adds, "And make it snappy."

"Are you feeling better?"

"Oh yes. I feel just like the moment the society page photographer shot me at my debutante ball. Dressed in a low-cut pink silk gown I was."

"That made you feel good?"

"He shot me, you fool. Aren't you listening? With a 45 just like Officer Franklin's."

"You're a cross-dresser?"

"No, a cross prisoner. Can we cut the head-shrinking mumbo jumbo and just let me out of here? And, by the way, did you really buy the pink dress bullshit? I mean, really."

"I'm Dr. Bernstein."

"And I'm Felix the Cat. Meow. Did they even have real medical schools when you were a kid in Mesopotamia? The crap you guys are taught and dish out, too."

No response. Just a kind demeanor.

"You must be deaf as well as ancient." Convulsed anew, "Let me go or I'll kick your two-thousand-year-old ass from here to kingdom come."

More patience.

Exasperated and sweating, but concerned this moment for the older man, "I might say you don't look that hot yourself, Dr. Béarnaise." Even so, unable to be a *mensch sans* wiseacreosity.

"Bernstein."

"Yes, <u>Bernstine</u>." Now changing tactics. Time for Mr. Good Guy. "<u>Are</u> you feeling OK? Why don't you sit and we'll chat awhile. I could use a little company. Would you mind first scratching my nose? Some fly, probably sent here by a right wing, neo-Nazi Luftwaffe, has been dive-bombing me." Laughs at his own jest, hoping to win over the medical sentinel.

"Here?"

"A little to the right. Ahhhhhhh. You <u>are</u> a healer."

In fact, feeling a little under the weather, the doctor sits on a blue taffeta chair and continues to wait for a hiatus in Daniel's rodomontade.

Now on the verge of losing it one more time, "Oh, I get it. This is the *Siddhartha* 'I can think, I can wait, I can fast' routine. *Entschuldigen Sie bitte! Herr Doktor.* I'm a little slow just now. As the CSN&Y song goes, 'I'm not feeling up to par' and do you think I need to cut my hair cause I almost did just before I jumped off Martha, the bridge that is! Ha ha ha ha ha ha ha." Now hysterical.

Bernstein rises, goes to the door, opens it and calls, "Linda."

Linda, a massive and entirely competent Irish hospital nurse, waddles in.

Dan, a veteran film buff, immediately makes a Kathy Bates-in-*Misery* connection. He rolls over on his left side and gives his still cellophane-wrapped gift Nipper propped upon the fashionable maroon-lacquered commode a final phony appeal. "Help! Please save me."

Man's best friend fails him, but a quickie Amytal and all is right with the world in deep and peaceful sleep.

An 8 AM Polite Knock At the Door

followed by a not-so-polite barging in.

"Hurry for breakfast, Daniel, the volleyball tournament starts soon," Elaine Bushkin, the resident LFOD recreational therapist – she likes to call herself – breathlessly announces.

Her strong Chanel scent violently grips him. "I'll have whipped cream licked off your breasts."

"I'm not on the menu, Danny," minces the still attractive and appropriately curvy 45-year-old natural – maybe – red-head.

The in-bed patient pleasantly finds himself unshackled, thereby propelling him to sit up and launch into banter. "Why would you screw my old man when you could have a young stud like me, Elaine?"

"I'm sure I don't know what you're talking about. Mr. Topler and I have a purely professional relationship."

Making the rounds, unnoticed, Dr. Jacob Q. sticks his head in the room.

"And what exactly is that profession?" smirks the now aroused young man patting the silk-covered mattress, "Lie down here next to me and give me a demo."

Bernstein surprises them both by his sudden emergence. "I see you're quite at home here, Daniel."

Not pleased at being served up as the curvaceous butt of his joke, the lady vanishes with an impudent toss of her rear but not without her own retort, "Now I understand what your father means when he says you have a head on your shoulders, Danny."

"What day is this?" Daniel says.

"Saturday. 9 AM. You've had quite a nap," Bernstein says to LFOD's regular visitor.

Now that they're alone, Bernstein sees Albert Topler's minions have already plenished the room with staples from Dan's Manhattan loft. He picks up a well-thumbed copy of Carl Rogers' *On Becoming a Person* from a nearby chair.

"Have you read this?"

To the new adversary in a condescending tone, "Everyone who ever took Psychology 101 knows this humanistic seminal work where Rogers treats patients as though they're intrinsically healthy. But, alas, there's no time for pleasantries. Nice of you to drop in. What did you say your name was? Sorry, I've got to be going. Ta ta for now, but duty calls. When the president begs for one to serve one's country, can one refuse?"

From experience, Dandy knows to find his clothes in the walk-in closet and hurriedly scampers from the king-sized bed and starts dressing.

"It's hush-hush, top-secret and on the q.t. Something about a scrofulous torso suddenly levitating from Kim Il Sung's tomb. You know you just can't trust those bastard Korean dictators to stay dead." Almost dressed now. "Where are standards, anyhow? And by the way, did my father have my car brought around yet?"

Without malice, a simple question, "Shall I call Linda?"

Sobered, Daniel sits on the bed. "No, that won't be necessary."

"Can we talk?"

"Do I have a choice? Do you mind if I smoke, uh. . . . "

"Dr. Bernstein. No, go ahead."

"Can I mooch a cigarette?"

"I don't smoke."

"Neither do I. Never touch the stuff. I hear it's bad for your health."

Dandy warily eyes his foe searching for kinks in the wall. He's highly trained for this sort of combat. Even with Dr. Bernstein's long years of experience, he's beginning to wear thin.

"Let me ask one more time. Can we talk?"

Dan warms up to the challenge. "Hey, sit down. Take a load off, doc. Sure, let's be pals, but it depends."

"Depends on what?"

"Well, on just what kind of headshrinker you are. My own preference leans heavily towards the druggies."

"Psychopharmacologists, you mean?"

"I love the green pills, but blue or yellow works for me if it works for you."

"That isn't my specialty, but I do prescribe psychotropic medication on occasion."

"I love the vocabulary you headshrinkers use. Did you hear the one about the old lady who goes to a German shrink and says,

'Doctor, I'm afraid I'm going to kill my husband. Oh, don't vorry about zat, Madam, he replies. In von month you von't be afraid to anymore.'"

Daniel cracks up at his gag and Bernstein joins him.

"Very funny. Your accent is decent, too."

"It is? I'm not sure I would have told it to you if I knew you'd like it."

"You feel you wouldn't have told me if you knew it would make me laugh?"

"Oh, oh. I feel a Rogerian coming on. Will my treatment consist of empathy, respect, unconditional positive regard and on-demand malted shakes with a maraschino cherry?"

"Carl Rogers helped many people."

"And just when I hoped that if you're not pushing drugs you might be my second favorite kind of voodoo doctor."

"Which is?"

"The gestalt-ites."

"Gestalt therapy has its place. Why your second favorite?"

"There's no analyzing your navel. I don't have to explain why I hate my mother and want to marry my father."

"You hate your mother?"

"Well, I feel it would be highly improper to hate your mother, don't you? I hardly know her." Dan's having fun. "Besides, when I was rudely interrupted I meant to append that my favorite therapy deals with the here and now. Let's go forward together for a better tomorrow and all that rot. Why go back to ancient history exploring the tragic times when my evil sister locked me in the family crypt without bread or water for days at a time? The worst part? My socks always stank to high heaven. Or when my Tanta Sadie ripped off my underwear and. . . . "

A knock at the door.

"That's enough for now."

"Why?"

"Because you're having guests just now it seems."

"But I'm just getting warmed up for your cure, kemosabe."

"Did you know that word originated with a boy's camp, Kamp Kee-Mo Sah-Bee?" Jacob knows he needs to keep pace with Dan's quick wit or lose his patient's focus.

"Yeah? Or is that b.s.?" Dan's interest gets piqued. *'Please don't tell me Methuselah has a brain.'*

"Pinky swear." Jacob goes to the paneled entryway. To the outside visitors, "Can we have just a few more minutes?" Sits close to Daniel. "I've examined your records."

"Pardon the girlish modesty, but I'm embarrassed at my accomplishments. Did you notice my high school record exceeding Jesse Owens' nine-point-four-second 100-yard dash? And he was black."

"Can you cut the crap now for a moment?"

Silence.

"Good. You're perfectly healthy physically, a little undernourished perhaps, and maybe slightly on the plus side of sanity and probably not a danger to yourself – unless you're drunk or under the influence of drugs."

"I've been healthier. And as for my alleged sanity. . . ." but the doctor firmly cuts Dan off.

"Be quiet," Bernstein almost shouts. "Any more of your nonsense and I'll call Linda and we'll start all over tomorrow when you wake up." Now perspiring for reasons unrelated to the discussion, Jacob's close to losing his professional demeanor.

Danny can see Bernstein's flaming cheeks and not looking too well. Doc probably has it up to here with him. "OK. I cry uncle." *This guy's going to be tougher to outfox than the others.*

"I'd like to tell to you about this discussion group I lead," Bernstein gingerly begins.

"Man oh man. Here we go with the group therapy," interrupts Daniel. "If I have to listen to one more sad sack tell me the story of his pitiful life, I really will lose my mind. Forget it, doc."

Gaining composure, "No, no. It's not like that at all," entreats the 74-year-old psychiatrist. "It's just a group of men getting together to kibitz. Really interesting guys. You'll like them," he tries to sell his patient.

Now Dan's darkly suspicious. He's in unfamiliar territory and doesn't like it one bit. And he doesn't like to be sold. Nevertheless, his curiosity has been aroused. "So what's the catch? I go and schmooze with some creaky stiffs and I'm out of here?"

"Not precisely." Jacob thinks he's almost got Dan on the hook.

"Not precisely?"

"We'll get together a few times, then. . . ."

"A <u>few</u> times!?" Now Dan gets worked up.

"Well, yes, a few times. More or less."

"More or less!?" Dan starts to rise.

Bernstein pushes him back onto the bed.

"Sit down. Now listen up. If you ever hope to get out of here you ought to consider my offer, young man."

Dan remains seated.

"Good. I want you to join the discussions in my senior men's group."

"Owens was a senior when he set his record, but I was just a junior when I lit up. . . . "

Bernstein gets up and briskly walks towards the door.

"Lin-"

Before Bernstein's call is fully formed: "OK. OK. All right already. I thought you could take a joke." Danny sensed Linda and her serum would have come next. Now changing horses. "You are kidding, aren't you? Me join this group?"

"We meet at Temple B'Nai Israel in Great Neck on Sunday and Wednesday nights. You'll still have to stay here when not at meetings."

"A temple men's group for dying people? This really is rich. Wait, don't tell me. You call yourselves A Better Tomorrow."

"New Beginnings. And maybe we're not as dead as you think."

"And you? You're the lead nefarious conspirator of the cabal?"

"I've volunteered to run the meetings."

"This is too much to ask of anybody. Why don't you just take my blood, for cryin' out loud?" Dan thrusts out his arm. "Here, open my veins."

Jacob coolly replies, "I have your college reports, too. Despite your corny theatrics, I see your elective acting courses at the Yale School of Drama prove invaluable to you."

Now talking turkey in his most steely tone, "When I talk to my dad, I'll ask him to take care of this matter." Dan taps Bernstein's knee. "I'll be out of here in nanoseconds. Fun time is over."

Dan has finished his comic performance for the time being. No pill pusher's going to push him around.

"The court put you in my custody. Besides, your father thinks it's a good idea. Well?"

"I've just given your business proposal the utmost careful consideration. No."

"OK. I'll be back here in a month when you've had time to reconsider. See you in June." Bernstein strides to the door. "Linda, Joe," he shouts.

Linda shuffles in followed closely by Joe, a six-six orderly, missing neck, two hundred eighty pounds if he's an ounce. Unmistakably the former NY Giants linebacker he was in his glory days. And they're carrying the dreaded straitjacket. They yank Dan from the bed and commence to wrap up the jejune loudmouth once again.

Dan, shocked at this unwelcome turn of events, reconsiders. "Wait. Wait. This is fucking blackmail. OK. I'll sit in on your mummified decaf coffee klatch."

Bernstein nods at his helpers. They untie the long-sleeved apparatus.

"Good decision," Linda says to Danny as they leave.

Dan sits. Trying to regain a smidgen of dignity, "Should I bring my own dentures or do you pass one set around for everyone?"

Ignoring Dan's intended insult, Jacob warns, "7 PM Sunday. That's tomorrow. Temple B'Nai Israel. We meet in the library. Be there or you'll be too tied up to attend the next meeting." He smiles at his quip. "Nurse Linda will give you a prescription later to help you sleep tonight. Do not, I repeat – do not take any alcohol or drugs here or you'll really feel like you're dying. And leave early. Traffic is a killer. And keep this in mind, as well. If you fail to follow my rules here, I'll have you transferred to Bellevue Hospital where they have more persuasive techniques for patient compliance. Then, addressing visitors waiting in the hallway, "Please come in. I think he'll be fine."

Pater Familias Et Soror

await to comfort the invalid.

"Daniel, Daniel, Daniel, how could you do this to your mother and me?" Albert's 260-pound body stacked on only five-feet-seven inches including elevator shoes ripples with the same emotion as his quivering voice.

"Again," elaborates Dan's not very adoring sister, smiling falsely. The siblings exchange drop-dead-asshole looks. Her forced presence and boredom casts gloom on the otherwise sunlit room. Daddy made Coco come to pay yet another visit to her sicko brother, but nobody can make her enjoy it (the promise of a new BMW convertible did ease the pain, however). "Dad, can we get this over with? Dan-Dan's just trying to get more attention."

"Oh, and is that your medical diagnosis, Dr. Coco?" Mere seconds with his sister suffice to ruin for Dan what has so far been a fairly interesting day. Turning to Albert, "And why is everything that happens to me always about you and mom?"

"What medical school did you go to, I'd like to know, Mr. Smart Ass? For all the awards you won at Yale, here you are in a high-priced nuthouse while I at least have a job." Coco stews inside herself. *Danny has some nerve spreading invective around when it's him who's always making trouble for the family.*

"Arranged by Dad," Dan counterpoints. She's scoring some flesh wounds, and it hurts a bit.

"You tell everyone that will listen to your horseshit that your big sister mistreated you when you were a snotty little kid. Now that you're a snotty big kid, I'm sorry I <u>didn't</u> beat you unconscious. It would have saved you the trouble doing it yourself."

For Coco, years of unfavorable comparisons to Daniel's prep school and college achievements still thrust up their ugly head.

Albert pokes his head out the window and catches sight of the activities director on the beach. "Say, this is a beautiful view, Daniel," he says, hoping to diffuse the familiar battle between his progeny. "Have you looked out today? Just gorgeous."

"You're licking your chops over Elaine, no doubt," the somewhat jealous son muses. "Is she on the beach bouncing her tits in volleyball?"

He hasn't scored a piece of her himself, and it's vaguely upsetting to be outdone by a fat septuagenarian, particularly if it's his own father.

"Don't think mom doesn't know about her, Daddy," Coco's brown eyes seem to turn yellow while piling on the new prey. Attacking a common enemy singularly unites bro and sis.

"That's very rude of you, Daniel. And I don't think it's funny one bit, Coco, for you to suggest that Mother has any reason to suspect me."

Albert's pressed to get to the point of the visit. He has a lunch date with a certain someone at an exclusive and secluded spot nearby and can't be late again. Subtly sniffing his underarms, I think she likes the smell of Old Spice.

"And just where is mommy dearest, daddy dearest?" asks the needling convalescent.

"She's not feeling well," lamely fibs the father.

"She's at the hair salon having her hair done, doing something useful with her time," reports his odious sister, delighted to make Danny feel small.

"Very unnecessary, Coco." Albert's aggravated at her, but now returns to the task at hand. "How can you throw your life away like this, Daniel? You, with every advantage in the world. Every possibility."

"Every possibility? Is it too late for me to be a penguin?" Danny's eyes gleam at upsetting papa.

"Your life is no sitcom, boychick. You should be ashamed to be so thankless." Dad knows the guilt routine will prove fruitless and decides to change tactics, "Why don't you come to Universal like your sister. We'll make you vice-president of something." Turning to his charming daughter, "What's your title, darling?"

"Vice President of Public Relations," 29-year-old cute-ikins replies dolefully. I'm heading right to the dealership before daddy reneges on our deal, she vows to herself.

"See. You can have a title just like that. And the pay's not bad either, honey, is it? One hundred grand a year will keep the wolf away as long as mommy and daddy throw in a little holiday bonus and a new car now and then. What about it, Daniel?" Albert's been through this a million times before with his baby boy but can't resist a millionth and first. My entire *meshpuchah*, the whole family, is on the dole, but I've got a son who wants to kill himself, anguishes the patron of the ever-burgeoning Topler family.

"Waste my life like you with junk and trash? Is that what I'm supposed to do?" This acid-tongued Demosthenes of Long Island instantly regrets the slur.

"Watch your mouth, son. My pitiful and undignified-for-an-Ivy-league-college-boy company keeps you here in luxury, and don't you forget it." Albert has pride in his success, son or no son. "I didn't have a father that gave me everything under God's creation."

"Why send me to a school like Yale if you just want me to take over the business some day?"

"He's thinks he's too good to earn a living like you did, Dad. He's pathetic and a loser. Let's leave. He can go kill himself if that's what he wants."

"God forbid. How can you say that, Coco, even in anger? What kind of kids did I raise anyway?" Real tears stream down Albert's face. He knows Coco will get married and leave Universal. Why did he spend his life building a junkyard colossus if his children don't take over? Albert doesn't know if the drops of lysozyme, lipids, and saline running down his cheeks have been shed for his son or himself.

He won't show it, but Dan is genuinely touched by his father's torment. They were so close before he got into drugs in his junior year at prep school and then deeper in college. Since then he can't talk to his father without an argument. Even he and Coco used to get along. As for mom, they haven't talked about anything but the weather in years. He knew his nanny better. Why do people have to have a family, anyhow? None of his college philosophy courses answered this question.

Danny sees his progenitor has reached the end of his rope and changes the familiar tune to a more pressing melody, "Pop, try not to get so worked up. You've always said that things have a way of working out." He eyes his father closely to see if he's a bit mollified before, "I'm glad you came, dad. Really." No sign of appeasement yet from Albert. "In fact, the funniest thing just happened. You won't believe it," lamely trying to whip up some frivolity at this funeral. "The shrink that left as you walked in says I've got to attend some *alte cocker* discussion group."

Generally speaking, Daniel hates Yiddishisms but isn't above using them now to describe old men for effect if the occasion arises. He knows how to hustle his dad when necessary.

"Isn't that a yuk-and-a-half?" Faked laughter from Dan.

But this time he miscalculates.

"I think it's an excellent idea, Daniel," beams daddy. "Dr. Bernstine. . . "

"Bernstein," corrects Dan, who – like all children – never wants a parental error to go unheralded.

"OK – Bernstein – and I chewed over it earlier. They say he's a highly regarded specialist for cases like yours, Daniel. It will be good for you."

Seeing Dan-Dan denied for once thrills Coco. Her face nearly breaks in two with pleasure.

"Now just a second, dad," panics the prisoner.

"No. You wait just a second, sonny boy."

Just recently, Dan's heard this condescending, noxious phrase but can't place where.

Daddy continues, "I've placed your welfare completely in the doctor's hands. Lord knows I've gotten nowhere with you. You always get around me and your mother, and look where you are. Whatever Dr. Bernstine. . . ."

"Bernstein."

"OK, dammit. Whatever Bernstein says. . . ," a caesura and a pointed finger in the air for their dramatic effect, ". . . goes. And that's that."

Dan's eyebrows rise of their own accord. Dan's amazed expression convinces Albert that he's finally taken the right path with his prodigal son and can't stifle a grin.

"Let's go, dear." Albert remembers he has other pressing business and, to Coco's amazement for its unfamiliarity, takes her hand.

"Father!" This completely unused word in Dan's lexicon when speaking directly to Albert punctuates his dismay at not manipulating his *pater* – as his mother refers to him – for the first time in as long he as can remember.

"I love it when you call me that. Don't forget to write," Albert joshes on his way out. Dad knows to leave in a hurry before he can be hypnotized as usual by his silver-tongued youngster.

Death By Boredom

fits this dump better than Live Free or Die, mumbles Danny. The dismal visit by dad and sister Coco washed over him, leaving him dry-docked. Feeling alone in his luxury cabaña, he meanders out of his room over to the Welcome Center and feels the real Nipper staring unblinkingly at him. "A stuffed dog in the lobby and these lunatics think I'm crazy," he says out loud – now an increasingly common habit with Dan.

"What's that, Danny?" asks Helen Clausen, the petite, outwardly refined receptionist of a certain age. Her still-sparkling blue eyes and Prince Valiant hairdo perfectly showing off her snow-white hair belie her truck driver mentality and the vernacular she's capable of.

Dan has loved Helen ever since the time when years ago two police officers in hot pursuit chased his car. Dan hid under the counter while she brazenly lied, "Daniel is in Africa," without blinking or a trace of a smile.

"Africa? What's he doing there?" quizzed the cops.

"Joined the Peace Corps," said Helen in a firm, no-nonsense timbre that also claxoned: I'm busy, and why don't you get going before I get rough?

"Guess we had the wrong tag. Swore I got it right," said the corpulent cop in blue to the dime-thin one as they backed away from her. It never occurred to the flatfeet that LFOD wasn't an ordinary residence and how in blazes would this old lady even know sixteen-year-old Danny?

"Just talking to myself, Helen. Do you have the keys to my car?"

"If you're talking to yourself, then maybe you really do have problems, Danny."

Dan sees that Helen's worried. "I'm fine. Don't you worry. The keys?"

"Even if I had them, I wouldn't give them to you. Doctor Bernstein said you had to stay here until you get better, except that you can drive to his group meetings on Sunday and Wednesday nights."

Dan reddens. By now the conspiracy against him has spread to his ally. "Helen, I thought we were friends."

"You're like a son to me, Danny. That's why we're <u>not</u> friends and you're <u>not</u> getting the keys. Your Porsche is in the lot when Dr. Bernstein says you can drive again."

Irritated and with an attitude, "OK. No *problema,* lady."

"Are you getting smart with me?" Helen's eyes narrow.

"No, no. I'll just be taking a stroll then." Helen is one of only a few people who have ever really scared him.

"Wear your hat. You sunburn easily, honey," returning just as suddenly to the lovable side of her vast personality divide. She can't help it. She's a mother – and Danny wishes she were his.

"I will," he lies. He learned early in life that the incontrovertible tactic with adults is to agree with them. What you do and what you say don't require an intersection whatsoever. Maybe I should go into politics, he speculates, as he wanders off to the beach. He's also thinking Bernstein's lined up the whole staff behind him. Pretty efficient for that old fart.

Pooling Thoughts

The newly renovated, outdoor no-horizon pool next to the freshly combed Long Island Sound sands beckons even this most cynical of ivied know-it-alls. Dan idles amidst the perfume of densely planted rhododendrons surrounding the pool and a pungent odor wisping from further up the beach. There lies Georgica Pond wherein their summer mansions East Coast hedge fund moguls converge with West Coast Wilshire Boulevard studio production heads and cocktail each other into nightly oblivion.

The fresh air and scents draw Dan to pause and reconnoiter. He puts his behind down on a green chaise lounge, waves to Roberto, the familiar, deeply tanned lifeguard – an ironic title at this joint, Dan reflects – and considers his next move.

Perhaps it's the fragrances, but a cheery thought occurs to him. The doting father of one of his prep school partners in crime, Bruce E. Langford II, has a Mafia-sized gated compound on the nearby pond where good old Brucie throws nonstop drug-friendly bashes starting about now in the season. I'll check that out tonight, he considers. Don't even need my car. I can just follow the shore.

A voice from next to him, "Hey, do you have to sit on top of me!"

"Well, I didn't know. . . . "

A 13ish-year-old girl in the next chair, "My parents said not to talk to anybody but my doctor. Are you a doctor? Cause you sure look like shit if you are," barks the 70-pound, aquamarine-caftaned strawberry blonde.

This youngster has a mouth on her, he thinks. Starts to get up and move away, "Sorry, didn't mean to crowd you."

"You didn't flash me like Suzie told me perverts do. She's almost a sister cause she has the same mole on her elbow as me and we have tons of sleepovers so I guess you can stay," she offers somewhat more mildly.

"I'm not a doctor, but that's OK. I'll just move a few chairs over here to the. . . . "

"Are you deaf or something? I said you <u>can</u> sit down."

Where have I heard this kind of rude talk before? Danny wonders and turns crimson at the answer. He sits as ordered.

"Sincerely, are you growing a beard? None of my friends likes them. I just love these magazines," pointing to the piles of *Girl's Life*, *Seventeen*, *CosmoGirl!*, *Teen People*, and on and on. "Some of my friends think they're too juvenile for girls our age but those jerks aren't cool at all. Besides, none of the girls but me and Suzie like to read hardly anything, so what do they know?"

Rubs his chin. Thinking he does need a shave, "Well. . . ," nearly getting a few words out.

"Mommy says there's perverts and criminals all over the place and not to trust anybody but you seem pretty much OK being an old guy. She'll be back tonight to visit me after she gets out of work. She makes a ton of money renting out offices to people. Daddy makes loads, too, mom says, but I almost never see him anymore. He's old like you. Even older."

"Old?"

"Gee, I didn't mean to make you feel bad, but you must thirty or something – nearly dead. But I guess I shouldn't talk since I was almost dead the other day. Do you like to swim? The water must be freezing but the lifeguard – I guess mom won't mind if I talk to him since he's supposed to keep us safe – he said the pool is heated. But I don't like it if the water's too hot. It's like being in the hot bathtub where I almost drowned on

Tuesday if it wasn't for our maid Elizabeth. She's Polish and talks funny. What's your name?"

"Dan. What's yours? What's this about being almost dead?" Dead has been a recurring word with Danny and it resounds loudly.

"Alicia, but you can call me Ally."

"Nice to meet you, Alice." Habits die hard.

"Is something the matter with you? I said my name was Alicia and you can call me <u>Ally</u>."

"Sorry, Ally. I've got a lot on my mind."

"Me, too. Elizabeth has me real worried, that's not her real name but I can't say her name the way Polish people do, Elzhbeatah or something like that, but anyway she really doesn't like Finster and I'm scared she won't take good care of him when I'm not there. Maybe I should've tried to drown him along with me since there'd be nobody left who loved him to take care of him like I do but he's as big as all get out – just humongous – cause he's a standard-sized poodle and all and won't get in the tub cause he hates getting a bath. Mom wanted to give him one of those fancy do's for doggies but I said no way. He's a boy dog and I think he'd hate looking like some girl dog though he sure likes to sniff 'em. Anyhow, I sure hope Elizabeth is taking good care of him."

For some reason trying to follow her banter, "Finster is your dog?"

Ally glares at Dan with contempt, "Are you here cause you're a retard or somethin'? Poodles are <u>dogs</u>."

"Yeah, yeah. I get it." Dan can't figure out why he's not changing chairs. She's kind of funny. Dan feels relieved other guests have taken chairs near them. A man sitting alone with a very young girl could start to attract unwanted attention. But the seemingly self-assured bon vivant feels lonely and wants to keep talking. His former private school friends have never been much help to him. Quite the contrary. And talking to

Ally takes his mind off craving more dope and then maybe again trying to permanently end the mental din clouding his every thought.

"Why are you here if you're not a doctor? Are you sick, too? All my friends say this place is for crazy people but I'm not crazy, are you? And anyway being crazy is not so terrible when you can have all the Coca-Colas you want by just shouting for them or crying a little. My doctor. . . . "

"Dr. Bernstein?"

"No, not that one. He's <u>really</u> old and never let me have Coke so I just cried and screamed my lungs out and told them I would try to kill myself again until I almost really did feel sick and then Mommy made them get me another doctor. But anyhow Mommy never gives me Coca-Cola at home. Bad for your skin she says and then boys won't like you cause you're already kinda fat. She also says I've already got loads of cavities and says the sugar makes kids hyper but I'm not that either. My new doctor, I call him the wolfman, he's nice I like him, says I can have anything I want until I'm feeling better." Now in a fake deep voice, "'The body makes its own sugar, so it can't, in fact, be bad for children,' the new doctor, what's his face, told Mommy right in front of me. She almost peed. I don't think she really believes him. He's old too but tons younger than Dr. Bernstein who must be a hundred, and huffs and puffs like he'll die any second. You wouldn't look so bad yourself if you didn't have all that hair on your face but I guess lots of rock singers think they're awesome like that but it's not really my type or Suzie's neither. Are you a rock star?"

"No, I'm not a rock star. And you're not fat at all. You look just fine, Ally." She's thin. What's up with her mom saying she's fat? he wonders. There's no monopoly on misguided parents, sinks into Dan.

"You really think I look OK, Dan? You're probably saying that just to make me feel good."

"Ally, let's make a deal."

"What is it?"

"I've never made this deal with anyone else so you can't spread it around. Agreed?"

Very excited to be sharing a secret pact with a new friend, "Oh no, Dan, I'll never tell anybody," whispers the girl. "I promise."

"No matter what we say to other people, we'll only say what's true to each other. Can you buy that? Deal?"

"Deal!" says Alicia as they interlock their right hand pinky fingers.

"All right then." Waits two beats for her complete attention, "Ally, you're fine. OK?" Daniel stares earnestly into her eyes.

"OK," she replies with visible relief.

"Mr. Daniel Topler, please report to Nurse Linda Shea's office. Repeat. Mr. Daniel Topler, please report to Nurse Linda Shea's office now for your medication," blasts over all the LFOD campus loudspeakers.

"Catch you later, Ally," says Dan, decidedly unhappy to hear his name trumpeted all over the Hamptons. What the hell is the privacy policy here anyhow, he wonders. As he heads for Nurse Linda, he turns to call back, "And remember. Don't tell anybody our secret deal."

"OK, Daniel Topler," Ally happily answers. She knows his whole name now – he won't elude her again. When he's safely out of sight she puts back on the tortoise-shell glasses she had removed when she had first spotted him. She lies on the poolside lounge chair for the next several hours magnifying the encounter and reenacting each word exchanged. "Pretty dreamy for an elderly person," Ally sighs.

Take Just One

of each at bedtime, the sumo-sized Irish nurse tells him. Earlier, sweet-talking Dan convinced Dr. Bernstein that contrary to customary LFOD rules, taking control of his own life – i.e., dispensing the magic potions himself – would be essential for his rehabilitation.

'I'm such a fabulous con man,' The Dandy Man congratulates himself. He nearly forgets by court order he'll still have to submit daily blood and urine tests to stay out of Bellevue. Danny repeats the instructions to Linda at her request. No driving and for God's sake don't take any alcohol or drugs. She wasn't particularly concerned about his disobeying the warnings since Dr. Bernstein had grounded Daniel. Where could he get those awful things here at LFOD? she must have thought. But, good old Nurse Linda didn't say <u>when</u> was bedtime or that he couldn't <u>walk</u> out of this isolated Eden for loonies. If it's noon here then it's got to be midnight or thereabouts somewhere. And if she had made these two conditions clearer? What the fug do I care. Danny tears to his room, shutting the boltless door behind him. His mouth's dry and he perspires from the lack of drugs he's used to stuffing down his throat by this time of day. I'm going to put a lock on this gate of hell myself someday, he tells himself. Who ever heard of an unlockable suite?

He puts his thumb in the motionless air to test the way the wind blows. Yes, *North By Northwest* it is and so time for beddy-bye, the film buff resolves. Now withdrawing one of two vials from the brown bag Linda gave him, he peeks in the translucent brown dispenser and takes out a tablet. Hip hooray! The green pill wins by a nose, mouth, tongue, esophagus, and eager stomach. He gulps it down. Dreamtime's coming soon.

Now for dessert. The other plastic bottle has teensy-weensy red pills. Despite the fact Daniel could qualify as a pharmacist by now, he can't divine their purpose. Take one at bedtime is all it says. He does remember, however, Ronnie's Rule of Remedies. Ronnie Schwartz was his other best friend besides Brucie and Chipster at the Bexley Academy for Boys in verdant Vermont. The simple tenet holds that the smaller the pill, the greater the kick. This theory almost never broke down – and if it did? Take another, Dr. Ronald advised. Second lozenge down the hatch and Danny lies down for the ride. It comes quickly.

A Full Moon

illuminates Danny's face. The sound of tinkling glasses laid to rest and a gleeful shout, "Full house, you suckers!" drifts in the open window from late night poker-playing patients and stirs Dan Van Winkle.

Jesus, I'm hungry, seizes the now fully rested boy. On with the lights. A quick dial to the maître d' of the three-star Michelin-rated on-site restaurant confirms that it is closed and, no, not even for a regular customer like Danny Topler would François open the kitchen for room service at 11:30 PM. I'm really losing my touch, floats to mind. Then he remembers Brucie and the sumptuous buffet probably waiting for him. A glance in the mirror confirms Ally's earlier *merde* assessment of his countenance. This sober appraisal leads to a shave, quick shower and other preparations needed for him to seem unconcerned by his appearance but elegant all the same. Despite his unreliable ego confirming a winning carriage in the cabaña's full-length mirror and his evident undernourishment, he really does look dashing.

Now remembering he's horseless, Danny threads his way to the lunar-lighted beach and, Tod loafers in hand (easier walking on the beach), makes a beeline along the shore for dinner, drinks of course, and the venerating crowd certainly hungering for his charm and wit at the Langford summer manse.

Unsweetened Coco

describes her better than the 29-year-old admits. The epithet publicly aimed at the debutante years ago by her baby brother amid her lavishly catered coming out party hit the bull's eye. It not only drew cackles but also continues to follow her as a stinging moniker used by the heiress circle that girdles her social life. Her MBA with honors from NYU four years ago didn't elevate her in either of her parents' esteem.

Harriet Topler, her mother, a five-foot-six, still-fit and head-turning ashen blonde, came from a generation when women gave birth then turned the offspring over to nannies, and wore white gloves to luncheons in swank New York restaurants. She never bought into the whole "career thing" for girls. Harriet – not a little proud that her face remains youthful and maturely appealing without the help of a scalpel – considers herself a true Yankee.

Unlike her husband's common Eastern European roots, Harriet's mother and father were born in Massachusetts, and her grandparents hailed from London and Salzburg. Her grandfather, Isaac Neustadt, an Austrian physicist himself, refused to Anglicize his name to Newton when he emigrated to America out of respect for the genius whose theorems he labored to master. Though Albert himself was born in Brooklyn – not a recommendation for the *Social Register* either, to Harriet's mind – his parents and grandparents were *Poloks* – excuse the expression – for goodness sake. In all, she felt socially superior to Albert and under former circumstances would never have considered him as a suitor. But the former circumstances were over. The family money was being rapidly dissipated through poor investments by her father. And a girl's got to eat. And eat well. Besides, Albert was handsome – at least ninety pounds ago – enterprising to beat the band, and frankly mad for her at first sight. Already well on his way to being a multimillionaire before thirty, Albert got Harriet to say yes to him on their third date. The rest is history in the accounting books of Saks Fifth Avenue, Harry Winston, and Mercedes-Benz of Manhattan.

As for dad, when it comes to scholarship Albert only shams having pride in Coco. After she couldn't get into Harvard Business School unless he "donated" the two million dollars ever so subtly suggested by the admissions office, she permanently lost face with him. Even for Albert, two big ones were a bit much when she had already been admitted to NYU – a safe school, i.e., where she was a shoo-in with a 3.85 average at Hunter College.

Albert now only sees his wife – the former love of his life – in passing. They meet mostly at the dinner table when Harriet's not on an "educational cruise" to say, India, with her new mentor, Dr. Florenz Castillia, a Distinguished Professor of Art History at Columbia University; or when Albert isn't at Universal Recycling or having an "important meeting" with whom and where he can never remember when asked. Harriet keeps a P.I., Norman Butterworth, on retainer. For some reason, so far he has been unable to pinpoint the details so badly needed for a large settlement in a divorce. The larger retainer secretly being paid to Norman by Albert for keeping the dirt quiet perhaps provides the explanation. Still, Albert knows Harriet is nobody's fool. The secrecy of his liaisons may have run its course.

Coco's starting to feel she's running out of time, too. While her friends drop like flies, she remains single – not even a recent steady (a deadly fact constantly thrown in her face by her womanizing brother). A very disturbing white hair had to be yanked out of her temple just yesterday. And the ticking of her damned clock practically deafens her. Independently wealthy from childhood trusts set up by her folks, she can well afford to live how and where she chooses. But Coco hasn't left the nest. She wants to set up her next digs with Prince Professional if she ever lands one. To boot, despite the over-blown bribes for her attendance, she resents getting dragged to LFOD to raise the family flag for her substance-abusing and befuddled sibling.

She first saw Danny in a Victorian wicker antique baby carriage postHarriet's return home from Mt. Sinai's mater-nity ward. Her first words reacting to little brat brother, "Oh, he's sooooo cute. When are you taking him back, mommy?" Her sentiments have remained intrinsically unchanged ever since. To this day though it sounds silly, Coco's convinced that her mother really did make such a promise. Her brother's excellence throughout school together with her Cambridge, Mass., B-School rejection shadows her as a constant Ivy League nemesis. Consequently, as far as she's concerned, they can take all Yale graduates and stick them where the sun don't shine up Harvard Business School's ass. If she hears her dad whistle the melody "Eli Eli Eli Yale" just one more time, she'll hire an ex-Irgun assassin to finish off him and then after the favor she paid her mother wait patiently for dear old mom to cash in her chips, too.

The Zipper Breaks

on the way down, forcing Albert to tear his pants in his pixilated frenzy to get it on with Elaine Bushkin at the Hampton Hideaway Motel adjacent to LFOD. Her job as the gung-ho "spa" up-and-at-em chieftess maintains for her a fit body and plenty of stamina, neither of which cards can be found in Albert's hand. Yet another session with his son Daniel has exhausted him. Just getting into position today leaves the junkyard magnate breathless and panting in the unromantic way.

"I don't think I can do it, doll."

"Again? Jesus, Al, you've got to go on that diet I gave you or you'll drop dead before your divorce is final and we can finally get married."

"Right. You're right, honeybun." Distressed at discovering his ripped trousers virtually unwearable.

By this time the "divorce proceedings" have taken two years off Elaine's life in her clandestine affair with the amiable, rich fatso. And she's not getting any younger. It was only three months ago when she had her own attorney check the courthouse records to discover there weren't any "divorce proceedings." Amazon women aren't called the fiercest warriors in ancient history for nothing, and as the saying goes, "Don't get mad, get even." Possessing normal womanly modesty, Elaine's frankly glad that Albert can't perform his manly duties today. Saves her the embarrassment of nude paparazzi pix – though not bad at all for her age, her tush isn't what is used to be. She's certain that the flash she saw outside the open window came from the camera of Harriet's new private investigator – the one she must have hired after Elaine's anonymous call informing dragon lady of this tryst's time and place. "And by the way, Norman Butterworth, your own P.I., is the other guy screwing you along with Albert," completed the call. Poor Albert had let it slip to Elaine how he had bamboozled the neglectful better half he married. Norman's on the take from Al. Divorce and a new marriage will land on Albert sooner than he thinks, Elaine sighs with no little satisfaction.

Albert points at the torn crotch of his pants. "Just look at this. How can I go home?" he pleads.

"Harriet's probably not there anyway. Just run in and say you have to go real bad if she asks, 'What's the hurry?'"

"You. You're like a shrink. You have the right words for everything, Elaine. If I only had a wife like you all these years," Al says hurrying out.

You will have a wife like me, Albert. Very soon, she comforts herself while watching him waddle off to his Mercedes holding his pants together. When Albert's left a trail of dust, "He's on his way home with torn slacks," completes Elaine's final furtive call to Harriet.

"Thanks for nothing, Elaine, you harlot," Harriet says and slams down the phone. *Does she really think I don't know who it is?*

But Elaine really doesn't care.

"The Dandy Man's Here"

shout Brucie, Ronnie, and The Chipster in unison, already well on their way to their own highly inebriated karma. Dan, magically it seems to them, has just materialized this witching hour from behind the gooseberry bushes. The three highly educated idiots sink to their knees and bow their heads to the ground in mocking obeisance to the infamous prep-school apothecary.

"Rise, grasshoppers," Dan commands. More to the point, "Where's the chow? I'm famished." Danny spies the feast just inside the glass French doors leading from the patio and pool to the ballroom. But he stops mid-stride away from the worshipers on the way to nourishment. "Who's that beauty at the table?" Dan demands.

Giving Ronnie a wink, "Why Dandy, you know Bertrand. He's been with us for years," Bruce replies with a straight face. "I didn't think he was your type."

"A joke on your lips is no laughing matter, Brucie. Not your butler. Introduce me immediately to that dark-haired mirage or I'll turn you into a man from the toad you are."

The knockout Charlotte Davison senses Danny's fixed gaze on her. Charlie's dressed to kill and dice into bite-sized pieces the sacrificial lambs who mistakenly think they're the jackals stalking her at this fête instead of the other way around. The long-haired brunette's hourglass figure requires no padded cups to provide shape for the dramatic pink, Givenchy floor-length halter evening gown with a plunging peek-a-boo slit.

This femme fatale's the sole heiress – when daddy dies, that is – to the G.F. Davison Vending Machine Corporation conglomerate, or rather the assets left.

G.F. himself had only by chance wandered into this giant of a going concern. He started as a regular summer intern for the former Piker Coin-OP Company while he was completing his scholarship-paid bachelor's degree in ancient history at Cornell. To his astonishment, old man Piker, a long-standing bachelor who treated G.F. like the son he never had, left the vast firm to him lock, stock and barrels of dough just months before graduation.

G.F., a sexually frisky widower despite his age of eighty-one, knows that Charlie has only pretended to take an interest in his business all these years. Consequently, he recently decided like many of the other independent NAMA – National Automatic Merchandising Association – members to sell out to publicly-traded Aramark, known worldwide for its ballpark hot dog stands and candy bar machines.

Charlotte had tried to be enthusiastic when G.F. took his little girl on trips to the many warehouses storing the coin-op's no-arm bandit cash. He couldn't understand why anyone, let alone his only daughter, wouldn't be as thrilled as he at the sight of heaping King Croesus mounds of cold, hard silvery coins – and millions of them – serenely waiting for the Brinks trucks to arrive for the weekly shipment to his Chase Manhattan Bank account. He correctly intuited she faked excitement to please her daddy. Oh well, a cool $2.1 billion will augment his coffers soon when Goldman Sachs, Aramark's investment bank advisor to the deal, puts the final touches on the merger. That positions his daughter in line for title of the most gorgeous and richest available debutante in the world, second only to perhaps a gal Charlie hangs out with – a well-known hotelier's daughter. And far more than all his other assets, Charlotte is G.F.'s dazzling prized possession.

G.F. married late in life to Andromeda Marie Jones, a magnetically gorgeous Broadway showgirl. He saw Anne (her stage name) background-dancing during an *Oklahoma* revival. She twirled so fast round and round in a long red gingham skirt and full petticoats that he could see her pink cotton bottoms. He lusted to see much more of her background thereafter. G.F. wooed her for four solid weeks. The other hoofers in the production began to complain when they needed to edge in sideways into the backstage dressing room for all the roses filling it – each blossom was tagged with a note begging for an introduction to the modest, small town girl.

When Anne finally succumbed to the flowered courting, many unhappy relatives who reasonably expected to gorge themselves someday on siblingless and bachelor G.F.'s estate became dismayed. The lovebirds wed thirty days later on the steps of the Greek Parthenon. To the shame of Anne's parents and much-holier-than-thou tsk-tsking by G.F.'s family, Charlotte was born nine months to the day after G.F. first met Anne. G.F.'s relations' sanctimony seemed rewarded when Anne soon died unexpectedly from childbirth complications. But to the forever-after-disappointed lives of G.F.'s cousins, nephews, nieces and other various and sundry relatives, Charlotte herself sprang like a miniature Amazon from her mother's loins full bloodedly screaming and healthy. The twenty-seven-year-old still can give full-breasted shrieks, including some later this very delightfully warm near-summer evening.

"Charlie, come over here and give this Romeo a break," shouts Brucie to the lilac-eyed goddess basking in the glow of Danny's obvious adoration. "Take this for good luck, Dandy Man," Bruce insists and slips a small bottle of white powder into Dan's pocket. But Charlotte knows very well her considerable powers over the weak-minded sex and transfixes Danny with her intensely violet eyes and beckons him with her little finger. Not a bad looking stud, she considers.

"Darth Vader couldn't do better," remarks Ron to Bruce and The Chipster. They take in the show as entranced Dan floats zombie-like toward her, past the amorous couples already strewn in and out about the grounds and boudoirs of the luxurious playground in varied states of sobriety and undress.

"Should we tell him her powers come from the dark side?" quips Ronnie.

"He'll find out soon enough," answers Bruce, who himself took a full eighteen months to recover from the heady elixir of her casual interest and then disinterest in him as a sex partner two years before. "Just wait until he discovers she's a black belt in karate."

Pirot stands nearby eyeing Danny and the rest of the crowd for possible future customers. He knows he's dressed ridiculously in a – somewhat shiny giving it a tawdry effect – tuxedo complete with blood-red cummerbund. But it pays to advertise. The same goes for his pencil-thin mustache. Brucie hires this procurer, a not-so-young-anymore sophisticated lout of unknown nationality, to score the drugs, book the musicians, and reliably supply willowy and willing young women for his parties. Just tonight, Pirot arranged for three beauties to alight here on a chartered plane from Philadelphia.

A Near Mating and Near Death

await the hero. The rest that Daniel soaked up in the last two days serves him well – for an instant. Though confronted by the presence of a real live deity practicing her arts over silly mankind, he regains his typical composure.

"Say, didn't you forget to give me change at McDonald's this afternoon? And I asked for onion rings, not fries." Despite his recaptured savoir-faire, his eyes rivet on Charlie's voluptitude bulging out of her low-cut pink silk gown. That her particular dress has a familiar design to it puzzles him.

Bruce thoughtfully ordered Pirot to tastefully arrange bottles of imported liquor and gold-plated razorblades tied by leather strands to vials of cocaine. They're placed on narrow antique Louis XV ormolu- and tulipwood-decorated bureaus throughout the downstairs. One in each of the eight palatial bedrooms, too.

All of his senses on full alert – gustatory notwithstanding – and not taking his eyes off this heavenly vision, Dandy two-fistedly gorges himself on the succulently laid out, but PC-deliberated, viands. Nothing but healthy California Certified Organic Farmer meatless treats for these cokeheads.

Although undisguised ogling of her more than ample bosom usually irritates Charlotte, she doesn't mind this time. Danny's new opening line unexpectedly makes her sincerely laugh – and this girl needs to laugh a little. All the better, he's spellbound. "Thank you, Sir. I hope I can find a way to make it up to you," Charlotte coquettishly replies. "Champagne?"

Was this scene in *Body Heat*? he tries to remember. Somewhere in the back of his mind Danny does recall that liquor might be verboten for the time being. "I'm Dan Topler and, no, I'm on the wagon just now, uh. . . . " he answers, fearing his wunderkind job at breaking the ice with this doll-and-a-half might vanish with a libation refusal.

"Charlotte Davison. Friends call me Charlie. So you're The Dandy Man? I've been panting to meet you. I'm on the wagon, too, Danny Boy." She presses her thigh hard between the two of his. Now isn't too soon for us to get very well acquainted, she decides. "Take just a skosh. You'll feel better and so will your wagon."

She opens his mouth with two deeply crimson manicured fingernails and pours a twelve-ounce goblet of Champagne Perrier Jouët down his throat. Dan's too weakened for more no's, and they continue to down drinks for some minutes as an intoxicated duel incites them to ever louder and more physically challenging parries and thrusts. He calls her ravishing and licks her ear. She dubs him her eternal slave while pushing him to his knees tight to the nether nexus of her designer frock.

As far as Dan, Daniel, The Dandy Man is concerned, the two of them have suddenly teleported alone together to a far away solar system. His initial firm control over himself and all he surveys has utterly passed and disappeared from view. For some reason, a few glasses of the bubbly have him spinning and a little nauseous.

"He's outmatched in this bout," Chip Siegel, one of Dan's Bexley Academy buds, wryly observes. Offspring of the very rich in this gang often simply refer to each other as children of corporate entities. The Chipster – son of Siegel Potato Chips, LLC, a manufacturer of many favorite highly-saturated snacks in the tri-state area – has become just one of a growing audience watching Charlotte make mincemeat out of Danny at the otherwise lacto-vegetarian buffet. Charlie's nightly conquests of one or another of Brucie's guests have become a spectator sport for the sotted crowd roused by occasional bets. The Chipster, surprisingly an inveterate gambler for an otherwise tightwad, shouts out, "One grand says she beds him tonight in the second round. Any takers?"

But no one covers the bet because Charlotte has already grabbed Dandy by the crotch of his twilled silk trousers and started leading him past the hanging Foreign Legion sword collection, up the circular staircase, complete with statued niches of naked Aphrodite and Hercules, to her favorite bedroom – the one decorated as a pre-Ayatollah Shah-era Iranian incense-scented harem – mirrored cylindrical ceilings and flexible double-tubed hash water pipe included. Dan has no problem with this arrangement since he's not on planet Earth in the first place and, in the second, a throbbing stomach pain now grips him in a growing panic.

At first, Charlotte hoped for more of a challenge from this sweet talker, but she's satisfied to saddle tight-butted Danny anyhow and shoves him forcefully to the Arabian linen-spread waterbed and rips off his trousers then jockeys.

"Tanta Sadie?" Danny calls out, nearly unconscious.

"Tonto said what?" she exclaims just seconds before The Dandy Man pukes all over her. Furious, "This is haute couture, you imbecile!"

"Bless you, Officer Franklin," are his last words before the ambulance arrives.

Earlier that day. . . .

The Posse Waits to Ambush

Albert as soon as his Mercedes speeds into the oval driveway of the Topler McMansion on the North Shore. Robert Sugarbush, Harriet's replacement private investigator, manages to cell-tel Harriet to be ready – how does she already know Albert's headed home? he wonders – and beats Albert there from the Hampton Hideaway Motel where the illicit lovebirds couldn't get it straight. A simple plan – Robert and Harriet will snare the tubby hubby just inside the front door. Harriet stands in front of the staircase like a menacing roadblock while Robert takes maybe a few hundred automated, rapid-fire Leica Digilux photos of Albert's underwear sticking out of his ripped trousers.

The extra pictures unfortunately are a necessity. Albert's torn pants made him trip just as Sugarbush took the shot at the motel. The P.I. hightailed it before he could get another good snap because he saw Elaine peering out the window in his direction. The photo of the groping couple shows the top of Albert's head and his pants, but not his face.

While not completely nude, the pose of Elaine's sexy, robust body could still manage a saleable foldout. A few snaps catching Albert running into the house with torn chinos will make the story zipper-tight. With or without permission from his clients, for a little extra vig on his gigs, Robert sells his digital exposés to whatever tabloid wants them. He also squeezes in a call to the *New York Post* Page Six editor, who instantly gives the photo sale a thumbs-up and will even use Robert's suggested headline:

Torn Trousers Topple Trash Tyrant Topler

Another job well-done almost in the can, Robert Sugarbush pats himself on the back while marking time patiently for his next victim in the Topler foyer.

Is this good for me or is this bad for me? Coco asks herself, watching her mother and the private investigator prepare her father's sacrificial bonfire. She's plenty bright anyhow, but it doesn't take a MacArthur Foundation genius for Coco to deduce what's up when Sugarbush sets his camera on a tripod facing the foyer. She has come home to surf the net and tie down the specs of the monster engine BMW dad pledged to her for earlier attending the gross display of her brother's ineptitude.

Now her MBA training comes into play: "Never forget, always do what's best for you – screw everyone else," her finance professor once said to her privately. On balance – promise or no promise – if her father gets ensnared, he won't be in the mood to buy the silver two-seater coupe she has in mind. Furthermore, she swiftly calculates, embarrassing photos complicate the property division between her parents in the sure-to-come divorce. She throws a little mathematical domestic game theory into the equation. Statistically speaking, Coco's better off with an even-steven property split in case she breaks off with one or the other in the inevitable offspring whose-side-do-you-take? tug of war between the parental units. This is bad for me, concludes her unsweetened self.

Ronnie Gets Yanked

in the door by Harriet's eager hand on his collar, crashes on the Perlino Bianco marble entrance, and gets automatically photographed fifty times before he knows what hit him. Ronald Schwartz's status as a forever friend of the family since his caesarean birth twenty-five years ago from the womb of Harriet's closet and long-lasting ally, Dolores, entitles him to barge into the Topler domicile without knocking. Since he was in the neighborhood he hoped that The Dandy Man might have already been sprung from the luxury looney bin.

Besides, Coco might be there. Ron has always been too embarrassed to tell Danny that he has the hots for the older sister unit. Once as a teenager he by-chance walked past her room and saw her *au naturel*, grooming herself in a full-length mirror, through her open – OK, he peeked between the crack – door. Ever since, he feels a rush even thinking of her. Now that they're both older, their age difference doesn't matter, and she's edgy – an inexplicable draw for him. Maybe he could see her on the sly without Dandy hammering him. As for Coco, while he used to be just one of the little trolls her brother hung with, Ron's muscular body has caught her eye on the few times she's seen him lately – how well he's hung seems more relevant now than with whom. And his recent early promotion to VP Marketing at Viacom brings added clout for this B-school grad.

Loud laughs at Ronnie's expense from Coco, absurd apologies of "I thought you were the maid" from Harriet, and No wonder you can't keep help thoughts by Ronnie precede Ron's polite boot out the door and Harriet's unmistakable command, not suggestion:

"Coco, why don't you and Ronnie go for a drive? <u>Now</u>."

This is my chance, simultaneously occurs to both sexes of the expelled couple. Coco slides into Ron's Jaguar convertible. "Ronnie, take out your cell phone." He obeys, knowing he's found himself in the eye of a Topler family hurricane. "Call this number and tell the man who answers to turn around and not come home today." A few rings and the deed's done. Both Ron and Coco's antennae crackle with the electricity of the moment. They peer deep into each other's business-trained eyes: "Have you ever seen the beautiful view of Long Island Sound from the Hampton Hideaway Motel, Ronnie?" Both engines, the XKR's and Ron's, roar into gear hell-bent for the sex snuggery.

Am I Too Old for White?

contemplates Elaine after her call to Harriet. *Maybe I should go for a hot pink wedding dress. Something daring but still demure.* She took the afternoon off from LFOD and now searches carefully for wrinkles in the motel mirror, to her satisfaction. Her daily pounds of hypoallergenic, citrus aurantium dulcis (orange peel oil) beauty creams have paid for themselves in near perfect skin. In addition, her regular dose of megavitamins, careful – mostly – dieting, and exercise routine casts from the looking glass the youthful figure of a woman at least ten years younger than her less-than-springtime real age.

Now the jackpot's paid off. Maybe big-time. The thought, Only God's CPA knows what Albert's really worth, brings goose bumps between her still creamy – thanks to gobs of Retin-A – thighs. Even if Harriet gets half, there's got to be plenty left. She takes a long very hot – then very cold – shower and considers what might be the timing of Albert's divorce and her marriage to him. Now turning to honeymoon plans while applying eyeliner: The poor thing needs a long vacation. With him it's either his business or seeing me here, which lately has been work for him, too. I thought he was having a Nelson Rockefeller heart attack the last time, and today his recently unreliable worm died on me.

The roar of a purebred, souped-up convertible motor outside her window interrupts her long dallying and daydreaming.

A man's voice floats its way into Elaine's room. "I can redial to find out if I want to. You had me call your dad, didn't you, Coco? Why?"

"Coco?" and why indeed? Elaine asks herself.

I've Been Betrayed

but by whom? ponders Harriet. She waits with Sugarbush until 9 PM for Albert's *coup de grâce*. Finally, a light bulb goes on and she calls security.

"Mr. Topler pulled in and turned around real quick like hours ago, Mrs. Topler."

Then her uncharacteristically unladylike to the P.I., "Don't call me again or send me a bill until you can tell me what's going on," casts the private investigator into the cloudy night with the Pella French door slamming shut behind him.

She methodically ticks off the suspects. Elaine? No, that *nafka* set it up in the first place. Sugarbush? No, not that dimwit, and he stood to make a nice bonus. Daniel? The dear can't know anything about this. And then drifting off to maternal matters, I just must pay him a visit at that place. He has to think horribly of me for ignoring him. But I've been so busy. I hope they keep him there long enough so that I can fit it into my schedule. Maybe I should at least call. Back to business. Ronnie? No, he just arrived by happenstance and, I think, actually believed I would grab my maid by the blouse and drag her to the floor. He's a bit stupid like his father. I don't care if he did land some fancy job in the city. Coco? Harriet's mind grinds to a complete halt.

Coco. Is Coco taking sides against me, her own mother? When she knows how I've suffered with that lout? Harriet's sorry now she didn't record the call from Elaine as evidence. In any event, Enough's enough. I'm getting rid of him and will take the bastard for all he's got. Harriet's machinations cease for now as she answers a call from a certain art professor who claims he adores her but has never proven it. She makes a mental note to call Dolores later to ask her husband, a prominent real estate attorney, for a divorce lawyer suggestion.

Only One Block

away from home – Albert hears a conspiratorial James Bond-like order, "Turn around and don't come home today." – but from whom? He suddenly torques his Mercedes away from some disaster – but what? the fugitive asks himself. He almost hits a fire hydrant and drives onto the grass of Fran Duckworth's house – he knows he'll never hear the end of his knocking over the old maid's fucking alabaster pink flamingos. A quick decision to call later to make amends. Al backs off the ravaged lawn and murdered plaster wading birds, then tears off out of the gated compound to find somewhere he can get plastered himself.

Whatever the particulars, he knows his and Harriet's marriage has finally gone kaput. He veers to the exclusive Northeastern Shore Country Club where forty years ago he was the first member of Polish background to be allowed in. Formerly only Yankee and German-Jewish families of culture passed muster, but expenses had risen dramatically, making admission of the newly rich seem more palatable. Besides, Jonathan Schwartz, a respected Island attorney, and his wife Dolores paved the way for the Toplers. Not Lower East Side Manhattan types, they personally vouched. And Harriet's lineage is prominently displayed in *The History of American Jewry*. Thusly, decades ago a junkyard man maneuvered onto the club's manicured grounds and now changes his torn trousers for green golf shorts in his seven-foot-tall oaken cubby at the rear end of the men's locker room.

Over time, Albert's open and sociable disposition made him a popular member. He's welcome on the golf course where he never fails to treat all comers to drinks at the nineteenth hole. He's retained the same gift of gab and sunny temperament that primed strangers to do business with him when he first set out for himself as a twenty-four-year-old. His winning personality still makes him popular wherever he goes – except at home.

A call to his links partner, Jonathan, "What now, Jon?" Albert takes the suggestion to stay in one of the few overnight guest rooms of the club and calls a recommended divorce law firm. Jonathan's no marital law expert, but he advises Al to stay away from any woman who could get dragged into the proceedings and maybe cost him tens of millions – and, "Yeah, of course I won't mention anything to Dolores. Geez, we're best buds and both men!"

Now Albert's thoughts turn to romance. Not see her? The thought of upsetting Elaine, too, makes Al reach for the Pepto-Bismol Chewable Tablets he's carried with him nonstop ever since their first steamy afternoon at the Hampton Hideaway Motel.

Dr. Bernstein's Not Smiling

this time as he leans over prostrate and nearly comatose Dan. "I could send you directly to Bellevue Hospital and lock you up in a straitjacket for the next year. Or I could tie you up and have Linda spoon feed you your meals. The former WWE pro wrestler who's been assigned to you as your CA will change your potty for you – when he remembers. Is that what you want?" Bernstein shakes with anger, making him feel as sick as his patient. "Don't you know you could have died right here in front of me, you little moron?"

"I liked you better as Dr. Frankenstein than your new role as Nurse Ratched," gasps Dan, coming to. The physical agony still pervading every nerve hasn't shaken the smart aleck out of him. "Doc, I have an urgent question."

"What is it now?"

"Do you think the Miss Universe that put me on this gurney will still go out with me?" Dan knows his priorities. "I upchucked all over her pink dress."

Softening a bit, "At least it's your favorite color. Why do you say she put you here?"

"I said no, Doc. I told her I couldn't drink and she poured spirits down my throat anyhow. Don't you love a gal that won't take no for an answer?"

Handsome Dan melts down the doctor's fury. "No, Daniel, I'm a sane adult. I don't love women who want to kill me." He walks to the door of the LFOD infirmary.

"No matter how rotten you feel, Daniel, you should be able to get up and shower in a few hours. I still want you to attend tonight's discussion group. This is your final chance from me or I'm shipping you off to Bellevue." He then leaves without another word.

"A Little TLC

never hurt anyone," Helen softly tells Danny while rubbing his hands. She waited until Dr. Bernstein's daughter picked him up and drove away before bullying her way into his room. "Don't mess with me," Dan overheard her tell the night attendant in the hallway who foolishly tried to prevent her admittance. Even in his sorry state, her threat made him crack up.

"You called the ambulance didn't you, Helen?"

"You're such a silly child. I knew you wouldn't stay put and peeked in your bedroom at midnight. When I saw the empty bed, I guessed you were probably at that ridiculous Bruce Langford's house drinking like a damn sailor. I called him to check up on you just about when everybody went apeshit about your passing out. Pardon my language, sweetie." The longshoreman posing as a gentle, white-haired old lady smiles at him.

"My buddies crack me up."

"Uh huh. They're not doing you much good. What you really need is love."

He takes a long look at Helen and nods off. "Thanks, Mom," he exhales, and then the sedative takes full effect.

Preparing for Battle

sums up his attitude. Dan finally awakens in his suite at 5 PM the next day. The phone gets him out of bed – a gourmet dinner's on its way, compliments of Monsieur François – but in fact paid for by Albert's house charge. He wolfs it down. He has no choice but to go to the meeting at the temple.

Before leaving, he picks up the flashing red-buttoned phone. A voice message from what sounds like a young girl, "Where the hell have you been today? Did you shave or do you still look like crap? If you didn't come to the pool today because you don't like me anymore then our (then in a whispered voice) secret deal is off and I don't like you either."

Oh, yeah. Ally.

The second message, "I just heard the dirt that they brought you back here in a police car cause you almost drowned in some pool around here but you didn't die cause some girl gave you mouth-to-mouth resuscitation which I coulda done for you if you wanted me to and needed it though that sounds kind of yucky but that you're OK now and still a spoiled punk. I almost drowned too so we're prob-bly better friends than ever huh so forget what I said before about not still having a you-know-what with each other."

A spoiled punk? For Christ's sake. Can't I even get sick and die without the East Hampton Stasi maligning me and alerting the media?

Third message, "In case you didn't know, the other two calls you heard where the person didn't say who it was was me, Ally. Ally from the pool. Nurse Linda said we could have a date I mean see each other tomorrow. OK? See ya."

At least somebody thought to call, Dan considers. I hope she's OK, he thinks, but decides he doesn't have time to call her back just now. The temple group's on his mind. I'll teach doc not to invite undesirables like me to meet his tired-out clique. The opposing ideas: Those meddlers should have let me die; and, But, I'm pretty lucky Helen called for help, scramble his brain. The key to his chariot lies waiting for him on the commode.

Later, traffic thins and he reaches fourth gear on the Long Island Expressway. The cogs in his mind spin endlessly about the past day and the meeting where he's headed. His own mental motor grinds to a halt. I don't know what the fuck to think anymore, ends the line of non-reasoning as he lays rubber into the Temple B'nai Israel parking lot, skidding to a complete stop. And it's a good thing, too. Just now Dan can't remember where he is or where he was going.

The Library

seems kind of cramped to Danny as he stands tentatively at the door, though only a few men lounge there shooting the bull. He scouts around before entering. A puffy couch and comfortably padded armchairs have been gathered in a circle in the middle of the room, evidently for the meeting. Dan's first impressions: The men aren't so old that the meeting seems like a visit to an old age home, but they're not young either. Two men appear to be of an age that he could imagine himself having a conversation with them without thinking that they might collapse mid-sentence. Evidently I came early enough so that the meeting hasn't started yet, Dan thinks. Rattled a bit. Will their rabbi be here?

Considerable relief no one wears a yarmulke or anything like that. In all, they're pretty much normal, casually dressed, some in khakis, others in tan or olive explorer shorts – the ones with pockets everywhere. Mostly overweight. Only one seems to be in decent physical condition. Sort of like a gathering of dad's brothers or his poker game. Men I would politely shake hands with if introduced to by Uncle Hy and then wait an appropriate time to sneak away without being rude. Not act rude? I haven't attended a family function in so long that I forgot I could behave like a nice guy when required.

Coming here fills Dan with a strange combination of pleasant nostalgia and vehement rejection. Years ago his dad coerced him into completing the whole Sunday school and confirmation razzmatazz through the tenth grade – not even

Albert with bribes of outrageous gifts could persuade him to
be *bar mitzvah*ed – the last time he ever set foot in a synagogue
until now.

The library measures maybe twelve by twenty, surrounded
on all sides by ceiling-height bookshelves with an eight-foot
foldout table along one wall. Delicious smelling coffee steaming in a large silver urn on the table draws Dan near. Thank
God it's caffeinated. He almost tiptoes so as not to be drawn
into the conversations.

"Daniel, grab a cup and come over here and meet the men,"
calls Bernstein. Dan hadn't spotted him when he came in and
now panics and comes this close to hightailing it out the door.
But he obeys instead and takes a chair as far away from the
others as possible. The men politely nod at him and continue
their conversations. Quite a large man updates the men on the
latest e.r.a. statistics for the Yankees and Mets rosters. A flesh-
and-blood Excel spreadsheet, Dan marvels. Travel and their
grandchildren now dominate the gab. A few more men wander in, exchange greetings. Then, "OK, let's get started. I think
everyone's here except Sam," begins Jacob Bernstein – Jack, his
friends call him. "We have a guest today, Daniel Topler, and, if
there are no objections, maybe for some more sessions." Dan
cringes in the spotlight.

Noncommittal glances all around. A hefty but intense,
confident, and intelligent-countenanced man of maybe seventy
offers, "Certainly, why not?" Glen Sobel appears younger than
his seventy-six years and holds the singular distinction in this
crowd of still working full-time, and non-stop at that. Ami-
ably taking off his Oakley glasses, "Jack, why does a young
man like him want to commune with old fogies?"

Effecting a just noticeable wince, the hulking stat-spewing
Barry approaches, vigorously shakes the newcomer's hand.
"Welcome. I'm finally not the youngster of this group."

"Only 60. A baby," cheerfully appends trim David Ansterman, an all-hair-still-in-place button-down-shirt preppy sort.

He projects the adman image he still lives – reduced pitches per day notwithstanding.

Jack signals that the discussion's about to begin. Dan feels he has at last been called to action. Under no circumstances will this tribal medicine man expose him as some raving lunatic. He can very well do that for himself and will. Danny rises suddenly to tell these geezers just where they can get off, "You all should know. . . ."

Jack springs up, "Just a second, Daniel. Let me give the introduction," guiding a somewhat unwilling Dan by the arm back into his chair. "Dan is one of my first-year medical school students at Stony Brook. He's considering gerontology as a specialty and I thought by meeting you cranky sons of guns I might discourage him." Laughs all around.

He's pulled a fast one on me, Dan realizes. Then – I didn't know he taught at medical school. Who is this guy?

"Why don't we go around the room and introduce ourselves?" offers Jack.

And then nap time on our blankies, Dan doesn't say aloud. Making fun of others has always been his best defense.

"Barry," simply responds the smiling, imposing man across from Dan on the couch. Maybe because the immense six-three Barry is half lying down with his hairless belly slightly sticking out of an orange Lacoste polo shirt, he reminds Dan of a moronic, middleclass Buddha. Still, Dan reconsiders. A dimwit? No way. This guy spouts sports data like a human calculator. Everyone there is in line to collect an automatic Go directly to jail! Do not pass go! card from worldly Danny Boy.

Next, athletic and still wrinkle-less, "David Ansterman. Nice to meet you, Daniel."

"You can call me Dan."

"I'm a PR man with a couple of clients left. Here's my card." David stands up, crosses the oval that divides them and hands it to Dan who pretends to read it.

From Robert Vitriol, a recently retired Wall Street trader standing at the urn, "Hey, does anybody know how to make coffee? There's only a little left and it's cold. There isn't any cream either. Can somebody go get it?"

"Yeah, your former secretary," shouts Morton Mavis, a wiry, goateed 71-year-old. "Have her bring us some danish while she's at it," he grins at the others. His comment and tone carry with them Morty's customary combo of humor and biting edge.

A startled Dan takes note that this evening might not just consist of discussing Dr. Katz's Seven-Step Guide to Prostate Health. Or is it three steps on the TV ad?

"I don't drink coffee anymore," begs off Harry Rosenthal, the 68-year old former CPA and comparative youngster in this group. Daniel unconsciously reaches up and touches his hair while considering Harry's round, bald crown, which gives the man a monk-like appearance.

"I think the coffee and milk are in the kitchen outside the door and to the left," suggests Jack trying to be helpful.

"Never mind. Never mind. I can go without," Vitriol replies a little too testily for a friendly gathering. He plops himself down near Dan. "So you're going to be a doctor, is that it?"

"Well. . . ."

Not waiting for an answer, "I've been a trader for almost forty years on Wall Street, very successfully too, I might add. I left my firm a month ago. I'm Rob Vitriol. They asked me to stay of course, but for what I ask you?"

"I think. . . ."

"I can just as well trade at home now with the internet. And my time's my own." Points a meaningful finger at Dan. "Do you see what I'm getting at?"

"Yes, you only bore yourself now," cracks Morty, garnering guffaws all around.

Jack regains control. "Thanks, Rob. Let's finish the introductions and, before I forget, remember we're meeting here

Wednesday at the same time." The group completes the informal formality of the intros, then Jack orchestrates the band of temple brothers. "Well, what should we discuss first?"

"Can we confer on staying relevant in our retirement?" suggests Harry, who left his CPA firm less than a year ago.

"Jesus, Hershel. We've talked that to death. Can we discuss something else for a change?" Rob interjects uncomfortably.

"Of course. What would <u>you</u> like to talk about?" Jack quietly replies.

"I don't care. Anything. Listen, I'm not trying to control the conversation or anything. It's just that we've been over the retirement thing a million times. OK, it's not easy not being the main guy anymore. We all know that by now. End of story. So let's move on. Let's talk about anything, I don't care." Rob shifts in his seat, avoiding eye contact with the others.

Trying to lighten up the meeting, "OK. Let's huddle on our main nemesis, our children," chuckles David.

Rob – now more agitated, "Dave, please. You're not one to talk. Everything's perfect in your life. Don't get me started talking about my child, Chucky. He's so infantile. Now I can't speak to him or even my granddaughter, Carol, anymore. We used to get together and have, you know granddad-to-granddaughter times, but she's clammed up now. Won't say two words to me."

"Well, Charles is your child, but you don't mean he's a real child, do you, Rob?" Glen asks.

"Yes, he is a real child. He's my son, but he's also a kid. He's getting divorced I guess, but still living with Susan. It's terrible for Carol. She's caught between her parents. He wants to change careers but doesn't know what and I think he's seeing another woman. Some divorcée, I hear. He had everything going for him."

Jack – evenly, "You can't help."

"No, I can't help. He's my son. Carol is my granddaughter. And I can't help. I can only watch."

An embarrassed lull in the conversation. Dan's engrossed. Wow. And they've just started the meeting. Dan takes in that Jacob knows what he's doing, leading the conversation along twisting, undetermined paths without dominating it. Danny's in more familiar territory than he had bargained for. At first he's glad he's not the focus or even part of the discussion, but then grates a bit at being ignored. It's not about him. As the evening wears on, Dan infers that, like him, this group has had a life of privilege. They're also educated, erudite. But, unlike him, they've had careers – and long ones at that. And they're accomplished men. Rob's on the American Stock Exchange board of directors. Jack, he finds out, has published *tanka* Japanese poems. Sam's computer programs helped design the Verrazano Narrows Bridge. And also unlike him, they've spent years catering to others – wives, ex-wives, maybe dead wives, children, grandchildren. And for all he knows, deceased in the last two categories as well. The concerns they express for these people unnerve him. He can sense the men's urgency and their diminished powers – their helplessness and their ingrained habit of taking command.

When Jack calls the meeting to an end, Dan realizes he witnessed no idle lawn social he could easily sneer at. But that won't necessarily stop him from trying. Dan scurries out of the library as soon as the men stand up and waits in the parking lot for Jack to come outside, although he doesn't really have anything he wants to say.

A Greeting

in the dim light. "Are you waiting for your father, too?"

Although it isn't completely dark out yet, even if it had been pitch black Dan's sexual radar would intuit by pheromones the question was posed by an angelic blond with hazel eyes. His internal tracking station doesn't fail to detect the substantial pair of parabolic reflectors filling her blouse either.

"Yep. Sure am . . . um. . . ."

"Laura," she says putting down her white writing pad.

"*Laura*. One of my favorite movies. Gene Tierney was very nearly as captivating as you."

Skillfully ignoring the compliment, "I don't think we've ever met. Who's your dad?"

"It's . . . him," pointing to Bernstein now coming out the main entrance of the temple. Under no circumstances will he volunteer why he's really there.

"Gee. I've always wanted to meet Dr. Bernstein's son."

"And now you have, lucky you and luckier me," he smiles widely, flashing the perfect teeth his parents paid so much moolah for. The sobering effect of the meeting has vanished – back to Mr. Charming in a nanosecond.

Bernstein approaches them while the other men pile out of the building, conversing with each other and heading for their cars. "Hello, sweetheart." Then, "Daniel, have you met my daughter, Laura?"

A year passes during Dan's three-second pause, "I've had that pleasure, thank you, Dr. Bernstein," pronouncing his shrink's name correctly. *There's nothing more to say. I'm dead meat.*

Bernstein nearly does a double take when called his formal name by this most difficult patient. *And so politely, too. Maybe we're getting somewhere.* But when he sees that Danny's surveying his little girl as might a lion prowling for a tasty gazelle, he hurries to his car, riding gunshot. "Let's go, sweetie. I need to get home right away. See you tomorrow, Daniel."

Laura Cheshire Cat grins at Dan with an ever-so-blameless soupçon of ridicule, slinks behind the wheel of the not very late model Chevy, purrs, "TTFN, Daniel," and speeds away without turning back.

"Can't get a break," Dan complains to the now starry sky.

Why Can't I Bring It Up?

David Ansterman asks himself, lost in thought on his way home as he leaves the Temple B'nai Israel parking lot. He pulls onto Lakeville Road, the main drag in Great Neck, then to the highway access lane, and finally onto the Long Island Expressway. Diane would be furious if she knew I did. Maybe they have some suggestions. These men are my comrades, after all. She and I used to go dancing. See a movie. She won the women's temple bridge championship a few years ago. And now she won't leave the house or speak to her sister. Won't see Jack, though he's like family. Hates it when I go. Sits in her room reading with the door closed. That's where she'll be when I get home and won't talk to me for hours.

Too deep in thought, the adman lost his bearings. It isn't until twenty-five minutes later, when his cinnamon-colored vintage 1967 Mercury Cougar pulls up in front of the tollbooth at the Queens Midtown Tunnel, that he realizes he drove the wrong way on the LIE. Can't turn around, and through the crowded tunnel the reddish-brown cat crawls. Congested traffic jam at the 34th Street portal the opposite way. Broken down car. David finally arrives home three-and-a-half hours later.

No lights on in the house. No response to calls of "Diane." He finds the four pastel-painted bedrooms of the conventional but large raised-ranch house vacant. Down four steps to the foyer landing and four more to the shag-carpeted rec room with wet bar. The new 42-inch HDTV has been tuned to channel one but muted so that he can't hear the pointillist static he's seeing on the screen. Anger and anxiety keep exchanging places in David's brain. Half-a-dozen phone calls. Not in any nearby hospital. Policemen arrive 30 minutes later. Perfect home, one says. Nice galley kitchen. Must be nearly two acres. Wish I had one like it. No sign of a break-in. Search the house. In the hall closet – the one with the walnut hard-core paneled door and ivory handle, behind the hanging winter clothes cased in sheets of dry cleaner plastic. Sitting on a rattan chair – one from the redecorated breakfast room. Facing the wall. Eyes wide open. Diane begins to sob.

Time for the Play Date

the following day, and Ally's so happy to see her new pool companion she forgets to take off her glasses. "Dan. Everybody's talking about you. Somebody said you're in group therapy with other old people and tried to kill yourself again. Did you?" She's practically breathless with excitement and nearly screams the welcome.

"Oh no, Ally. The word's out. Killing yourself isn't cool anymore," thinking, that's just great. Maybe they should erect an LED signboard so this entire circus can keep up with the news on me.

"It isn't?"

"No, it isn't. How could we sit here together and rag on the other inmates here if we were dead?"

"I never thought about it that way," Ally suddenly realizes <u>he</u> is seeing her with the specs on. She yanks them off. Defensively, "I don't really need them."

"Put them back on. I like women in glasses. It makes them look intelligent."

Women? She's just been elevated non-stop to heaven. Well, if that's what my <u>boyfriend</u> wants, she reflects and puts them back on.

"Good. Just perfect."

A lull – then, "Dan, you know the other day when you didn't come here I thought that maybe you didn't like me anymore or that I really pissed you off when I said you're old. You're not really all <u>that</u> old and even if you were my dad is older and Finster is nine years old and that's seventy-two years old in dog years and I still love him so you being the age you are is OK cause it wouldn't mean that I don't love you." Turning crimson, "Not that I <u>do</u> love you cause we hardly know each other and we haven't even gone out on a date – yet. Anyhow, if I thought we couldn't be friends or something anymore I would kill myself I really mean it."

Ally's intensity finally wakes Dan up to her feelings. He's panicked by the deep water he's in. *Holy shit. What the hell did I get into?* Now grabbing her arms, "Listen, Ally, don't you ever ever again even think about killing yourself. Do you hear me?" Dan's frightened at the terrible thought of her killing herself and now aghast that he gives a rat's ass about some little girl he knows zilch about.

Ally shakes free. "Hey, take your mitts off me. You might be my boyfriend but my mom says if another man ever hits her again she'll shoot his fucking brains out for him and I should do the same."

"Sorry. I'm so sorry, Ally. I'd never hurt you, but you really scared me." Also concluding, *Whoa, Helen Clausen and this girl must have been sailors together somewhere.*

Crying now. Anxious that she might frighten him away. "Dan, don't leave me. I won't do anything you don't want me to."

Not getting it. "We'll always be friends, Ally."

For all his prowess with women, Dan has missed the mark by a gazillion miles with the young girl. Fluttering her eyelashes at him as she thinks movie stars do. "Oh, we're much more than friends, <u>Daniel</u>," coos Ally.

Daniel? The lightning bolt finally makes its way through his leaden egocentric head. He's headed for an immediate meltdown of his own when. . . .

Saved by the Bell

Dan gratefully thanks God as, "Mr. Daniel Topler, please report to Dr. Bernstein's office. Repeat. Mr. Daniel Topler, please report to Dr. Bernstein's office for today's psychiatric treatment," booms across Long Island.

"I'm going to find that woman on the loudspeaker, thank her, and then strangle her with my bare hands," he thinks he's said to himself.

"Would you really kill her? And thank her for what?" Ally inquires.

"Just kidding. Catch you later."

"Why won't <u>they</u> ever leave us alone?" exclaims Ally pressing her forearm to her forehead.

A fine Garbo imitation. That girl's got a movie career ahead of her – if she stays out of bathtubs. Can't be late for Dr. Brain-Nuker, Dan ruminates while he makes his way to his daily psychiatric appointment.

The mini-blinds have been let down and adjusted so that minimal daylight creeps through the narrow slats. The dimmer switch has set the recessed lighting low. Dan takes it all in. He deduces Bernstein thinks he's the spider and I'm the fly. The doctor points to a comfy, deep purple wing chair for Dan to be seated, which he does but in so doing wiggles his derrière ostentatiously in the descent for a bit of comic relief. They both sit silently for a few seconds. Although Dan has never played this particular Freudian parlor pastime, he thinks he gets the point. Whoever talks first loses – verbal *zugzwang*. Danny likes conversational gamesmanship.

A moment later, "I don't like games, Daniel." The utterance zinging him so soon rattles Dan in his tufted leather perch. "I don't care who talks first, I just want to help you," Bernstein says without a trace of irony.

"OK. Since you talked first, I'll talk second. What's your daughter's telephone number?"

Bernstein coolly resists the temptation for an argument.

We're going nowhere fast on that traffic lane, Dan concludes. Now uncharacteristically serious, "I met a girl here at LFOD, Alicia, who says you're her doctor. What's her story?"

"I'm aware you're not telling the truth to me since Ally ran up to me earlier in the day asking about you. I know you know I'm not her physician anymore. She's very taken with you, it seems."

"OK, you got me. You're not her doctor. But what's with her? She's a sweet kid. Why's she here?"

"Why are you here? You can't adjust to life's realities. I can't discuss my former patients, but how much harder would it be for a 13-year-old child to live in a highly dysfunctional family than for a 24-year-old? Some people aren't wired to cope without a little help. Be careful, Daniel. She's fragile and not a championship games player like you." Changing the subject at hand, "Tell me your impressions of last night."

Dan takes his time to analyze the board before making the next move. He decides retreat is in order, and maybe some bonding will pave the way to the answers of his questions. Embrace the enemy. "Rob is having real difficulty dealing with his loss of influence and control over his son's life. Your bringing him to say so aloud was undoubtedly therapeutic." A dramatic hesitation, then in a staccato tempo echoing a TV medical drama, "Good work, doctor. I'd pat you on the back, but I fear it might go to your head." Continuing while assuming a Central Casting physician's demeanor, "He needs to let his granddaughter know it's OK if they just sit together quietly or see a movie without speaking. She'll come around when she's ready. Tell the whole family to take two aspirin and call me in the morning."

"Amusing. Still, you prove you have the intelligence to be a top-notch psychiatrist, Daniel. But intellect isn't enough."

"Who said I want to be a shrink? Or any kind of MD?"

"I know for a fact you were a joint psychology and biology major at Yale and got into your first choice of medical schools. What happened?"

"What happened? I didn't want to be one of those idiots going to a trade school for fixing mental faucets. I'd rather be a real plumber. Speaking of plumbers, did you hear the one about. . . . "

"Please stop. I don't believe you. You don't have to defend yourself. I'm not attacking. You possess superior verbal abilities. But they're not helping you. You use language as a weapon and a shield. But your only war is inside of you where words can't help."

Feeling cornered, "I'm surprised at you. Don't you know that therapy is supposed to take months, years, maybe forever? Laying it all on the table so soon isn't in the psychiatric playbook is it?"

"This is no game, and I'm not playing with your life. The next time you jump off a bridge or mix drugs and alcohol you might succeed in preventing a brilliant career, a wife, children. Death is forever; it can wait its turn."

Dan waits impatiently for the session to end. He considers tapping his toe loudly to rudely demonstrate he's about done with this nonsense – but doesn't. He can't laugh Bernstein off.

"Tell me about your depression."

"What are you? Some kind of mind reader? First I'm a lost lamb headshrinker. Now I'm a depressed nutso."

Bernstein says nothing.

"What do I have to be depressed about anyhow? I've got a trust fund. Accessories to my crimes of non-stop partying. A beautiful home away from home here in zombieville. This is the life."

"What kind of life is it? Try to stick to our regimen, if you possibly can. You'll start to feel better. Then you can pull your life back together again."

"Yeah. Sure." but Dan's only pretending not to listen carefully.

"Why do you attempt suicide, Dan?"

"Why not? I was top of my class at prep school and valedictorian at Yale despite my habit. But then I needed more of the stuff – and more often. I was too zonked the first few weeks of med school to even get out of bed and dropped out. What should I do now, Doc? Spend my life whoring half the time and asleep the other half while my former classmates actually live a life?" Dan takes a deep breath. There, I said it, he thinks with uncustomary relief. Where the fuck did that come from? he wonders as he brushes away a tear.

Bernstein says nothing. A beat while Dan waits for more of the homily. It's not forthcoming.

"See you tomorrow."

"That's it?"

"That's it. For now."

"Can't we analyze why I dress in kangaroo suits only on J. Edgar Hoover's birthday?"

"Daniel, I'm too busy for nonsense. Our time left is all we really own, my boy."

Mulling it over and halfway out the door, "So, why isn't intellect enough?"

"Because caring has the greatest healing power, Daniel."

"See, I knew it! You are a Carl Rogers disciple."

"He was my mentor. Authored some peer-review articles together. We were close friends and colleagues."

"<u>You</u> were a close friend and colleague of Carl Rogers?" then darts out of the office, suffering from the embarrassment of openly showing how impressed he is. Bernstein's question, "What happened?" burns in his mind.

Brucie's Call

awakens Dan from a troubled nap. He needed to lie down after the session. A mixed metaphor – eating crow isn't my cup of tea – snuck into his mind and made him laugh just as he nodded off.

"Ahoy there, matey. Pretty rough sea you found yourself in. You OK?" inquires Langford the second.

"Arr, couldn't be better me hearty," evoking a respectable Wallace Beery *Treasure Island* imitation. "'Twas the grog that did me in, you scurvy dog."

"I think it was the wench that keelhauled you, Dandy Man." Dropping the pirate lingo, " Say, we missed you at my quotidian bash last night, old man. A certain temptress wants another shot at you, though she didn't get the shot from you she expected."

"Trying to sandbag me, aren't you, Brucie?"

"Cross my heart and hope everyone else dies but me, Dandy." Realizing the faux pas, "Uh . . . no offense." Even among his wisecracking friends, Dan's suicide attempts aren't considered fair game for humor.

"No offense taken. Do you think Charlie will talk to me again?"

"I don't think that <u>talk</u> is what's on her mind. Fornication fits the bill somewhat better."

Interested, "Yeah? Will she be there Saturday night?"

"With bells on her cloven toes."

Reconsidering, "I don't know. I probably should pass this one and finally dry out, Brucie. Having your stomach pumped isn't the fun it's made out to be."

"Not a problem, Dandy. You should stay away. I'll just tell her you consider her an unworthy slut and she ought to take up with me again."

"Is she the Charlotte that nearly drove you to sobriety?"

"That very seductress. Thanks for dropping her in my lap again. There's no rutty tomato like the one rebounding from throw-up on her dress."

Knowing full well his folly, "OK, Svengali. You've sweet-talked me once more into attending one more of your low-brow soirées. By the way, you don't know a girl by the name of Laura Bernstein, do you?"

"Do you mean the one who lives in Stony Brook? How would you come to know the name of an honest woman?"

"That's the one."

"When it comes to female company, I thought you avoided the element, old chap – your element that is."

"I'm waiting, Brucie. You won't like me when I'm angry. I turn Godzilla green."

"I don't like you much now. Anyhoo, she's a Ph.D. candidate in English at Princeton. She and Charlie met while they were both at Stanford. We all had lunch together last summer. Quite the budding literary lion, I hear. Already had some fiction published in the *Sewanee Review*. Besides her darling face, she's sweet, wholesome, intelligent, and it seems to me a consummately decent woman. In summary, not at all your type, Dandy Man – in any respect."

"What's her number?"

"Don't know but I can ask Charlotte for you. Shall I?" Then innocently, "Or do you want me to invite her so that Charlie can introduce you personally?"

"Don't be an ass. You underestimate my powers, Brucie. I can see you smirking on the other side of this phone conversation. No, don't invite Laura. Make up one of your ready fibs about why you want the number. And <u>don't</u> tell Charlie it's for me."

"Your wish is my command, Sahib. What else do you seek from your lowly conjuror? "

Now in earnest, "Brucie, would it be a terrible imposition if you didn't serve liquor Saturday?"

"Not even this magic genie can prevent it, old bean. Not to hint for a token appreciation from a thankless chum, but most of it appears as offerings from invitees."

"Not a problem," Dan lies without being believed. "Catch you later."

Bruce hangs up, delighted to be in the middle of such a yummy melodrama. "Bertrand," he calls to his father's servant, "Call Hampton Catering and double the amount of Perrier Jouët for Saturday." A second thought, "And buzz Pirot. I have a special assignment for him: extra snow for Dan Topler."

Just now, Bruce Langford II feels damned good about himself. His boss at Morgan Stanley didn't mind his leaving a tad early in the afternoon – after all, the summer season has almost begun on the Eastern Shore. The helicopter ride to his own landing pad from the MS worldwide headquarters on Broadway in Manhattan, made possible through a grandfather clause in the local zoning laws, means that he can stay at his desk until four. Brucie resents the recent critical grimaces he gets from some of his neighbors over the noise. Now that the *nouveau riche* routinely take five-hundred-and-twenty-five dollar one-way choppers to the East Hampton Airport, unfairly he's become the poster boy for the insufferable *Apocalypse Now* racket the denizens must now endure here in paradise.

Though he lacks the prerequisite MBA, his undergraduate degree from the Wharton School at UPenn, and more importantly his pedigree from the blue blood of his parents, qualifies him for perks not ordinarily given to new hires. His family has been listed in The Blue Book of the Hamptons for decades. A few phone calls to dad's friends from the even-the-local-movie-moguls-can't-get-in Maidstone and Shinnecock Hills

Golf clubs had already put Brucie and his firm in the middle of the two biggest corporate mergers this year – the ichor of Morgan Stanley's corporate finance unit. Investment bankers in the airless stratosphere of the top-tier firms clasp to their breasts a secret invisible to the great unwashed: rolodexes run the world.

"Speaking of the Devil's Handmaiden,

just how are you, scrumptious?" Bruce flatters Charlotte when she calls. He had just finished his conversation with Dan. "Any fresh kills today?"

When Charlie originally enrolled at Stanford, her plan was to mine West Coast contacts for an eventual legal career in Hollywood. She was a junior and Laura Bernstein a freshman when they met at a Stanford Film Society screening. An instant friendship began then for the two New Yorkers. Later at Columbia Law School, a feminist professor drew Charlie into a wholly different career. Defending woman's rights presented itself as a higher calling, and now she's well on her way to becoming partner in one of the most feared family (read divorce) law firms in Manhattan.

Contrary to the managing partner's experienced business advice, Charlotte represents women only. "Not good for your career or the firm's revenues," he warned. In fact, a sizable chunk of the money in the divorce legal racket nowadays comes from fees paid by wealthy errant husbands to their female counsels. A jury's natural sympathy for an injured damsel can often be mollified or even evaporated by the appearance of a persuasive counsel that happens to be wearing a well-tailored skirt. Charlotte's fame has risen so rapidly that the mere mention of her name frequently brings the opposition immediately to the bargaining table in a quick, favorable settlement for her client.

A plaque on her office desk declares Bobby Fischer's famous dictum:

I like to see 'em squirm.

That goes for her dating habits as well.

"Bagged a ten-million-dollar cash settlement from a wife-beating pig who controls the largest global reinsurer registered in Bermuda. Also landed his five-acre villa near the Southampton Princess Hotel."

"What a shark."

"He got off easy. He cowered like a frightened schoolboy caught with his hand in the cookie jar. We could have reeled in his yacht as well."

"Why didn't you pluck that, too?'

"Yachts are just another name for money pits. Maybe it'll capsize with him on it. Say listen, Brucie love, do you remember Laura, my friend from Stanford that you met last summer?"

The serendipity never stops a-comin' for this bonus baby. He silently licks his chops. "Yes, of course. The homely one with bad breath and buck teeth. How is the dear thing? Ever land a date?"

"If you had asked her out one more time last year, Brucie, she would have started charging you dial-a-porn rates."

"Oh, <u>that</u> Laura!" He knows his chances are slim, but she can't slap him over the phone. "Speaking of dates, any chance you, oh sprite of the underworld," now singing the 70s song intentionally off-key, "*Voulez-vous coucher avec moi ce soir?*"

"If you were only as big a dick below the waist as you are above it, we'd still be lovers, darling."

"Ouch! I've always revered your dead aim at one's privates, dear." Thus exhibiting yet once more the source of the awful rhyme often repeated by Brucie's cronies:

Bruce's breeding made him uninsultable,

a trait his friends find fun 'n lovable.

Charlie wants to get to the point. She's still bustling at work, pounding men into the ground like they were railroad spikes under a titanium cudgel. "Anyway, for some ungodly reason she found you droll, in an uncouth way of course, and thought we might all lunch again sometime."

"I have a much better idea," springs the trap. "Why don't the two of you come to the pond house Saturday night? You can show her how the base upper class demean themselves."

"Perfect. She can use you degenerates for one of her short stories. I'll twist her arm. We'll be there," and hangs up without a goodbye.

It all goes to show you how wonderful life can be if you live right, Bruce congratulates himself.

New Beginnings

may sound like a men's club, but it's not far from group therapy, considers Dan. He's on the expressway halfway to the Wednesday night meeting. But, why not? They're among friends, no pressure to bare their chests, and they can just talk sports and the market if they want to. Kind of like getting together with Bruce, Chipster, and Ronnie without the booze. Or maybe it's more like talking to Ally, except the two of us gossip about movie stars and how weird some of the other "guests" behave instead of the Yankees and the Dow Jones Average.

When he's not reading in his room or giving one of his three-times-daily mandatory urine samples, Dan spends most of the last two days with the teen, though it's been tricky to keep it platonic. Just this morning she pretended that "Hey, why don't we just go to my place and fool around" just casually occurred to her then instead of the well-rehearsed line she'd been practicing for days.

Dan sensed that a suggestion like that might come from her and that she'd try hard to fake nonchalance. He put her off by treating it as farce. That's all I need, races into his mind. Trade Long Island for Riker's Island. If she persists along that line, I'll have to stop hanging out with her. Hate to do that. She's a nice kid. Funny, too. And all the other prisoners here are either bats or comatose.

Sam Blotkin, the club member who was a no-show for the last meeting has already taken a seat by himself as Dan strolls into the temple library. Why does Sam sit by his lonesome?

Dan asks himself. Though he didn't say much at the last get-together, Danny feels more comfortable this time sitting next to one of the other men. In truth, Dan also feels a bit like a little boy in the presence of these seasoned survivors. He finds that their company has an unexpected calming effect on him.

"Hi, Dan, good to see you again. I'd really like to hear more about how you like it at Stony Brook," Harry warmly says to him. "I have a niece that's applying to med school. Maybe you can give her some pointers."

"Sure, love to." My bit roles in college plays come in handy now and then, he laughs to himself.

Jack begins, "We're all here. All of you remember Daniel, I hope." Polite nods to Dan from all points on the circular seating compass. "I'd like Harry to start off the meeting tonight. He's prepared an introduction for a possible starting topic tonight."

But Harry doesn't seem all that prepared. "Well, you know. One of the issues we've deliberated before is kind of getting ready . . . um . . . prepared for not being well or facing poor health. Or going through an operation that could be scary. Stuff like that." Harry's having a hard time expressing himself. "Anyhow, as you all know, Jack has to have surgery for the tumor they found a month ago, and why don't you take it from there, Jack?"

"Two tumors," Jack begins calmly. "The X-rays show one wrapped around the left kidney and one between the renal artery and kidney on the right. They must complete more tests. I'll be operated on soon thereafter."

Dan takes in the deadly silence. For a man his age, this could be a death sentence. Dan's mind floods with the news. Bernstein never once mentioned he was ill to me, but I'm not a friend. Am I now? He hasn't looked well; I should have guessed he's sick. He wouldn't simply start talking about himself even among close friends. He had Harry make an introduction to maintain the appearance of impartiality at the meeting. Proper. Dignified. What the hell am I doing here?

"My physician has recommended a surgeon at Columbia-Presbyterian Hospital. What really scares me is that I don't know any of the doctors there. I've known all the Stony Brook medical staff for years. And now I'm just a stranger, another patient at a hospital I haven't yet visited." Jack just barely maintains composure. "I thought I'd share my experience with the group since we all might have to face problems like this."

"Are you seeking counseling to help you, Jack?" softly asks Morty, whose typical bite is wholly missing in the question.

"Yes. Mary, a psychiatrist at Stony Brook, has recommended me to her friend, a counselor at Columbia-Presbyterian. That doctor will introduce me to my surgeon and the rest of the operating team. I don't want anyone to operate on me who doesn't know me."

"You have your daughter to help you, too," David suggests.

"We're very lucky," interjects Harry. "We all have children that we can rely on." Trying to humorously cover up the possible slight, "Except Barry, of course, who's a lucky bachelor."

"Children? I don't have any children I can rely on," muscles in an agitated Morty.

Glen tries to reassure him, "I probably shouldn't talk since I have a young child, two adult daughters and a third wife I almost never see, but you have your two grown kids, Morty. If you have trouble, you can call them."

"You, Glen. It's you I'll call if I'm sick. Not my children. I hardly talk to them now. Do you all remember when I got *bar mitzvah*ed again? You all were there. My kids couldn't believe a hundred people showed up. They thought nobody would be there except them. That nobody likes me just because they don't."

"There's your sister you could call if you were ill," suggests Barry.

"We haven't spoken in over a year," Morty bitterly replies and turns off his receptors for the rest of the meeting in isolated contemplation.

The group conversation retreats into happier, more comfortable gab – the book club they also attend on other nights, summer travel.

Later, Dan again leaves the building first, but for a different reason. Even the weight of Bernstein's earlier disclosure hasn't made him forget his new goal.

"I almost never lose phone numbers, yet what can I say?" Dan teases Laura outside. "The pressure of daily life – corporate board meetings, press interviews, et cetera et cetera. They suck the life out of you." Dan tears out a page from the note pad she was writing in and a pen from his pocket while transmitting his most winning smile. He's not trusting to luck that Brucie will come through for him. "Please give it to me again. Not too fast, cause I'm a little slow."

"You're as fast as they come," says Laura laughing. "But since we're brother and sister you can ask our father if you've forgotten the number."

Oh, yes, the little detail of my miniscule fib, remembers Danny. He hesitates. *I don't know what Bernstein has said about me.* "What did daddy-o say?"

"Daddy-o didn't say anything at all about you, Daniel."

Bernstein had departed the temple and blindsides Dan-Dan from behind. "What shall we say?"

Dan realizes that his psychiatrist has skillfully turned the tables on him. "I'm a patient of Dr. Bernstein's and enrolled at the Live Free or Die rehab clinic in East Hampton. He kindly has permitted me to sit in on the New Beginnings meetings so that I can witness the real difficulties and pleasures of life and aging. I can't take drugs or alcohol. The combination with the medicine I'm taking could kill me." There's no defense like a good offense.

"A concise confession and self-analysis. Excellent, Daniel." To Laura, "Well let's go, honey. I need to get up early."

"Your number, Laura?" Dan persists.

Bernstein pulls Dan aside. "Let me talk to you for a moment, Daniel." Out of ear range, "You're my patient and still in danger, it seems to me. Furthermore, now is not the right time to pursue romantic interests. You must focus on recovery."

"You don't think I'm fit to see your daughter, Doc, is that it?"

Firmly, "That's exactly it. Don't call her."

"Are you speaking as my doctor or as her father?"

"Frankly, both, Daniel." Then getting in the car, "Let's go, honey."

A sad you-know-how-parents-are mug to Dan from Laura and they're gone, leaving Dan alone in the parking lot.

Maybe because he's already asked Bruce to get Laura's number, but other thoughts occupy his mind. Community means so such to Jacob. Meeting the surgeon has more importance than the threat of the surgery itself. *I never did find out why Sam sat by himself and said nothing all night.* In analyzing the night's conversation, Danny's yearning gonads have temporarily been forgotten on the drive back to his posh prison.

"Patients Are Funny,

Daniel Topler," the doctor in a white coat says to him, as the lad approaches the pool area the next AM.

"You know my name? And why funny?"

"The doctors know all the guests here – you know we have to call them that, God forbid we call them patients. Have a seat, Daniel."

Dan sits as told. He needs to take his mind off last night. "Do the MDs here have meetings to dissect us, doc?"

"Please call me doctor. I'd know you anyhow. You always pop up from your seat next to that little dish you always talk to when your name is called. Why funny? Well, for example I have this one . . . uh . . . guest, who never arrives on time. I can't tell you his or her name of course – confidential. He's a control freak. Coming late is a way of showing me that he calls the shots around here."

Dan beams, "Have I joined the medical staff?"

The doctor returns the smile, but perhaps not so warmly. "So the last appointment I say to him when he comes in twenty minutes late, 'You're a bit tardy again. Why do you think that is?' Very chatty and low-key. I'm not threatening him a bit, you see. By the textbook professional with all that rigmarole I learned at Harvard Medical School."

Impressed, "What did he say?"

"What did he say? Why he says he's not late at all. That's what he says. Can you imagine it?"

"Well, some of us here need psychiatric help, I'm told." Dan jests and gives the doctor a gentle nudge with his elbow in a familiar way. "Then what did you say?"

"See, that's what I mean," pointing at his poked rib. "You patients here take liberties. I'll tell you what I said. 'My time here is valuable. I can't waste it waiting for half-wits like you to wander in when they feel like it.' That's what I said."

"Pretty strong stuff."

The doctor rises and leans so close to Dan that he feels the physician's breath. "Now this patient says, and what gall he has – listen carefully, 'Twenty minutes is nothing.'" The doctor's face gorges red in the telling – his voice rises – "So I say to him, 'Maybe twenty minutes is nothing to you, Lars, God-damn it. . . .'"

"Never met a Lars I didn't like," Dan says.

" . . . but the good Lord Yahweh made the Earth in seven days. . . ."

"Six, really," Dan offers.

Now waving his arms around wildly like a windmill and bellowing red-faced with rage, ". . . and twenty minutes is enough time to fill the waters with fishes and make our blessed earth green or my Jehovah-given name isn't Dr. Jacob Q. Bernstein." His dripping saliva wets his white frock.

Danny considers his best option: Run for his life or, since he's not in all that great shape, cover his vital parts and scream bloody hell for the CAs. Too late he noticed the man's bunny slippers.

"Lars, I'm glad I found you," the real Dr. Bernstein says, taking a friendly but solid hold of his patient's shoulder. "Daniel, please excuse us. I'd like a chat with this guest just now."

Now suddenly soothed and apologetic, "Sorry I'm a bit tardy, Doctor. I think I'm only twenty minutes or so late to see you."

"Not a problem, Lars," as Bernstein leads him away, "Twenty minutes is nothing."

"He's One of the Perverts

Mom's always telling me to watch out for," Ally says to Dan. She points at Lars led by Bernstein as they go inside the *Helper Campground* where the doctors have offices. "Always sitting across the pool from me and staring at me like a weirdo."

Now that Lars has gone, Ally has the courage to come up to Danny and whisper to him, "I told mom about him and she said to tell the CAs if the creep ever bothers me to kick him in the balls and run like a bat outta hell but he's never done nothing but stare so I just kind of ignore him. I don't think he likes us talking together cause he always has this freaky frown on his face when you sit next to me so then I sort of give him a too-bad-if-you-don't-like-it-asshole look right back and then he turns away and pretends he's wasn't watching me like I see you look at Elaine. Funny, huh?"

"Yeah, very," Danny says, thinking it's not one damn bit funny.

"So you <u>do</u> think Elaine's cute or somethin'? I know she's prettier than me and got big you-know-whats and I'm still sorta flat but mom says she didn't fill out until she was. . . . "

"Ally, you're A-OK by me."

Nearly in tears, "No you don't think so. You don't think that at all."

"Do you remember our deal? What did we say?"

Eyes cast down and maybe still not believing it, "That we'd never lie to each other."

"OK, then. So that's that."

Brighter, "Well, if I'm really A-OK why can't we. . . . "

"Ally, do you want me to go to jail? You're thirteen. If your mom or anybody here thought we were even having this conversation, I'd never be allowed to talk to you ever again."

Nearly in tears again, "I bet you have a girlfriend you like better – who's cuter than I am."

"I don't have a girlfriend. Or maybe <u>any</u> real friends." Dan recalls the vial of coke Bruce slipped into his pocket at Monday's binge. "Sometimes I think you're the only one I can talk to and I don't want to lose you, OK?"

Feeling thrilled by this revelation and taking on a phony, mature tone, "Certainly, Daniel. We'll always be friends." She pats his knee, assuming her take on a therapist's comforting role. *What fun I'm having* makes her tremble with excitement.

Daniel again? At least I think I'm safe for now, Dan concludes. "Catch you later. Got to go," one second before. . . .

Over the loudspeaker, "Mr. Daniel Topler, please report to Nurse Linda. I repeat. Daniel Topler, please report to Nurse Linda for your morning urinalysis."

Calling behind him, "I know you've got to go," Ally giggles. "They make you pee three times a day into a bottle, don't they?" she says practically falling off the chaise lounge with glee.

Vexed at the intrusion, Dan remembers Bruce's dad has a Beretta at home in his library. Showed it to me once. I have an alibi. I'm already in a nuthouse so. . . . mumbles Dan to himself as he pokes along on his way to Nurse Linda to prove himself on the path to rehabilitation.

"Goodie, My Favorite,"

exclaims Dan clapping his hands together in a rather lame imitation of a circus pinhead.

Although forewarned of tomfoolery for this daily session, Bernstein decides, I'm going to plow ahead with my standard Rorschach test with this over-the-edge comedian.

"Tell me the first thing that comes to mind, Daniel."

"Sex."

"No. I mean after I show you the ink blot."

"It won't change. It'll still be sex."

"Listen to me, if you can. I'm trying to help you, and you're intelligent enough to know you need it or wouldn't be here in the first place."

"All right. OK. I'll try to be good."

Bernstein first takes out a red, orange, and white multi-colored card. Although the inkblots theoretically shouldn't represent any particular object – it's the patient's interpretations of the images that count – in Bernstein's experience, sooner or later this particular flower-shaped blot evokes a vagina response from most men.

"Well?"

"Which part of the picture do you want me to X-ray?"

"What difference do you thinks it makes?"

"Observing the projection of my personality onto the pictures is the point of the test, is it not?" inquires Dan.

"Yes, that's correct. I see you've done some reading on the subject."

"Well then. Are you interested in the anal part of my personality that deals with just a small portion of the inkblot? Maybe I should focus on the human forms of the upper half or perhaps the terrifying savage forms on the lower half. That's supposed to tell us if I'm alienated."

Tiring of the sitting-down stand-up routine he's hearing, "Just tell me what the whole picture says to you, would you please?"

"A porcupine."

"At last some cooperation. And what is the porcupine doing, Daniel?"

"It's playing with its vagina."

Thereby ending this day's session with Dr. Bernstein.

"Live Your Narrative,"

Professor Elmer Blodgett exhorts *ad nauseam* to Laura, the Graduate English department catechumen and doctoral candidate at Princeton under his worthy wings. "Write what you know" describes the same advice she was taught in undergrad composition. Laura has begun to take the counsel to heart. While one of the up-and-coming stars in the department, she believes her sheltered life – living at home and still technically a virgin – prevents her blossoming into a full-fledged literary lioness.

Deep in her inexperienced psyche, Laura has come to a fundamental crossroads – she must begin to live, with a capital L. On the way home with his daughter, Jacob Bernstein at first bravely resists attempts by Laura to get the skinny on Dan. He tries to maintain the professional confidence of privacy concerning Daniel, with the same result any father would have with his darling, loving, and unimaginably persistent baby girl. He fails utterly, and completely spills the beans on Dan.

He informs her that the arrogant and brilliant Daniel has suffered from a directionless and drug-addicted life. He's become suicidal. Jacob has carefully raised his stable and thoughtful daughter since his wife's death ten years ago. Now that she knows about the young man, it's inconceivable to him that she could have interest in hearing from his troubled patient – ever.

"You're absolutely right, dad. Not my type. I won't speak to him again," she reassures daddykins. Laura's attracted to Dan's wit and has a strong physical attraction for him. But she's also inflamed to think he's the possible link to the more thrilling life she seeks. Her thoughts, What universe does dad live in? and, How can I get my number to Dan? fill the time on their way home from the temple. The latter question now occupies her mind most of her next day, too, as she slaves over her thesis:

Deranged U.S. Presidents – A New Theme Trend
For Twenty-First-Century Short Stories?

Then a call from Charlotte, "We're still on for Brucie's shindig this Saturday aren't we, Laura?"

"Wouldn't miss it." Charlie's invitation to go to a lascivious party of spoiled socialites is just what the doctor – though definitely not her father – ordered. And she needs to take her mind off Dan.

"I also want you to meet my next sex slave if he can manage not to puke all over us."

"Who's your latest conquest?" Laura relishes that Charlie's personal and professional life is diametrically opposite hers. It only enhances their close friendship. To Charlotte's amusement, more than once her sexcapades appeared only with name changes in Laura's stories. But now Laura seeks to shed her inhibitions and create material for a spicy memoir instead of ersatz literary journalism.

"They call him The Dandy Man, and he is."

"He upchucked on you?"

"Must have been a stomach virus or something. They had to call an ambulance. And just when we were *in flagrante delicto,* I might embellish." Charlie has no idea Dan's in rehab. Bruce didn't tell her. Though they don't hesitate to jibe The Dandy Man to his face about his frequent sojourns to LFOD, the prep school fraternity brothers maintain their childhood pact to keep secrets that concern each other.

"You lawyers have a Latin word for everything, Charlie. Are you serious? You were in bed together when he got sick?"

"You know that cute Galliano pink dress?"

"Not that one?!"

"I should make the dickhead pay for it. And speaking of dicks, he's definitely got the goods and a slim, trim bod the way I like it."

"Wait a sec, I need to take some notes for my next *roman à clef*. What's his name?"

"Later, Laura, got to take this call. Pick me up at 10 PM on Saturday.

Tout à l'heure, dearie."

Laura's thoughts return to Dan, whose appeal magnifies every minute. Maybe I should pay an unexpected call on dad at LFOD just to say hello, suggests itself.

Laura writes in the full-sized white pad she uses for future story notes:

"Seeing the impoverished, handsome, and needing-a-caring-woman John at the mental clinic by coincidence would just be an act of mercy. He practically begged for her telephone number."

She nearly forgets to substitute "John" for "Daniel" and will take care of the syntax later. She'll "accidentally" run into him on Saturday and can share the adventure with Charlotte that night at the party.

Humiliated and Depressed

without the help of drugs or champagne, Dan tells himself, I can't go on this way. He's had criticism from judges, psychologists, and the police before, but in his entire dissolute life he has never suffered the sting of rejection from someone he respects. It's Friday afternoon and Dan's still reflecting on Bernstein's treatment of him Wednesday night.

Despite his smart-aleck demeanor, he admires the doctor. He can't shake off the recurring thought that this man considers him unworthy of his daughter. That cute stuff. Laura. Hardly had a chance to talk to her. Beautiful. Sweet. Got to be smart if she's Bernstein's kid. I bet Laura loves movies. Maybe I should try graduate school. Get a job. Bernstein would beg me to date his precious little girl, Dan fantacizes. Stay away from my prep school playmates. Somehow even with an occasional white line in their nostrils or a drunken binge they've managed careers.

Dan knows if he goes to Brucie's again he'll melt under the lure of the champagne and cocaine, a rush that lifts him up beyond the solar system and then casts him over a void into an exploding nebula. Just the thought of it makes his mouth dry with anticipation. And there's Charlotte – Bruce says she's waiting for me. He's met many temptresses and ravished all of them with an equal dose of suavity and dispatch. But Charlie. She must have been born in a different galaxy, he broods. While his education, prep school, and family wealth pushed Danny into his current orbit, Charlotte has the intensity and power of a different species altogether. As soon as they met, Danny sensed she's a warrior sex goddess.

I hope to Christ she's there Saturday, now captivates his tired mind. Whether or not he takes the little tiny red pills that will make him violently sick if he imbibes or takes drugs, he knows Charlie will pour death down his willing gullet again if she gets the chance. The fleeting thought of a career and normal life speeds away to Alpha Centauri. The cacophony: Charlotte – cocaine – Laura – champagne – march in an endless parade echoing throughout his cerebellum. At least the disgrace of Bernstein's repudiation has receded.

Still, not even with his depression, and maybe because of it, does Daniel lose his grip on his savoir-faire. He met Lars for the first time only moments earlier and now banters with Nurse Linda as he hands her a urine sample. "Did you catch that guy outside going berserk on me? They have some real psychos here, don't they?" Her look-who's-talking stare back at him gives him the reaction he hoped for and provides him with a well-needed laugh.

In Linda's windowless office he can taste the pungent smell of medicine on his tongue – and he hungers for it, as might any junkie. Dan checks in at the gym for his treadmill routine: 10,000 paces at a 12-minute-per-mile clip, and then push-ups and calisthenics – part of the rehab. Dan knows Bernstein would keep his word and tie him up again like a doggie at a rodeo if he blows off the prescribed regimen – death sounds better. Anyhow, though he's feeling down, the exercise works its own curative. Dan can feel the physical strength of his college years returning, and he's gained a pound or two. Then shower and off for the pool area where he knows at least one real friend waits for him – spectacles and all.

The Alarm Rings

loud and clear noon Saturday when the female competitor enters her turf. Her feminine instincts have matured beyond her juvenile emotions. Maybe the smell of a new perfume in the air set her sixth sense in motion. Ally knows before Daniel has a clue that a she-wolf hunts for him on the LFOD grounds and that she, Alicia, must protect the lair.

Laura approaches a young girl at the pool and inquires about Dan's whereabouts.

"Daniel left for the South Pole," she tells Laura.

"The South Pole? What's he doing there?"

Danny told Ally just yesterday the funny police chase story about his lasting gratitude to Helen for saving him. But this ugly blond woman with huge knockers – why does this type always follow her boyfriend around? she wants to know – poses a much bigger threat for her Daniel than the police would. When the monster asks Ally if she knows Dan – it hurts to hear another woman say his name – and which cabaña is his, Ally sees the woman's eyes grow just this much wider and brighter. Ally knows this old lady means trouble. "The peace corn. He joined the peace corn." Man, she looks like a school teacher or somethin, Ally says to herself to stay calm. Nobody can be interested in one of them. Now the situation grows graver. This grandma laughs at her.

"Peace corn? You're really funny. What's your name?"

The defender of the LFOD territory sees what's coming next – Dan's coming. Now the ancient female ogre – who does have MTV-sized thingies – catches his eye and she smiles real big.

"Hey, Laura. What are you doing here?"

The end of the world has come for Ally. Daniel appears from nowhere just as I might have had this booger on the run. And he knows her! I might as well be invisible. He never looks at me like that. Ally's on the verge of tears.

"Thought I'd stop and say hello to my father. Haven't done that in a while." Not bad with his shirt off. I should have brought my swimsuit, too, Laura muses. Dan's exercise program and tan make him glow, regardless of his confusion. I can't let this catch get away, she thinks.

Dan and Laura explore each other's faces and acknowledge the excuse they both know is a lie.

Ally can't quite read their expressions, but not for a lack of trying. "Oh, yeah? Then why were you asking for Daniel? She's a liar. Tell her to go away! We don't like liars here, do we Daniel? Remember what we said?"

The urgency and the danger to Ally can't be clearer to Dan. "Have you met Ally, Laura? She's a <u>very</u> good friend of mine here," and puts his hand meaningfully on Ally's shoulder.

Laura sees Dan's worried expression and the tears forming in Ally's eyes. "We've met. Well, glad to see you, Dan. I've got to be going. Just want to say hi to dad and then I must leave. Nice to meet you, Ally. Maybe we can be friends, too." Laura takes comfort in the triumph on Ally's face and knows she did the right thing. She turns and slowly walks away.

Ally's right eyebrow rises in involuntary skepticism of the truce offer. She puts on a fake smile for Dan, blinks back the tears, takes a deep breath, and watches Laura disappear to be certain the enemy has retreated. Ally also notes that Dan has closely followed the sway of Laura's rear in leaving. *I can walk like that, too. Just need practice,* and unconsciously wiggles her behind. She knows she must watch her Daniel more carefully now.

As for Dan, the thought, I'm going to lose my mind, makes him shiver in the bright June sun.

The Red Pills
on the Counter

whisper to Danny every night before he goes to sleep – take me or die. The Dandy Man keeps a secret stash for himself. Doc wouldn't budge again on the rules for this lozenge. Nurse Linda must witness that he take the little red watch guard. But he's been through the drill often enough to know how to hide them under his tongue while he's watched. If he's desperate for a drink, he won't let this nuthouse kill him – he doesn't need the tablets' help. So far he's listened to their siren call and taken one every day since his latest trip to LFOD. Without their wails of warning he already would have found a way to quench the thirst for coke and liquor.

Bernstein's threat of hospital incarceration for noncompliance looms over him as well. Dan's carefully watched by Linda when he gives his urine sample. No chance to switch vials in the loo. That Valkyrie practicality strip-searches me before I go in. Missing the opportunity to commune with Laura poolside has dampened his mood into hopelessness. Tonight's Brucie's weekly Saturnalia celebration. The Dandy Man knows he hasn't a vodka-on-the-rocks chance in Hades to abstain in the midst of the licentious East Hampton pagans.

On his way out of the cabaña, headed for the bash, Dan considers that either way he's a goner. If he doesn't take the pill he will either jump off Bruce's roof or get locked up by the good doctor. And if he takes it, the physical pain will make him wish he were dead. Do I deserve the pain? In it goes. Sinking deep into his gut, the red demon spreads through the stomach lining into his veins and waits to do its job. Danny sneaks out into the night toward the beach again – but this time he doesn't go unnoticed.

A Gothic Bacchanal with Platinum Twin Concubines

fits the bill exactly, Brucie told Pirot – his talent booker – as he thinks of the unusual pimp and drug pusher. What a fabulous suggestion. Tiffin and Adelle arrived from Holland in the late afternoon. It cost the young host a pretty penny for Pirot to convince the Amsterdam owner to agree to cancel their immensely successful weekend show at the Blue Bell Nightclub on the Thorbeckeplein, famous for its revelry. Pirot knows Bruce has too much refinement – and too much dough – to inquire what his take is on the deal. Just the sort of client he tries to cultivate these days.

Contrary to what might guide common sense, Dandy Man's near fatal collapse *au naturel* last Saturday only enhanced Langford II's reputation as a delightfully depraved host. For the past week, dozens of neighbors, friends, and friends of friends have hounded him for tonight's invitation. Bruce won't let his public down – the lucky ones, that is. He tells security to open the gate to the partygoers starting at 10 PM. Unfortunately, Ronnie, the fourth member of the dissolute preppy confederacy, begged off. Too bad. Said he had a date, of all things, and wouldn't say with whom. How strange, Bruce thinks.

Bruce informed Pirot that The Dandy Man would likely surface from behind the shrubs again and had him train klieg lights on the likely bush. Dan arrives on schedule at midnight through the gooseberry boughs and faces the spotlight and applause of the already drunken assemblage with aplomb but a weary heart.

Maybe I've had enough of this nonsense, he thinks as Pirot leads him upstairs, followed by Brucie and the guests who can still walk to the mansion's largest bedroom.

Pirot throws open the door for all to see the room flamboyantly decked out just for tonight's festivities as a medieval torture chamber – chains and all. Danny, the willing puppet so far for tonight's amusement, balks however. Tiffin, one of the magnificently endowed silver-blond twins (triplets in truth, but the third sister found a sugar daddy) hangs naked – save for fishnet stockings and a gold lamé Harlequin mask – loosely tied by satin bindings to a puffy silken pillory. Adelle, somewhat more modestly adorned with only a transparent bra and lace panties, starts to undress Danny, who tries to pull away without making a spectacle of himself and seeming a spoilsport.

Bruce waves two oversized martini glasses – nothing but the "perfect" mix of Gordon's gin, equal parts of Noilly Prat dry *cum* sweet vermouth, and a dash of water for Brucie's invitees – in front of now shirtless Dan and braless Adelle. She caresses Dandy Man's chest with apparent real lust just as Bertrand the butler escorts two new guests though the padded bedroom door.

"Charlotte! Laura!" Brucie too warmly welcomes them with a phony oh-my-goodness-gracious in his voice. The Chipster takes a shine to the more demure blonde. Just his type. Maybe Brucie will introduce them. Laura grasps both the danger to Dan and an opportunity to write the first page of her memoir. She proceeds to heighten the risqué merriment with an impromptu burlesque of her own.

"Take Out the Trash,

honey, before you leave. It's pickup day," Dolores calls to Jon from the bedroom as he shaves, "and I need to ask a *wittle* favor from my big strong lawyer husband." With that cue, the Toplers' closest friends gird their verbal loins for the approaching domestic skirmish. Harriet's call to Dolores the day before has the bosom crony worried. She can't put off fulfilling the promise to help.

"What the hell's the matter with LaVerne? Got a broken leg?" He tries to change the subject, but he knows what's coming.

"She doesn't do trash. She's an inside maid," says Dolores coming into the "his" bathroom. She let him choose the colors for the tile and Kohler fixtures only in this one not-so-tiny corner of their 14,000-square-foot home. Brown, brown, brown, and brown. Men are so hopeless. Dolores avoids entering his sanctum sanctorum so that she won't have to endure the infantile color coordination of Jon's john (except when she enters to pinch the emery boards that he hides in his doppkit). But her best friend's dire situation demands a woman's persuasion.

"Do tell. Well, I'm an <u>outside</u> employer. If she doesn't like it, she can find another job outside of the Schwartz house."

Now's the time to mention her name. "We should be grateful to even have LaVerne work for us. Harriet keeps telling me how hard it is to keep help."

"Yeah? Well, it's no Goddamn wonder. Ronnie calls me yesterday to say that he knows for a fact Harriet waits for the maid at the door and drags her to the marble foyer floor if she's late. Takes pictures of it, too. No kidding, Dolly."

It's hard to believe that a real company like Viacom would hire my little boy when he's such an idiot, Dolores thinks, but instead says, "It's wonderful to have an imagination like our Ronald." Changing the subject, "Jonnie," stroking his arm, "seriously, dear, do you have any ideas who Harriet might call for her own personal legal matters?"

Like all long-married couples, Jonathan and Dolores speak to each other in their own private code. Ignoring the signal flare, "Yeah, sure. Ben Friedman," as he sprays his under-arms with Right Guard – the Classic scent he's used since high school. "One of the best estate attorneys in the business. It's about time for them to plan what happens when she and Al wake up dead someday. The kids could get socked for mil-lions if they don't set up the bowling pins now." Stall for time before it hits the fan, Jon figures, as he dresses as fast as he can for a possible getaway. He takes a last glance at his thinning hair. Maybe I should get a transplant fleetingly worms into his precise legal mind.

No more lovey-dovey, "OK. So I'm stupid now. Giving me the business, huh? You know, and I know you know. Just look at your red nose. Whose side are you on? Certainly not that cheater's. I bet you hear all the dirty little details."

Dolores can get worked up in a hurry, but Jon can pull his pants on even faster. "OK. All right. I'll do it," he disingenu-ously agrees. A temporarily pleased Dolores foolishly steps away from blocking the bathroom door. "I will take out the trash," Jon yells to her as he runs down the stairs and out the door to freedom.

"You sure the hell better have," Dolores calls downstairs to the slammed front door. But he didn't.

"Maybe We Can Get A Twofer Price

from Bleeder's firm," Jon lamely jests. He's not laughing.

"You think so? He quoted me $750 per hour, wants a fifty grand retainer, and the big shot can't see me until next week," whines Albert. Like most truly wealthy men, Al doesn't care a whit about blowing ten thou at a casino, but wasting money on attorneys practically constitutes a sin worthy of an eleventh commandment prohibition.

"No, I don't think so. Movie stars use him, for crissakes. Raoul Bleeder and Associates is the best, Al. Protect yourself. And you've really put me in a difficult position, old golf partner. Dolores reads me like a book. She claims my nose grows longer and redder when I lie to her." Jonathan checks the mirror of his chocolate-brown Lexus with coffee-dyed leather interior on the way to his office to see if his schnoz has regained its normal size and complexion. "I'll be lucky if she talks to me for the next week. I didn't suggest an attorney for Harriet, but that won't stop her for long.

"What should I tell. . . ."

"Please, Al. Don't reveal anything about you and what's-her-face. Harriet will squeeze it out of me like a lemon into her boiling tea." Jon pulls into the midtown Manhattan garage and his assigned parking space (only for partners). "Talk to you later." Jon hangs up and remembers that he forgot to take out the trash, adding more tension to his morning. And a hangnail on his right-hand index finger bothers him. He couldn't find his emery boards. I'll bet that snoop LaVerne told Dolores where I hide them, he fumes, nearly spoiling the fun of escaping Dolores' crafty machinations for him this morning.

Jon didn't help him much. Idling humming the Whiffen-poof Song, Albert sits sadly in his comfortable but unpretentious Universal Recycling office surrounded by family pictures. He carefully considers his next move. Should he call her? Jon said not to and he hasn't yet spoken to the divorce attorney. He hated moving his clothes out of his house. Everything had worked so well for so long. Why did it have to suddenly end? It's lonely at the club, and the lack of pampering at home or from Elaine elsewhere doesn't suit him at all. He's a homebody at heart and eating out, no matter how *haute* the cuisine, can't beat flank steak, iceberg lettuce salad with Thousand Island dressing, and a baked potato for the down-to-earth entrepreneur. Albert picks up the phone. "Darling?"

Elaine's innate self-control over her eating and exercise habits extends to her temperament as well. She'd like to say, "Where the hell have you been for the past three days?" but demurs. "Darling, I've been so concerned about you. What's happened?" As if she didn't know.

After his long-winded explanation and pledge to call her every day no matter what some high-priced mouthpiece says, she lays out her plan. They'll meet tonight at the White Plains Marriott in Westchester County across the Whitestone Bridge, where neither of them knows many people – definitely not in Manhattan. Elaine knows she's taking a risk and that Jon's admonition to Al not to see her sounds prudent. But a whopping, newly available fish-out-of-water like lonely Albert with gold-digger female sharks all around needs her protection. She's got a crucial investment to safeguard, and investors have to take risks now and then. She also makes a conscious decision not to tell Al the conversation she overheard between his

Coco and some salivating twenty-something boy at the motel. She might need that info for herself sometime when it could come in handy. Elaine left not long after they arrived and doesn't know the young man's name but feels it safe to assume it isn't "Deeper, Deeper," the words Coco screamed at the top of her lungs in the adjacent room.

"I Don't Need
This Just Now,"

Jacob Bernstein says to himself as he stares out his LFOD office window. Tears come to his eyes as he watches his daughter pull out of the parking lot. There's only one reason why she came here and didn't see me. He sits down. The surgery will be in a few weeks. The pain from his tumors has been growing worse, and now other quandaries grip him. Laura has no mother. If I die and she takes up with that troubled boy, then what? I can't threaten or bring up the subject. She'll assume I'm spying on her. She's never been around an alcohol and drug addict like him. At least I don't think so. No. No.

I know she hasn't. He should be incarcerated. Locked up somewhere else. No. That's not best for him. Perhaps they'll talk to me about it. Come to me for consultation. Why not? They should. I'm her father and his doctor.

Jacob's drenched with perspiration and doesn't have another patient for an hour. He lies down on the couch usually reserved for clients and falls into a troubled sleep. When he awakens, the nap has provided no respite from his fears.

"No Half-Dead Lady
Will Steal My Boyfriend

if I've got anything to say about it," Ally sleepily jabbers aloud to herself. But jeez if the mosquitoes don't bite like all get out. Why don't they spray or somethin' around here?

Ally's nightly vigil hiding in the bushes outside Daniel's cabaña so far has kept her reassured he's not cheating on her with another girlfriend. If she sees Laura again with him she's prepared to scratch that she-devil's eyes out – at least that's what she heard she's supposed to do from her friend Suzie who ought to know since she's eight months older.

"What have we here, precious?" wakes Ally whose thin legs stick out from under the shrubbery in the moonlight. Since last week when Helen found Dan's bed empty and luckily called an ambulance for him, she does a little night checking herself to make sure he's there. It's nearly midnight and she knows this hour on Saturdays lures Dan from his warren as lemmings are drawn to the sea – and with much the same result.

"My doctor said it was OK to sleep here, Helen. Please let me stay."

"Your doctor said no such thing, young lady, and you know it. Take my hand and I'll walk you to your room." The two leave without the distracted Helen checking Danny's now-empty bed. This time the emergency response team won't save him.

Off Comes Her Blouse,

shocking Dan, Bruce, and Charlie, but not the other crocked guests who assume Laura's part of the performance. Chipster's so taken with Laura, the reticent twenty-six-year-old who normally won't try to kiss a girl before the third date fantasizes he's Dan and takes off his own shirt. The attar-of-roses scent permeating the candle-lit room augments the crowd's gaiety. The surprise addition to the Dutch twins' performance takes the two filled-to-the-brim humongous goblets of perfect martinis from Bruce's hand, downs one herself in a gulp, vigorously rubs her breasts against Dan's shirtless chest while giving him a long-tongued French kiss that could be seen from a spy satellite, then throws the other glass all over the front of his pants, drenching him.

"Jesus Christ! What did you do that for, Laura?" The Dandy Man protests.

"Catch a ride home, Charlie," Laura tells her stupefied Stanford friend as she drags Danny by his belt out of the room.

Brucie can't be more pleased with himself as he delights in Charlotte's lost expression. Pirot, on the other hand, worries that Langford might have found another society pimp to replace him.

"That Was a Close Call,"

Dan whispers to Laura as he kisses her ear while they tiptoe to his room. They spent the last hour petting in her car, parked in a secluded sector of the LFOD lot. Both instantly grasp the precarious circumstances as they watch Helen lead Ally away from the front of Dan's cabaña. Neither wants to be separated again just now.

"She really likes you, Dan."

"I know. It scares me. Shall we go into my chamber of doom to discuss it? And by the way, did I thank you for saving my life? Your dad says the little bitty red ones can sometimes be fatal with alcohol."

"It cost me my favorite blouse," the still tipsy writer responds.

"And now your bra and undies, I fear," as Dan opens his lockless door.

"Is It OK to See Sonny Boy

now, Doctor?" asks Albert bright and early the next morning. Al's feeling rested and calm after his drive back from the Marriott. Elaine couldn't have been a better tonic for him. Have to see how number-one son's getting along, he thinks while he sings, "Bulldog, bulldog bow wow wow," on his way to LFOD. When he arrives, he peeks into Dr. Bernstein's office and is pleasantly surprised to see him already at work.

"He's making much better progress than I hoped for, Mr. Topler," not truly hiding the irony in his response as he leads Albert to the door of his Danny Boy's plush cabana.

"I see what you mean, Doctor," grinning broadly at the sight of his naked son lying asleep next to an equally unclad, very cute what Al-assumes-to-be a because-she-has-what-looks-like-naturally-blonde-hair *shiksa*. "Is this part of the treatment?" Albert asks Bernstein altogether in earnest. *Who knows what these shrinks do nowadays.*

"No, it's <u>not</u> part of the treatment," Bernstein says startling the sleeping couple awake before dragging Topler outside. The sight of his daughter lying nude with Daniel made him nauseous and near tears. He collapses onto a bench outside. "That's my daughter."

Albert senses the discord and vexation in the doctor and wisely voices a solitary correct word for the tense situation, "Oh."

Inside the room, Laura takes one of Dan's jerseys from the closet, dresses without looking at her lover, and leaves without a word. By the time she's out the door, both Albert and her dad have left.

"John and Margaret didn't know whether to laugh or cry when they were caught by their parents in their torrid, forbidden liaison. She slowly left his desolate garret room without a turning back, knowing she could never see her impoverished demigod again," the hopeful author writes in the white pad she never fails to carry with her.

Should I Go?

Dan asked himself a hundred times today as he lounges by the pool Sunday chitchatting with Ally. Bernstein didn't say not to. I have every right to date, if that's what you can call it, any girl I want. If I don't go, then I'm admitting I did something wrong. He did tell me not to call her. But I didn't call her. She grabbed me. Maybe he'll think I think that I can get away with not going to the meeting tonight since I slept with his daughter. But if I don't go he can use my not attending to get even with me and put me back into a straitjacket. I'd better go, he continues to agree with himself on the drive to Temple B'Nai Israel.

Now he massages the appropriate greeting to Dr. Bernstein. Hiya doc? Way too familiar. Good evening, Dr. Bernstein? Stilted, and the group might wonder why the formality. I'll try to get away with just nodding, Dan finally concludes as he pokes his head into the temple library. The gang's already here, seated and schmoozing around the circle in the middle of the room.

"Hi, Daniel, glad you could make it. Have a cup of coffee if you want to and join us," Jack says.

What a pro. Bernstein practically gave up the ghost when he saw me this morning and now I'm his med school disciple again, Dan reflects. "What's up, guys? Nice to see you all," Dan struggles to say pleasantly, leaning on his childhood training to be a nice, well-mannered boy. Even in his own West Village co-op, Dan still puts the toilet seat down in case a lady should need to use it. Some good habits die hard, too.

"Good," Jack says. "Let's begin the meeting. I thought that perhaps we would discuss depression tonight. Some of us, I'm sure, have suffered through it, and maybe by sharing our experiences we could all learn to cope if it's a problem now or perplexes us in the future."

Silence, and a stiffening in the room. Then finally. . . .

"Well, sure. We've all experienced it, haven't we, men?" Harry says, searching around and getting nods from all but Sam, whose stony expression says no comment.

"When I first got out of college I was laid off from the accounting firm and couldn't get a job for months. I felt like a failure. Here I was an honor student in the NYU business school and I'm unemployed. I was already married, and Frances was pregnant with Marc, our first one. I didn't know what to do. Stayed in my room and didn't talk to her for days at a time."

"I had to start taking Zoloft just two years ago," interjects Rob. The group members now lean back in their chairs, feeling comfortable speaking frankly with men they trust. Dan leans forward, engrossed in their confessions. "I don't know why I was so depressed. I couldn't work and started making mistakes in my trades. Wrong symbols, and buy instead of sell. The other guys in the trading room started looking at me funny when the operations head caught obvious mistakes and called them to my attention in front of my desk partner. I feel much better now."

David jumps in. "I guess I'm just lucky. I've never really felt that down, but I know my wife has from time to time. It's a good thing I still have a couple of publicity clients left. It keeps me sane. I couldn't do like some of you and have every day completely free without any schedule. My weekly bridge game helps, too."

"Yes, I know what you mean, David," Jack says in a faint voice. "My consulting at a rehab clinic and the one medical school class I still teach at Stony Brook helps me to contain the fear I have over my coming surgery."

"Who's going to lead the discussions while you're . . . uh . . . recuperating, Jack?" Barry tentatively asks.

"Daniel has volunteered, if you all don't mind."

"That's great, Daniel." Barry shakes his hand. "It will be good to keep some young blood in the meetings." The group smiles in approval.

"You know, when we first started New Beginnings ten years ago, the wives joined us," volunteers Morty.

"Has it been ten years already? Barry asks. "I was just a fifty-year-old kid then."

Now the normally aloof Glen. "But their issues weren't the same as ours."

"So we threw them out," Morty says, completing the thought.

"Now he'll really give up on geriatrics, huh, fellas?" Harry says to chuckles from the others.

I've been had again, rattles inside Dan. "Thanks for the totally undeserved vote of confidence, men," he tells them. Never at a loss for words, at least.

The rest of the conversation eases away from life's real difficulties to the latest French film – Dan never considered that men their age had ever seen a foreign film – and the new Asian exhibit at the Met in the city. Jack concludes, "If there's no other business, let's break until the Wednesday meeting, fellows."

"I've had depression," Sam gloomily erupts out of nowhere just as some stand to leave – his first comments to the group since Dan joined. "I want to kill myself. I would if I knew it wouldn't hurt my family so much. Just step in front of a car or something. There's no point in continuing. I just want it to end."

For a few seconds Jack doesn't know how to respond. The time is up, and these meetings technically aren't therapy sessions. The men retake their seats.

Dan takes the lead. "Thanks for sharing that, Sam. Is the operation on your leg getting you down?"

"I can't walk without this cane now," holding up the object of contempt. "And I'm bored. Bored to death. I don't do anything all day except watch TV."

Jack surveys the faces and sees that despite the compassion the others have, it's nearly 9 PM and the gang is restless. Time to go. "Can we talk about it the first thing next time, Sam? Would that be all right?"

"Sure. Why not?" Sam says, casting his gaze down away from his friends' faces.

This time Dan takes his time leaving the temple. When he gets to the parking lot, the slam of Bernstein's passenger car door reverbs in Danny's head. Laura sadly turns her head away from her lover with what he perceives as a final goodbye and drives off. Daniel Topler knows now what he must do.

This Funeral Seems Even More Somber Than Usual,

divines the Very Reverend Francis X. Pilatus as he completes the eulogy. The clouds have blackened the skies in the gray overcast afternoon and now lightning strikes make the crowd want to run for cover. *I don't much like Monday wakes anyhow. I could have begged off. A prior meeting with the church council.*

He delivered his best performance the day before in his sermon at the renowned Riverhead Episcopal Church. But, today, he can't whip up any enthusiasm to deep-six this near-stranger. Offering memorial prayers at the burial of a man he hardly knows no longer has appeal at this point in the career of the distinguished cleric. *I wouldn't have agreed to perform the service except for the colossal donation his daughter handed me yesterday. What a piece of work she is. She specifically tells me not to mention Jesus or say "in the name of the Father, and of the Son, and of the Holy Ghost." And she put a coin in the corpse's mouth. This could be my first pagan service,* he tells himself, nearly laughing out loud while watching a long line of he-has-no-clue-who sprinkle dirt on the lowered bronze casket.

Most of the sizable crowd want the ordeal over with. A monster, black-anvil, cumulonimbus cloud crackling with thunder hovers directly over the head of the deceased man's daughter. Dressed in a diaphanous white tunic, she stands elevated on a grassy and flowered hill next to her father's resting place. Her ethereal yet powerful appearance dominates the assemblage and makes the word *awesome* mean what it says.

To her right and slightly below, Laura Bernstein stands holding her hand. The assembled scores of G.F. Davison's relatives and business associates certainly do feel solemn – but for a dissimilar reason. To be sure, some openly sob as the final spade of black, fertile soil on the sarcophagus tops the mound, since it signifies no hope forever of inclusion in G.F.'s sizable will. The fountainhead of their grief looms above them – the witch lives – and, from the aura of her vitality, maybe forever.

Seven Goldman Sachs bankers stand in a row, identically nattily dressed at this obligatory business – for them – convocation. Even the singular woman wears a dark blue suit with a Windsor-knotted red-and-black-striped power tie. They stare with wonder at the formidable offspring. The corporate playmakers struggle to hide the intimidation they feel at her presence. The worldwide head of the structured finance department himself came to offer condolences, note the underlings.

All for a good reason – good old G.F. kicked the bucket before signing the merger documents with Aramark. Now they need the approval of a warrior deity who, by the way, doubles as a dreaded divorce attorney, to earn an over one-hundred-million-dollar investment banking fee. They feel certain that heaven will not forgive G.F. for this transgression against their nearly-as-mighty firm.

Reverend Pilatus concludes the burial with "May God. . . ." Hesitation for a second. I can say <u>His</u> name, can't I? ". . . rest his soul, and let us all leave now with hope for the forever after." The reverend's own spirits brighten with the thought, I also pray Peggy has that egg salad sandwich with pickle and curry the way I like it ready when I get home. Then he scuttles off before he has to make small talk. The Very Reverend's hungry.

"You must be Zoë, my dear," startles Charlotte. No one but Charlie's dad used her middle name.

The stranger, something of a giant teddy bear, approaches and takes her hand. He's a bit overweight perhaps, but his handsome, chiseled features and powerful physique remind her of the statue of Zeus in her father's home on Central Park South. He warmly smiles in a way that only an older man can that tells a woman he's sincere and not making a pass. The heavyset man's well-made, but disheveled, clothes hint at his academic career.

"Ganymede and I were great friends. I hope now that he's gone you will give us your permission to acknowledge your father's generous anonymous contributions to the university's Classics Department over the years. Columbia University, that is."

The multiple revelations catch the normally prescient heiress by surprise. How is it she never knew what her father's first initial stood for? He always laughed off the question. Dad loved to read over and over Thomas Bulfinch and Edith Hamilton's mythology books, but not once did he mention gifts to the study of the subject or bring up this man. A man who, although he doesn't resemble her father whatsoever, somehow reminds her of him. "You are?" Nevertheless, she maintains some caution.

"Please forgive me, I'm Professor Blackmun, semi-retired professor of Greek and Roman history. Your father would be so happy to know that you're dressed as you are, Zoë. In the ancient Greek tradition of white – celebrating the immortality of the spirit. Not in black – mourning a passed soul." Stepping back to take her in, "He often told me over a glass of wine that his daughter is beautiful, but I had no idea how understated his words were. I should have guessed as much from the mouth of a man named for the most handsome among mortals and cup bearer to the gods."

Charlotte can't remember how long it has been since a compliment pleased her. Flattery arouses her fierce and combative instincts. But these words aren't blandishments – they're the reflected thoughts of the only man she ever loved. And he's dead. But this strangely appealing man isn't. "Perhaps, we could. . . ." she begins.

"I'm sorry to interrupt, but I have a meeting downtown and I just want to say before I go. . . ." the worldwide head of structured finance starts to say as he grasps her arm. But Zoë takes back her limb and turns, her cheeks flushed with anger, to sternly face him. She appears to physically grow in stature as he stumbles back, nearly wetting himself. Her ice-violet eyes mirror into his a lightning bolt from the ominous cloud looming above them and a fear he had never known in his life grips his heart. "Another time, Miss Davison. Another time," and Davian Corbeille, more accustomed to inspiring terror than experiencing it himself, practically runs away amidst the roar of the resulting thunderclap.

"You were saying, my dear?" asks the gentlemanly professor, sublimely oblivious to the fright of the fleeing man.

Turning back to Blackmun, the hole in his brown jacket – no doubt from his favorite meerschaum pipe – makes Charlie giggle. The red ire in her cheeks turns to a girlish pink. "Perhaps, we could get together at your office or dinner to discuss how I could continue dad's love of antiquity."

"But, of course, Zoë. How sweet you are to consider it. And who is this charming friend of yours, may I ask? Do I know you?" he says turning to Laura, who thoroughly enjoyed witnessing the financial world leader scramble before her best friend.

This familiar-looking prof has won her over, too. "I'm Laura, Professor."

A gleam comes into his eyes. "You know, seeing you two marvels together, with glorious blonde and dark hair, reminds me of the myths of the conflict between fire and ice." Realizing the possible gaffe of comparing the young women to rivals, "But this is not the time for such tales." More thunder, and a light rain starts to fall. "When shall we meet again, Zoë, in thunder, lightning, or in rain?" Blackmun's Macbeth allusion makes all three laugh despite its impropriety at a funeral.

"Why don't I pick you up at your office Wednesday at noon and we'll have lunch."

"Splendid. You can find my disheveled college haunt on the college web site, I'm told," and he ambles away sprightly muttering about the Viking tale of the fall of Ymir and Surtr begetting the birth of the world. Charlie follows his departure with wonder, as if he were an apparition.

"Thanks so much for coming, Laura. It meant a lot to me to have a real friend here."

"It seems that you have two now, Charlie. Or is it Zoë?"

"Charlie. Zoë was the pet name my father used for me."

"The professor called you Zoë."

Thoughtfully, "Yes. He may if he wants to." Attention back to Laura, "Why don't we have dinner some night to catch up?"

"Can we make it Wednesday? I have to pick up dad that evening since he can't drive at night anymore," a true enough excuse. But though she's made a promise to herself not to betray her father's wishes again, Laura wants at least to see Daniel.

"Wednesday it is. I need to find out what you did to my latest conquest, the one you stole from me Saturday night – and how he knew your name. I don't give up my trophies to just anyone. Please don't bother to walk me to my car. I'm going to stay here for a few minutes."

It just now strikes Laura who The Dandy Man is that Charlie referred to days before. "I'll call you," and she leaves Charlotte standing silently alone next to the grave of her father as the wind picks up.

The sad woman considers the loss of the only man who ever cared for her. She has extraordinary energy and an uncanny ability to dominate most people. But, except for her friend Laura, she feels alone and vulnerable as she never has before. Her thoughts turn to the commanding presence of Professor Blackmun. The first man other than her father to treat her as just an attractive young woman – not some imposing freak of nature. Someone who could show her a normal man's affection. Perhaps as an ordinary woman's lover. The rain continues to fall, but somehow not on Charlotte Zoë Davison. As if it didn't dare.

"Is That Two-Timer Still Seeing Her?"

Dolores asks with just the right amount of compassionate indignation required by the best friend of an injured woman. Still, she knows better than to come down too hard on Albert Topler. Harriet wouldn't be her first friend to reconcile with her husband, and she could find herself and Jon dining with both of them again at the club. Rain, thunder, and lightning or not, they're meeting at their favorite luncheonette on Long Island's North Shore this Monday to avoid the chance of being overheard by either one's maid.

"Sugarbush hasn't caught them yet. They're too clever," Harriet replies.

"Sugarbush? You've kept that incompetent bloodhound? I thought you fired him, dearie," as Dolores squeezes the last drop of lemon into her scalding tea with an Olympic-wrestler ferocity.

"They're all incompetent. I told him he's not getting paid anything until I get results."

"I hope that strategy pays off. I'm so sorry about Jonathan. Men are thick as slimy thieves."

"Don't worry yourself, Dolores. I called Albert's bookkeeper and said I was asking for a friend. The dummy recommended what he heard was the best divorce firm in New York City. Maybe anywhere. I'm seeing a senior partner Wednesday."

"How's Danny?"

"He's just fine as always," Harriet says lightly, not having the slightest clue of the truth about her son. Trying to seize her server's attention, "Waiter, I asked for no butter on my toast." Pedro keeps walking past the tea room's frequent and infamously low tipper, nevertheless. My eye not so easy to catch, he sniffs.

"He is? I heard he was arrested after he attempted suicide again and was committed under court order to Live Free or Die."

"Oh that. Just more of his childish foolishness. I wish he would grow up already. He's making quite a nuisance of himself and here I, his mother, have real problems to contend with."

"Hmm," not quite buying the offhand explanation. "And do you really believe Coco betrayed you?"

"I don't know what to think. I haven't seen her since I told her to go out for a drive with your Ronnie last week. Came in while I was out, got some of her clothes and makeup, and left a message on the answering machine saying she's finally going to get her own apartment."

"Strange. I haven't heard from Ronnie either in a few days." The two women look up at each other waiting for the other to say something. Neither wants to commit to expressing the same possibility on their minds. Moving on, "But I'll hear from him. I'm so glad that when we set up a fund for Ronnie, we kept ourselves as trustees until he's forty. It keeps the return phone calls coming."

"I'm furious at Albert and our estate attorney. Al and I still haven't gotten around to a will. But, no, that can go on unattended to. Years ago they agreed that we must endow a trust for the children and let them have control at twenty-one." Nearly crying, "Now they're both independent big shots and I can never get a straight answer from either of them."

Dolores sympathetically takes Harriet's hand. "Children are so selfish."

"Just Awful News,

my dear Harriet," consoles Dr. Florenz Castillia, chairman of the Art Department at Columbia University. "I'm terribly sorry that it's come to this between you and Albert." And he means it, too. His loaded patron just informed him of her intent to finally dispose of her cheating husband.

"Very confidential. I'm sure you'll keep this *entre nous*. And perhaps we shouldn't take that trip to India until after the divorce. But then, Florenz, perhaps we could spend <u>much</u> more time together," intimating more than she said and more than the professor wants to hear. He's the second confidant to know her plans after Harriet earlier spilled the beans to her best friend, Dolores.

"Damn it," he says to Billy, a 27-year-old art department grad student lying next to him.

"What's up, Professor?"

Ignoring Billy, Florenz jumps out of bed wearing only his zebra-skin jock strap and speaks to the classic *Faun in Repose* male nude statue as he hangs up. Gazing at the statue's privates as if posing the question to them, Could there have been some *sous-entendu* intended when she said "keep this between us"? No. Of course not. Not like Harriet to be witty – or even subtle for that matter. Christ! I'm getting so paranoid around her.

"Any trouble with my getting an A in your course?" the young man nervously asks.

Florenz examines closely the paintings in the living room of his well-appointed lodgings just off Christopher Street in the

Village. He and Billy had just returned them to their rightful positions on the walls from the closet after Harriet's recent visit there. Nary a scratch on my beauties, he determines. What a pain in the butt for her to come here, he laughs at the unintended pun. I should have told her years ago. It's an open secret in the department after all.

The professor has enjoyed her company on many an excursion to exotic destinations where he's given impromptu discourses on the native art. That the Topler Foundation pays for these junkets more than makes up for the fact that, considering the long days and nights they have spent together, the time would have been far more enjoyable had she been of the right gender. Trouble between them was brewing anyway. Although Harriet Topler's quite the proper lady of good breeding, Florenz senses that the still attractive woman is becoming increasingly upset that he's never made a pass at her. More an insult to her feminine pride than an expression of lust for the slight, sixty-five-year-old man with thinning black hair.

By this time she should have guessed that my solo overnight shore expeditions weren't primitive artifact explorations. And I'm damned tired of hiding this favorite sculpture of mine and replacing my nude pictures with art that won't offend her when she visits my pad, the last word reflecting his sadly outdated sixties' flower-child vocab.

At this point he's a little indignant at her naiveté. In his opinion, an educated women of her social status should prefer a gay traveling companion who allows her to dally with a handsome stranger if she were beautiful or rich enough. And Harriet's both. They first met when she attended his lecture on Hindu art at the Metropolitan Museum of Art. He could tell she was swept away by his descriptions and the sight of the erotic imagery of the Hindu artifacts there. She nearly fainted from the longing thrill of seeing the 13th-century *Loving Couple* statue depicting a full-blown *maithuna* – a sexual union, as it's called in Sanskrit. Since then he can scarcely keep Harriet off the topic. It's always tantric sex this, tantric sex that with her. As if the sexual rites of generating transformative bodily fluids encapsulate the complex, rich spectrum of Indian art. No doubt a fallout of her failing marriage, Florenz concluded some time ago. Now he feels that a mention of his engaging in any alternative to heterosexual love might be terrifying for her.

Florenz lovingly fondles his favorite work of art in his chambers as he considers possible strategies with his patron. *Perhaps I should seize this opportunity to tell her the truth about me and the hopelessness of anything but a platonic relationship between us. Then we could go ahead with the trip to the Ganges we've been planning forever. We'll be free to explore substitute partners for the nights.* A pause in his thoughts, then facing reality. *No. Not Harriet. And she might yank future funding for the department chair she's promised. Maybe there's some other way to prevent the impending disaster of divorce.*

A somewhat sordid idea that makes the Art Department chairman simultaneously strangely recoil and gaily burble comes to him that June afternoon. He places a call to an odd fellow introduced to him just the other day at the Russian and Turkish Baths enterprise on East Tenth Street. Only in New York can you meet a man dressed in a threadbare tuxedo at such a place.

I Make More Stripping

by the hour than I will as an attorney, the svelte but well-stacked Karen Bladner thinks as she twirls naked and upside-down around the vertical dance pole at the Kit Kat Club along the West Side Highway. It's late afternoon, and for a Monday already unusually packed with hungry eyes. Her long auburn hair and sensational, albeit somewhat asymmetrical, body has guaranteed her another prosperous summer job while she completes her law degree at Harvard. After an ex-college boyfriend happened to spot her dancing at one of the few remaining clubs near Boston's former Combat Zone, she decided New York was a safer venue, career-wise.

The monotonous rhythmic music stops and the high school gymnast and varsity college squash player known professionally as Carrie Blade gracefully steps down from the small circular stage and begins working the crowd. Some girls slip on a waist-long gossamer blouse first, but it hurts tips she's discovered. She slithers between the closely packed tables, smiling at the naughty boys enjoying a night out on their expense accounts.

As Carrie approaches the customers, they cease to chug their watered-down mixed drinks. Face-to-face with their sexual fantasy on display, they're too embarrassed to leer directly at the normally hidden parts of a woman's body that interest them most, and gaze into her eyes instead. The suits in this upscale gentlemen's club who boisterously whistled at her a minute ago now meekly stuff fives, tens, and even a few twenties into her glittery, cubic zirconium-encrusted garter belt. She pulls the strap just a tad from her gam. The narrow gap gives the vein-bursting males a chance to place the bills between the fabric and her stunning leg and ever so slightly glance her perfect skin with their sweaty hands.

Karen smiles invitingly – she's thinking about the thirty-percent-off sale on designer Coach leather goods at Blooming-dale's tomorrow. This well-paying job permits her to indulge herself in her own mania – she's a confirmed bag-o-holic. Meanwhile, chills ripple through the Wall Street brokers and lawyers and their out-of-town clients at this forbidden touch. Two bull-necked bouncers – judging from their bulk, probably former wrestling pros – serve as shamuses. Their passive expressions and searching gaze serve as a warning to see-and-not-touch the tempting merchandise.

Not too shabby, Karen aka Carrie decides as she counts the performance take and returns to the spare, shared dressing room in the back of the club. She answers her ringing cell phone, "You want me to go to a castle in Florence next week?" The caller corrects her. He was saying the man's name. "He's a confessor? Oh, a professor." *Whew. What if I ran into one of my old parochial high school teachers by some bad luck?*

She writes down the time and address. Pirot's combination of a slight sibilant and foreign accent always makes it a little difficult for her to understand him. He's calling from a bois-terous party and she can scarcely understand him between the din of the bash and the ambient noise from the Kit Kat-ers out front. Consequently, one can hardly criticize her for think-ing she heard Pirot say, "Tie him up and just whip him," when Pirot in fact said, "Can't talk now. I'm tied up. Just kiss him."

Pirot introduced himself to her a few weeks ago at the club and since then has provided Karen with even more lucrative bookings on her days off. Mostly to tantalize business clients. All strictly watching, voyeurism with a little S&M thrown in for good measure. She was brought up as too much of a liberal to criticize others' peccadilloes. But no physical sex. She's a nice girl, after all – just needs a little money to get by and pay for the outrageous tuition, her fashion fetish, and an occasional latte at her favorite Barnes & Noble café uptown.

"Should I Have Asked for Her Number?"

The Chipster asks his professional household manager – he prefers this moniker to butler – in his spacious new flat at the Time Warner Towers. He was so breathless watching Laura take off her blouse at Brucie's he nearly followed her and Brucie out of the mansion.

"I don't see how you could have, Sir," Frederick replies. "It seems as though she had her mind set on the Topler gentleman." He can't bring himself to call the boy Chipster.

Charles R. Siegel III inherited – so to speak – the imposing six-foot-two-inch, beagle-faced Frederick, along with a black-stretch classic Bentley landau limousine and an embarrassingly Baroque, gold-flocked wall-papered, six-bedroom, five-bath, expansive dining and living rooms, study, and billiards room plus ballroom co-op on Park Avenue. The assorted authentic Jean Ingres and Piero di Cosimo paintings, et. al., therein never suited his taste, but he bore his late Great Aunt Lizzie's art treasures too in good humor.

Fifty million dollars in cash and negotiable securities also rode along to The Chipster in the bequest from the nonagenarian maiden great aunt. When the family's attorney and executor read her will and testament to the astonishment and outrage of other equally, if not more closely-related, relatives assembled in the stately quarters, he pointed out that it wouldn't have been any skin off their collective noses to have paid the old biddy a visit now and then – like her favorite great nephew did.

Good old Auntie Lizzie was the only child of one of the cofounders of the Maribyrnong Defense Explosives Factory built in 1909, safely hidden away in the western suburbs of Melbourne, Australia. Down Below, as the munitions plant was called, supplied both badly needed explosives for the free world in two world wars and immense wealth for future generations of Siegels – the latest beneficiary being The Chipster. And he genuinely looked forward to calling on his aunt. The loquacious lady loved to tell him stories of buying black market jewels from waiters in Spain just before WWII, and her childhood rides on her father's private train from DowBel, their mansion in Newport, Rhode Island, next to the Breakers, the Vanderbilt summer cottage, to his office near Grand Central Terminal in Manhattan. And oh the parties she attended as a young debutante there. Chip never really filled her in with details on the parties he went to. He knew she wouldn't have approved. Different generations never really understand each other, for the woman could have easily one-upped him with her own dalliances. The worldly woman often thought, but never said, that from all appearances her great nephew should get laid more.

Chip certainly couldn't invite his friends to the gaudy Park Avenue museum his aunt called home, so he sold her co-op and moved to more contemporary quarters with an impressive view near the top of the tower looming over Columbus Circle, from his not-exactly-a-dump-either apartment on the Upper East Side. When he moved, Chip felt obligated to bring along Auntie Lizzie's aging butler as well.

For Frederick's part, although the English butler and chauffeur wasn't precisely wishing for the old lady's demise, he's happy to enjoy the company of the tender young man who's not nearly so demanding. Boiling hot lapsang souchong tea – imported from the Fujian province of China from her contacts in the Far East – no lemon and certainly no milk, the withered hen demanded. Furthermore, the stipulation her refreshment be served to her at precisely three o'clock in the library every day had begun to take an irritating toll on the not-a-kid-anymore servant.

Boring work as well. No one much came to see his former employer for some years except her great nephew. And if he had to hear one more time about her splendid trip to Austria where she slept in the Schönbrunn Palace as a teenager, he might have murdered Elizabeth Siegel himself.

In fact, Frederick expected the dowager to outlive him. Never a cold; no trace of rheumatism, arthritis, fever, heart congestion, or any other damned infirmity; his employer enjoyed perfect health – at least for a very old lady.

On a cold day in October, Elizabeth Siegel – "Ma'am" Frederick invariably called her – decided of all things to buy a diamond-encrusted platinum happy face she saw in a *Times* Tiffany ad. For the first time, Frederick thought the canny woman had at last lost it. From the vantage point of the limo, he and The Chipster, who had been invited to lunch after the purchase, watched her march across Fifth Avenue at 57th on her way to the famed jeweler.

"What an Amazon your aunt is, Sir," Frederick said with a smile to Chip.

"Only a meteorite falling on her could do her in." Frederick happened to glance upwards. " . . . or a piano."

The Steinway grand being hoisted by a crane to a penthouse co-op snapped the cable – proved defective in the finally settled lawsuit two years later – flattening the otherwise hardy senior citizen, legs sticking out à la the Wicked Witch Of The East's from Dorothy's house. To Chip's credit, the additional one cool mil he collected did not assuage his loss. In many ways she'd been practically a mother to the boy who had lost his own when only a teen.

These days, Frederick considers that if he can ever learn how to use one of those computers his new employer's always toying with, he'll ask one of his cronies what a "professional household manager" exactly is, as Charles likes to introduce him to his friends.

For Chip, now that The Dandy Man's incarcerated for the most part on Long Island, and Brucie and Ronnie are so wrapped up in their jobs, he doesn't have any guys to shoot the bull with anymore. No one for a game of squash at the club, to putter around with at a Matisse exhibit at the Met, or take in a late afternoon stroll in Central Park. Last night wasn't a disappointment only due to his watery plunge. Although she seemed a bit too keen on sniffing dope – he only pretends to take any of it himself – Laura Bernstein's just the kind of girl he's hankering for: comely, educated, and apparently romantically willing but not so much so that's she some kind of tramp. In all, what every man secretly desires – an intelligent, eye-candy, sexually experienced virgin. Although she would be considered the wrong persuasion for him as far as his Methodist family's concerned, Danny Boy – that lucky son of a gun, he thinks.

Even though The Chipster's a bit tightfisted, he's sprung for a noted interior designer to decorate his lodgings with élan. He's a shy man lusting for the right girl. Chip seeks a woman who only after he's convinced that she likes him for who he is – a decent young chap not encumbered with a boring job – he can properly regale in style. Most women Chip meets nowadays want a trophy beau – some kind of captain of industry. He can't see why really. His business courses at Babson College proved frightfully boring, though useful at times. He did learn to use his pc to find quotes for his fixed income securities on Bloomberg dot com.

As for the other women he usually meets. . . . They're gold diggers. Chip certainly wouldn't want to show off his handsome co-op to a date in this category. Mom, thankfully, had warned him against this odious breed (his dear mother – a former waitress – met his father in the Times Square Nathan's Famous Hot Dogs where he was slumming after a formal bash. She tripped – she swore – and spilled mustard on dad's tux). Or some rich blithering tanorexic idiot who's mostly interested in her next boob implant and trendy basement bar dives. Such a vulgarian would want to transform his comfortable living quarters with gold-plated faucets and glittering déclassé frou-frou. The kind one might see in a tour of a rich and famous real estate tycoon's home.

Chip feels that the hour or so a day he spends reading the *Financial Times* and monitoring his bond portfolio should suffice to prove to any potential conquest the serious and business-minded side of his nature. I'm hardly some sort of fussbudget coupon clipper, he snorts. A few times he used the line, "I'm a professional investor," to keep a girl interested. Their eyes would open wide at the conversational gamesman-ship possibilities. They imagined gossiping with their frivolous girlfriends that their beau's a hedge fund manager. But invari-ably they'd ask specifics or on occasion recommendations about a particular stock they're considering adding to their IRAs. Then the jig's up. How should I know? I'm not some Ernst & Young bean counter.

Frederick helps him pick out just the right slacks, from one of the three cavernous cedar-lined walk-in-closets, for this sort of hot weather. A subtle greyhound gray color. Ah, the wood scent. It really gets the blood boiling.

"You know, Frederick, I want a woman who wants me for what I am."

"And what exactly is that, Chip, Sir?"

Unsure if he's detected a hint of irony, "A perfectly respect-able man with a bit of time on his hands. I'm off to get a book I ordered.

"I'm happy to fetch it for you or take you in the Bentley."

"Frederick, there are some things a man must do for himself."

"Don't forget your lip balm, Sir," his professional organizer tells his employer as he hands him a Vicks tube.

"Thank you, Frederick."

Although he's not gotten to the financial section of the *Times* yet, he decides to toddle over to the nearby pharmacy to get a cold inhaler. Can't be too cautious with this change of climate, he thinks. What with buying the occasional can of lime-scented shaving cream, picking up his shirts from the Chinese laundry on the East Side – he's not sure if he can trust the West Side to do an adequate job – and finding just the right cheese for lunch from Dean & DeLuca, he wonders how other single men find the time to spend all day at a desk on Wall Street.

Nowadays Chip has an additional task. Finding ways to keep Frederick busy. Lately The Chipster has a bit too much free time after letting his household manager do some of his pressing errands. It's only correct for both of them to keep Frederick occupied doing something or another.

Flavored lip defender and inhaler firmly in his pocket, Chip wanders uptown toward his favorite café at Barnes & Noble at 82nd and Broadway. On the way he discovers a discarded Siegel's Potato Chip bag – six-and-half-ounce size, sour cream and onion variety, he notes – right in the middle of the wide sidewalk. He feels humiliated that his namesake company has contributed to the visual blight in his neighborhood, albeit inadvertently to be sure. He removes one of the blue plastic *Times* wrappers he carries with him in his pocket just in case of such an emergency – lest he soil his hands – and, holding his nose, deposits the offending sack in a blackened metal trashcan. I wonder why they can't keep our waste containers cleaner and more attractive? the public-spirited man asks himself and resolves to write a letter to the editor of a newspaper. He'll seek Frederick's opinion later about which publication would be most suitable. A missal to a local journal would help to solve the pressing problem in my own little corner of the world. Yes.

He stops his journey and stands still at Eightieth and Broadway to consider his proper course of duty. *But perhaps that would be selfish of me.* Lately he's noticed other litter scattered in his path and thinks quite rightly that it's a bigger problem than just Columbus Circle's. *Maybe I should write to a national paper, or the International Herald Tribune?*

Satisfied that he's done more than enough work for the morning, he enters the bookstore where he happens on the latest issue of *American Angler* magazine. *Have got to try the sport someday,* he thinks. And now up the stairs to the café on the mid-mezzanine level. He orders a simple coffee, thank you very much – he's not one of those doppio dopes who lay out extra good money for some fancy who-knows-what. The Chipster remains thrifty, and proud of it, despite the trusts from his parents and, of course, Aunt Lizzie's kind gesture. *I'm not a tightwad, and fifty million may seem like a lot of money to some, I suppose. But it doesn't hurt to save for a rainy day I always say.*

As he takes a communal seat by the window, he tilts up his contemplative head from his magazine and spies an auburn-haired beauty directly across from him. She's reading *The New Yorker*. *Chuckling at some witty cartoon,* he surmises. *Probably educated. Why can't I meet a girl like that?*

"Pardon me, Miss. Would you mind passing the salt?" he forays.

"For your coffee?"

What a dolt I am! he reacts. "It improves the taste by bounds. You should try it sometime," the Chipster replies as he lightly sprinkles a dash of sodium chloride into his joe. "No kidding."

Karen Bladner manages to keep from laughing at him. *I've heard some lines in my time, but this takes the cake.*

An obnoxious odor breezes into Chip's nose. A sweaty, unshaven man in grimy work clothes sits down behind the well-dressed and poised young lady he's taken an interest in. Karen sniffs, her eyes cast suspicious daggers at Chip, and the long-legged nymph takes a seat at another table.

Bloody hell, the Chipster rages internally. We Siegels won't take this unjust calumny lying down, and jumps up. Understandably incensed, he strides over to Karen, "It wasn't me," he says, pointing to the pungent perpetrator. "You see, Miss, it. . . ."

She tentatively inhales in his direction. "OK. It's not you. But you think I'm cute, don't you?"

"Well. . . ."

"Of course you do. Why else would you follow me to tell me you don't smell? I get it. You want to meet me. Please sit down," she says. She's a bit lonely herself. With her night work and overtime duty for Pirot, she never gets to meet men her age as Karen Bladner.

"I didn't mean to intrude. I. . . . "

"Have a seat. I'm getting a stiff neck looking up at you." He seems harmless enough, sort of cute, and not badly dressed, she thinks.

Already smitten, young Siegel plops down. "I'm Chip. You were laughing before. A cartoon?" he asks.

"No. An amusing piece about strippers in New York."

Siegel's no prude. "Well, a girl has to eat, doesn't she?" he says understandingly.

"Yes, she does," and likes her table companion even more. If she ever sees him again, maybe at some point she could tell him about her night work.

"Very pretty bag you have. Saw one like it in the Sunday *Times Magazine*."

He's winning some big points with me. I hope he's not gay, she thinks. "Are you?" she says out loud.

"Am I what?" he asks. "Did I spill some coffee on myself?"

"Are you gay?"

"What?" he says and stands up.

"No man has ever complimented me on my bag before."

"Just because I read the complete Sunday *Times* cover-to-cover including the Styles section doesn't mean I don't prefer women. I chased you to this table. Remember?" Chipster's enamored of this woman but won't lightly be taken for playing on the opposite team.

"Sorry. Please sit down. It's just that well-dressed, handsome men often are."

"Well, then. I see. A natural mistake," and sits again. Chip's not immune to flattery.

Then he considers taking a big chance with her. He might as well find out her attitude now about dating a jobless man. He fantasizes the conversation. I'll say, "Not everyone's as fortunate as I am. I spend my days like this. Having coffee, reading the paper, going to an exhibit at the Whitney, playing a round of squash at the club. Pretty dull, huh?" Then she'll say, "Not in the slightest. It's to your credit if you enjoy it. I'd love to have a happy man of leisure at home waiting for me at the end of the day." She interrupts the happy fantasy. . . .

"What do you do?" Karen instantly regrets her commonly asked question. She doesn't want him to make the same inquiry.

"I'm a witness." He doesn't want this one to get away like Laura did. Chip rented the movie *Witness for the Prosecution* last night and it's the first thing that pops into his panic-stricken mind.

"You're a what?"

His mind whirls around, "You know what I mean," angling for time.

"Not really."

"Well. During a trial they call expert witnesses to help the jury decide who's the right fellow to get the award and so on. I'm one. An expert."

"An expert on what?"

He hesitates answering for a moment. The Chipster regrets not reading the entire article in the *Financial Times* this morning. He tries to recall the story, headline news about some Brit cell phone company buying a near-bankrupt one in Bangladesh or some other blasted third-world country, but he can't get his mind around it. "Telecom," he finally replies simply. "Yes, telecom. Very big, you know. Very, very big. They're always going broke with all those wires, antennae, and other such thingamajigs. Highly technical. Mostly night work. That's why I'm free just this moment. I won't bore you by delving deep into it." But he does dig himself deeper into it.

"Wow. I'm a third-year law student, so that's really interesting to me. I don't want to go into litigation, but. . . ."

Indignant at the very thought, "Of course not. A nice girl like you."

She gapes quizzically at him, "I mean I don't want to practice litigation . . . as an attorney."

"Right you are. I'm with you now." *She must think me a complete birdbrain*, he shudders.

"But even corporate lawyers need to know evidence and torts."

"What would evidence be without a tasty tort? I always say," and emits a little chortle. What the dickens is a tort? Chip wonders.

Pretty stale law school gag, she thinks. "What are you working on now?" she inquires, noticing his magazine.

He peers down at *American Angler*. He's forgotten all about it. He sees a large pink fish on the cover. "A little research. Seems the Alaskan salmon chew their tiny, sharp little teeth into TV cables. They cut them clean in half. Can't get a good signal anymore in Fairbanks. Salmon have become a major telecom issue. And yet we need to protect the poor critters, don't we? A conundrum. They want my opinion. Confidential. Please don't tell anyone about it, Miss, . . . "

"Karen. Karen Bladner. I won't. Lawyers have to maintain confidences," she smiles. He's the first person she's told her real name to this summer in New York except her landlord. The Kit Kat Club and Pirot pay her in cash.

"Pleased to meet you, Karen. That is, if you don't mind my calling you by your first name. It's seems to me that one of the troubles in this world. . . . " but his coffee confederate interrupts his speculations on the pernicious freewheeling use of familiar names between perfect strangers.

"Not at all. Please do."

"So. If I'm not being too nosy, <u>Karen</u>, what's a brilliant young woman like you doing between school terms? Interning, I suppose, at some prestigious law firm in the city, no doubt."

"Yes. It's an evening job, too. Researching financial predators." *And that's exactly what the Wall Street crowd I titillate nightly should be called,* she thinks.

When they part an hour later, she demurs at giving him her phone number but takes his. "I'll call you," she says. "Or perhaps we'll run into each other again," Karen tells the disappointed man.

"Perhaps," he replies downcast. Once again it seems to him that his good luck in accumulating wealth doesn't extend to women. Drat. Probably won't call, he pouts. They never do. She thinks I'm a telecom expert. I could have at least come up with something adventurous – war correspondent, or dog breeder maybe.

Awhile after Karen Bladner leaves the bookstore, the soon-to-be Carrie Blade wonders why he didn't tell her his real occupation. That expert witness lie's the silliest fabrication I've ever heard. We all have our secrets, I suppose. Kind of a mysterious guy. Interesting. I'll call him soon, she decides as she leaps on the number-one subway headed downtown to the Kit Kat Club just before the doors slam shut.

"Which One Talks About Our Fees?"

Chung Fat, the new quant man recently transplanted from the sixty-eighth floor of the Goldman Sachs office in Hong Kong, wants to know. When he arrived back from the Davison funeral, Davian Corbeille called for a 7 PM, all-hands-on-deck emergency meeting at the Broad Street headquarters.

"The fourteen business principles upon which the foundation of our firm rests has nothing to do with fees, young man," Davian calmly rebukes. "For example, take our first one, 'Our clients' interests always come first.'"

"That principle ends with, 'Our experience shows that if we serve our clients well, our own success will follow,'" reminds grey-templed Mason Rextal, a suave veteran banker with his eyes never off the table's chips.

Davian's cut on the fees and the resulting year-end bonus will pay for the little island and château off St. Tropez that his wife's been nagging him to buy. The maybe twenty million dollars at stake here for his wallet amounts to nearly a year's pay – not peanuts even for him. "Malcolm, what's Charlotte Davison's personal cash flow estimate?"

"With daddy dead, and combined with her trust funds, something like two hundred and twenty five big ones a year," responds the Oxford-trained financial analyst.

"Big ones?"

"I mean million not billion," forgetting this is a Goldman Sachs meeting.

"Debt?" asks Davian.

"Maybe five hundred."

"Million?"

"No. Just dollars. She likes to pay in cash."

Davian's nonplussed, "You mean this dame owns a coin-op worth two billion smackers and she owes five hundred bucks?" his Bronx origins shining through under the unusual stress.

"Yes, Sir. And that's just an average of her monthly credit card bill. It could be less." Breaking stringent company rules, Malcolm Bennett begins to sweat. He sees the logic of the question. Pursuing this implied strategy can't succeed.

"Who was that Alaskan bear talking to her at the funeral, Bhadra?" Davian asks the thirty-two-year-old woman from New Delhi in charge of personal backgrounds for this transaction. Not all deals warrant this kind of coverage, but Davian's nothing if not a detail man.

"B. L. Blackmun, Distinguished Professor of Classics at Columbia University. A friend it seems of G.F. Davison, judging from the photos we have of them together. Always gesturing toward buildings and statues near the park."

"Why would anyone do that? Perhaps demented. Get a full background on him. When we leave, we all must do a full court press on this case. What about Charlotte herself? Any peculiar habits, friends?"

"Likes to party. Big-time athlete – a karate black belt who regularly wins competitions. Divorce attorney, as you know. And plenty good at it, judging from her clients' awards. All women. She won't hesitate to go to court – and she wins every time," Bhadra tags on.

"That's just great. A monstrously rich, kung-fu, tightwad, litigating ball-buster stands in the way of this merger," Davian moans.

"And pretty scary, huh, boss?" Malcolm smirks. He surreptitiously peeks at the time on the Bloomberg trading machine.

Bad form to be caught at it. The meeting's diverting, but he's late for meeting a drinking partner at the Kit Kat Club.

Corbeille's very displeased at the impudence of the junior associate. "I told you. I wasn't feeling well at the funeral. An upset stomach or something." Each member of the cabal sitting around the large circular table scrutinizes the others. They were all there as witnesses. None of the subordinates will say that the worldwide head of structured finance is full of crap – not to his face anyhow.

"There He Is,

Ms. Davison, on the corner," Charlie's chauffeur tells her on the appointed Wednesday at lunchtime.

"How are you and how are your grandchildren, Thomas?" Professor Blackmun asks the balding septuagenarian driver as he settles into the black stretch Lincoln limousine. After decades of service, G.F. couldn't bring himself to let go of Thomas. Not working would kill the loyal employee, though his G. F. Davison Vending Machine Corporation pension had more than ample assets to keep the senior citizen in comfort forever. So G.F. continued to let Thomas drive him, praying to the gods that the two of them wouldn't get killed or injured due to Thomas' declining vehicular skills.

"Everybody's just dandy, Professor. You're lookin' mighty fine. Makin' time with the coeds?" the driver jests.

"You're making me blush, Sir."

"The usual place?"

More secrets, Charlie sighs. Everyone knows this man but me. Resigns herself. "Where are we going? I thought I was taking you to lunch. You date your students, Professor Blackmun?"

"Thomas teases me because he knows I'm a confirmed bachelor, Zoë. Men my age aren't only unattractive to young women, we're invisible. See right through us. I can't imagine a young woman having the slightest interest in me."

I'm not so sure, considers Charlotte.

"Please, Thomas. Yes, the usual place. I thought we would dine, my dear, where your dad and I used to sup. I hope you'll enjoy the finest of New York's *haute cuisine*."

"I thought only your daddy called you Zoë, Ms. Davison," Thomas remarks, obviously intrigued as the limo pulls up in front of 51 Madison Avenue.

Blackmun spots a familiar-looking, tasseled red tarboosh before reaching the destination. "Greetings, Achilles, how's business?" says Blackmun in Greek.

"You bring me always good luck, professor," answers a spindly, middle-aged merchant with a thick Balkan intonation. "I knew you would come soon. This week fortune shines on me because of your visit.

"What is your pleasure, Madam? As my guest of course," asks Blackmun as he and Charlie stand in front of a Greek gyro and spanakopita cart. Charlotte allows him to treat though it's always been her immutable practice to never let a man – except dad of course – pay for her even on a date.

The two walk toward Madison Square Park a short distance away and the professor turns and points upward. "There. This is the best vantage point. Do you see the gorgeous golden pyramidal roof? And the splendid spandrels and gargoyles? It's the forty-story New York Life Insurance Building designed in 1926 by Cass Gilbert, who also was the architect for the Woolworth Building. Made from Indiana limestone. Gothic-styled with 72 gargoyles and 2,180 windows. The first flag on top was unfurled by a button pressed by President Calvin Coolidge from the White House. After today, my favorite architecture in the city."

"Why now your favorite?"

"Because it's the Life Building. And Zoë means "life" in Greek, I'm sure you know." Blackmun reddens a bit over his explanation. On entering the park, "Over here on this bench. We'll sit where your father and I liked to converse."

She takes a bite. "This is a delicious sandwich. I'll never have a gyro anywhere else and only with you, professor."

The two linger over the pushcart delicacies for an hour discussing what additional help the university Classics Department could use. "Ganymede told me you are an attorney. What kind of law do you practice?"

"A divorce attorney," she hesitates in answering, unsure of his feelings in this sphere.

He smiles admiringly at her for a few moments, "Just from knowing your father and the short time I've known you, I'm sure you do your best to reconcile the parties. To at least try to find a balance and harmony between husband and wife. I am correct, am I not? I know I sound naïve. I'm not a modern man."

Charlotte's watch buzzes, "I'm terribly sorry, professor. Let me answer your question another time. I must be going – appointments with new clients." Charlie's relieved to have an excuse to change the subject. "Let me have Thomas drop you off."

"Not at all, dear Zoë. I'm headed for the New York Public Library to study a rare book on Norse mythology they have. I'll take a stroll from here on this beautiful afternoon. I look forward to seeing you again whenever you think you can tolerate the company of an old man."

"Sixty is young, professor." Seeing his puzzled face, "The internet."

"Of course. We're all so public nowadays. I am young," he says with a vigor she hadn't seen before in him. "Thank you for noticing. I pretend I'm old so people your age don't think me foolish. *Adieu*, sweet girl," and departs uptown with a strong stride. Fifty feet away he turns back, "And, Zoë, please call me Barry," then resumes his journey at a faster clip.

Charlotte waves down Thomas, who's been circling the park during the lunch. Time for the meetings with the firm founder, Raoul Bleeder, to discuss a new case and one with another senior partner. Her father died only a few days ago. Work will comfort her best. But her thoughts linger over the physically imposing Professor Blackmun – Barry – who's really not that old at all, she decides.

"You're Not
That Old at All

for a guy your age," Ally tries to reassure Dan while they have
a late lunch at the LFOD bamboo shack that same afternoon.
"It'll be months or even years before you're really *deecrept*."

"She's a scream. How did I live without her?" Dan, in an
old varmint's inflection while he reaches around his shoulder,
"Why shucks, Ma'am, you're really sweet to say so. Ouch!
There's goes my back, gol darn it. Guess they'll have to shoot
me like they did my horse, Trigger."

"Daniel, you're soooo silly," giggles Ally in a bogus deep
tone.

"Maybe they'll stuff me and put me next to the Nipper at
the Welcome Center," roars Danny. He's made up his mind to
forget both Charlotte and Laura and feels better for it. Yak-
king with the tart-tongued girl cheers him up and helps to clear
some cobwebs. Maybe the New Beginnings meetings aren't so
hard to take. Interesting even, sometimes. He sometimes pictures himself in Bernstein's shoes, helping others to find a way
out of their problems.

From behind, "You didn't tell me you were Charlotte's
lover, Dan." Laura couldn't wait until this evening to see him.
She wouldn't be able talk openly at the temple anyway with
her father there. "Excuse us, Ally, while the grown-ups talk."

"Who's Charlotte? What does she mean, lover? Is this your
girlfriend, you liar? You promised me you'd never see this
bitch again."

"Ally, be reasonable. I never said. . . ."

"You're a big fat fucking booger. That's what you are, and I hate you both," and she runs away hysterical.

"Maybe I should go see if she's OK."

"You're one of the patients, remember, Dan? This isn't the temple meeting where my father lets you pretend you're a medical student. They have real psychiatrists here to help Ally. If we're ever going to talk this over, for me it has to be now."

Lars still skulks after Ally. He's been taking in the unfolding drama from a few tables away. Now Dan sees him stand up and trail the disappearing teen. Dan takes off, "Be right back, dreamboat," he says to Laura.

Fifty yards away, Lars sounds sane for starters, as his custom, "Would you like to talk about it, Ally? I'm a doctor."

Dan catches up, "No Lars, she wouldn't."

"Would you two old guys just beat it," Ally says.

They both watch Ally stomp indoors to the HDTV lounge, ignoring both of them. Dan waits by the door and tries to stare down Lars. But the other patient glares back.

"You're not exactly on the outside of this zoo looking in a glass window, are you, my boy?" says Lars with a smirk.

"You've got to lose this doctor crap, Lars. They might put you in a real jail."

"I am a real doctor, young man. I told you. A psychoanalyst," he replies with a steely look.

"Such crap," Dan counters. But he's not so sure just now.

"Oh? A dazed, directionless drug addict who's never done a lick of work knows what's real? Don't you realize many psychiatrists choose their career to solve their own problems? Jack Bernstein often asks my advice about cases. Get a hold of yourself before you criticize me, you junkie. At least I'm a has-been and not a never-were like you, Dandy Man. Isn't that what they call you?"

Dan blanches at the insult. Lars hit his mark. The maybe-doctor sees it's no use hanging around and shuffles away – bunny rabbit slippers and all – without a further word. Daniel watches him go and wonders if Lars is telling the truth about his MD and working with Bernstein. One thing's certain – for a madman, Lars sure clocked him. He returns to try to find Laura. But dreamboat has sailed away.

A Mischievous Elf

describes nearly everyone's first impression seeing Raoul
Bleeder, the founder and head partner of the feared Raoul
Bleeder & Associates law firm. With his bald head – except
around the sides – and his full, close-shaved gray beard and
pointy eyebrows, he could double for a Shakespearean Puck
grown up to be a seventy-year-old divorce shyster.

The infamous leader claims – legitimately, perhaps, though
if untrue wouldn't stop the boast – to be the first lawyer to
inveigle the benevolent and honorable divorce court of the
State of New York to deny all property, alimony, and child
support claims to a legitimate and faithful pregnant-again
wife on behalf of his cheating-husband client. Wild party after
the decision – in the good old pre-lady law-partner days –
including soft and maybe-not-so-legally-compliant feminine
consorts booked by a young and upcoming tuxedo-clad specialty talent agent for that sort of thing – a certain Pirot (no
last name known). And all arranged by the firm but paid for
by. . . . Whom else? "You," Raoul once told a callow yet well-
heeled client.

The opulent décor of the office-building lobby upset him.
And now the new client, Albert Topler, detests sitting in the
forty-by-twenty-foot mahogany-wainscoted conference room
at a thirty-seat, oval cherrywood table waiting for Bleeder
to make his appearance. Could those be real Picassos on the
wall? he asks himself. He's looks at his watch. It's been twenty
minutes. The side table stocked with numerous choices of hot

and cold drinks, an overstuffed fruit bowl, and a sizable plate of miniature mandelbrot and rugalah only confirms suspicions that his retainer of fifty thousand dollars will have to be replenished often. He knows it's the clients who pay for this extravagance.

Finally, in walks Bleeder accompanied by a luscious – Albert thinks – but somewhat severe young woman in a black suit. "Raoul, is there some mistake?" she asks after seeing Albert.

"Mr. Topler? Very happy to meet you," Raoul addresses Albert, who politely stands when a lady, even a young one, enters the room. "I'm Raoul Bleeder, the firm's founder, and this is Charlotte Davison, one of our rising stars. Charlotte normally handles only our female clients, but I've been trying to persuade her to branch out to the weaker sex." Albert smiles weakly at the small joke.

"Topler? Are you a relative of Daniel Topler, by any chance?" Charlie asks. Nothing but revelations lately, it seems to her.

"Do you know my son, Danny? It's very sad. My handsome boy's brilliant, but he's in a rehab clinic on Long Island. He would have gone to medical school if it hadn't been for that junk he takes. Maybe that's why Harriet and I have had so much trouble." Albert plops down, all choked up. He can't help spouting out his boy's problems, though they aren't really anybody else's business. His daughter's on his mind, too. Hasn't showed up for work in days. "We used to have fun, the two of us, Harriet and me. There used to be a balance. Harmony in our marriage. But now. . . ." Al's voice trails off without completing the thought.

Raoul doesn't have much hope of converting the stunning protégée into representing the other gender on the firm's cold-blooded attack team, but in his long years of experience it never hurts to try. He's used to winning. Still, he's taken aback when Charlotte sits down next to the roly-poly client. She'll take on a male client? he asks himself.

"Perhaps I can be of help to you, Mr. Topler." Albert's sentiments echoed the professor's. Maybe next time Charlie can tell Barry more about her law practice without having to change the subject.

"Meet Harriet Topler,

she's a new client for our firm, Charlotte," says Evan Roth, the second attorney to join Raoul Bleeder's firm when it first started over thirty years ago. Neither of the Toplers has been registered yet in the large firm's client database, allowing for the mishap of opposing sides in the proceedings to be invited for simultaneous prelim conferences.

Charlie's meeting with Albert continued in her office for an hour, and he had left a few minutes before. She discovered where The Dandy Man got his charm and gift of gab. The saying's true: appearances can be deceiving. The fat senior citizen has a winning demeanor and no small flair for keeping up his side of a conversation. He must have been quite a ladies' man in his day, she laughed after he left.

By this time, Charlotte's beyond surprise. There are no coincidences, her dad once told her – only the unwinding of the cloth spun by Clotho, the sister of the Fates who spins the fortune of mankind on divine thread. Charlie startles Evan and Harriet. "I just met your husband, Mrs. Topler," thereby beginning a new chapter in the billing statements of Raoul Bleeder & Associates. "Perhaps I can be of help to you.'

"Let's Start Where We Left Off,"

Jack was going to say, but then realizes Sam hasn't arrived yet. The discussion was supposed to begin with the problems of facing depression that Sam expressed at the end of the last meeting. It's 7 PM, so Jacob decides to begin the Wednesday night session promptly, anyway. "Dan, since I'll be having surgery soon and you'll be leading the group, why don't you take over tonight?"

"Well, I . . . uh . . . don't think. . . ."

"Come on, my boy. We're all comrades here," Barry says with a warm smile.

Dan notes that the sociable Goliath seems particularly forthcoming and dressed a little more put together tonight. It's hard to say no to such an imposing guy. "Well . . . depression can hit any of us as we grow older," draws laughs from the men. "OK. OK. I'm not as old as the rest of you. . . ."

"Not by half," interjects Sam as he limps into the library with the help of his cane. "Sorry I'm late. I almost didn't come at all. I told you last time. I don't want to do anything – sometimes not even see you guys. I'm not young and healthy anymore like Dan here."

"You'd be surprised," Dan replies somberly, "Even at my age it's not that easy. I have to force myself to get out of bed. Not get dragged down by negative thoughts. Figure out why I should live each day." Dan feels the men's eyes on him. Probably questioning how a young man like me has any problems at all. What could possibly concern a young medical student?

Sam unloads his suppressed anxieties. "I don't do anything. Here I was a big deal at Bell Labs for twenty-five years in solid-state physics – a department head. We filed over 100 patents. Dozens of everyday products we all use wouldn't have happened without me."

Dan leans forward, absorbing the fact that this pathetic-sounding man had a dynamic career. "The last few years I didn't enjoy it anymore. The constant change in priorities. New division bosses. But I was terrified to quit. I didn't know what I'd do if I didn't have an office to go to. Since my operation I can't get around very well. They said it would heal. I don't know. Sometimes I turn the TV on and I don't know what the hell the program was an hour later. I just stare. My mind blank."

"Do you see your grandchildren, Sam?" Dave volunteers. "I love to play with mine," glancing at the others to seek cheerful confirmation.

"They're babies. They make noise and run around. I know we're not supposed to say this as grandparents, but my grandchildren are a pain in the neck." Sam sinks more.

"Like W.C. Fields, a man who hates babies and dogs can't be all bad." A little relief from the tension. The men welcome Glen's levity. "As for me, I'm working harder than ever. My international tax practice takes me all over the world. That's why I guess my third marriage didn't work out, either. I thought a commercial real estate agent might have a better head on her shoulders. I haven't seen my daughter in months. I'm seeing several women. Nothing serious of course – I'm already a three-time loser. For relaxation I go to the Cosmopolitan Club in the city to play billiards or poker."

"I'd like to do that, Glen. How can I join?" asks Sam.

"Well, it's . . . uh . . . not easy to join. It's expensive, for one thing."

"That's not a problem. My pension's done well over the years."

"I had my law firm sponsor me. You need several recommendations from existing members. It's very hard to get in." Glen has made it clear to everyone – he won't help. His friendship stops at the clubhouse door.

Sam knows to drop it and turns to another friend, "And you, Rob? What are you doing now that you're recently retired?"

"I go to my club, too. I'm an Elk."

An Elk? wonders Dan. "You mean like a Moose?" he says to Rob. For Dan, it's like hearing a man describe ancient history. He's never met anybody who said they belong to what he thought was a relic from another century.

"Yes, like a Moose, but we're Elks."

"Are they the ones with the funny red hats?" Dan can't leave this alone.

"You're thinking of the Shriners, Dan. I didn't know you're an Elk, Rob," Harry says.

"I don't hear much about the Elks. They're still around?" asks Barry.

"Of course. The Benevolent & Protective Order of Elks does loads of philanthropic events. Fundraising for needy kids. Stuff like that. We got our lodge clubhouse renovated not long ago. Pretty nice. The wives come too, sometimes, and we put on some music and dance."

"Sounds good. What do you normally do when you go there?" asks Sam, trying to find something tonight to hang onto.

"We sort of, uh, stand at the bar, chew the fat, and watch TV. The drinks are cheap. It's great. But I only go for an hour or two. It's not something you can spend the whole day doing, you know."

"Oh, yeah, I see."

A dart from Morty, "Who are you kidding? You guys just watch porno movies all day."

Ignoring the jibe, "I'd be glad to introduce you, Sam. We're always prospecting for new members."

"Thanks, Rob. Let's do that," Sam replies politely, making it clear that he has zero interest in pursuing it.

For the first time Dan wholeheartedly enters the conversation in the men's group, "If you don't mind me asking, guys, is a lack of visibility a problem in retirement? No office or daily routine?"

"Morty and I are on several community projects," Harry answers. "I have more visibility than I ever had. Now my neighbors know who I am. When I go into the pharmacy, five people say hello. I used to not know anyone because of my work hours. The more help the merrier, Sam. I'll keep you so busy the time will fly. Nights, too, when a lot of the civic association meetings are held."

"The committees keep me alive, too. Get on board, Sam. You know, I used to be a senior business consultant. I loved it. I got to push people around without having to do the work," glows Morty. "Now that I'm retired, I push planning board members around. They'd get rid of me if they could. But they can't. They need me cause they know I'm right, and some of the meetings are open to the community anyways." He speaks his mind half in jest, but only half.

Morty's hard edge shows itself to Dan even in public service – a tough nut. Dan goes back to Sam. "What would you <u>like</u> to do if you could?"

Sam smiles sheepishly, "It's dumb."

"You men just told this youngster that we're all friends here," cajoles Dan.

"Well, I love baseball. I've always wanted to. . . . "

"Spit it out," says Morty.

" . . . run a hot dog stand at Yankee Stadium. See the games. Everyone's glad to see you. Stupid, huh, for guys like us?"

"Doing nothing is what's stupid," Morty says – never one to sugarcoat.

"*Carpe diem*, Sam," Barry urges in his characteristically urbane manner.

"That sounds fun. Why don't you just do it? Forget you were a corporate pooh-bah," David chimes in.

The group breaks for a ten-minute coffee break and pit stop. Meanwhile, Dan takes a book off the library shelf and starts to read until Jack calls for order. The conversation drifts back to Shriners and Masons.

"What does thirty-second degree mean? I always get the third degree from my wife," one of them cracks.

"Weren't they mentioned in *War and Peace*? Tolstoy has several characters, such as Joseph Alexeevich, discuss Freemasonry extensively," Barry volunteers.

They all feel relieved to retreat from the real, hurting problem of a member. "Time's up, men. See you Sunday," concludes Jack.

I'll Wait Here
Until She's Gone,

Dan resolves, and lingers in the temple library. But not long enough. Outside, Bernstein signals to Dan that he needs to talk to him in a minute. He's standing next to Sam's car and leaning in the window talking to him when Danny exits the building. Giving Sam some extra propping up, Dan thinks, and walks over to Bernstein's car.

Up go the windows on the driver's side, shutting out the possibility of apology. I had to leave her earlier in the day. If she knew how Lars dogs Ally, she'd understand. Won't turn in my direction. Pretending to read a weathered, torn magazine that lay on the back seat moments ago. Now both Dan's heart and his Porsche engine race. Convertible top down – pedal to the floor and speeding away before speaking to Bernstein. But thoughts of Laura travel faster than he can rev the motor. They refuse to be left behind.

"I'm Sorry You Can't See Her,"

a prim, fifty-something, prematurely gray nurse tells Dan. She examines the filed nails on her outstretched right hand with approval. It's way past visiting hours and this rude, agitated man isn't family, anyway, she says to herself.

"Dr. Bernstein already saw her and left a little while ago and I don't care if you are one of his medical school students. She's been screaming to see her father, can't be contacted it seems – but you're certainly not him, young man. And no, Ms. Alicia Sobel isn't in room 203, Mr. Smart Mouth, she's in 307."

Oops – no matter. He's not getting by this gal and we've got plenty of hall monitors. The night nurse follows the obstinate fellow down the corridor and out the exit and with satisfaction watches him head back to his car. The Stony Brook University Medical Center doesn't let its guard down, she congratulates herself as she returns to the emergency room station and settles back into her swivel chair.

Helen had stayed up to tell Danny the news when he returned to LFOD from the temple – what Bernstein wanted to tell him in the parking lot. "Ally tried to kill herself again. Breathed in what must have been a quart of water. Overflow from the tub spilled out the cabaña alerting a CA walking by." Dan didn't need to hear more. He headed immediately for the hospital, but not before some preparation first. He's no stranger to hospitals and knew he wouldn't be allowed to see his distressed friend. A burglar in the night, the thief made off with the prize. Thank God the lunatic's asleep and the doors aren't locked in this asylum. Or else putting my hands on Lars' M.D. white coat might not have been so easy, he thought.

Dan watches Our Lady Saint Of No-Way-You-Can-See-Ally leave the hospital entrance to return to her desk. He slips on the white coat. Dr. Topler will have no problem making his way to Ms. Sobel's room. Ms. Sobel? It hits him. As in – reserved and intellectual Glen Sobel who hasn't seen his little girl in months? The *bon vivant* dating tons of women? The gambler playing high stakes Texas Hold 'Em and lagging for the break shot on his club's billiards table? The father who can't find time to visit his suicidal daughter?

By 6 AM the next morning, Ally had been watching Daniel sleep in the visitor's chair for an hour. Exhausted after the sedative they gave her, she's still hurt and plenty mad at him. Nevertheless, she loves her man and he's back. An eye opens. "Nipper got soaked, too," she laughs. "Did he make it?"

"It's a Trap,

honey, don't fall for it," Elaine desperately tries to keep her composure. Albert and her mortal enemy talking calmly and quietly together ranks with him dropping dead right now on their Marriott queen-sized bed. What if wifey tells him how she knew to ambush him at home? Rubbing the inside of his elephantine leg squeezed next to her, "Mediation just means that the money-grubbing law firm can legally collect fees from both sides, sweetheart. Don't you get it?"

Albert sits up, nearly pushing the activities director onto the hotel chain's typically bland but adequate-for-business-travel carpet. At the end of the day, he's going to end up paying for Harriet's legal fees no matter what the settlement is, that's for sure. Maybe those mouthpieces just found a way to skin both cats instead of one. "It's all been very sudden." Catching himself – unaware Elaine knows there's no filed divorce – "I mean, we've been working through the proceedings all along, and now there's a new wrinkle. You should've met this gal, Lainey. Very intense. I couldn't say no to her." It's a crying shame she's not in the junkyard game where she could make a fortune, occurs to him.

While Elaine, heated-up-but-not-from-love, reckons, Saying no to <u>me</u> is what will get you in trouble, you idiot.

"Then get a load of this, Lainey. They call me on my cell after I leave their artsy-fartsy office. And let me tell you, doll face, you know the Toplers aren't cheap. I could spend the same dough on my office. I can afford it as well as. . . .

"Al, will you just get on with the story, for crying out loud?!" Now's not the time to digress for this tigress.

"Yeah, sure. What's eating you? Anyways, Mr. Divorce Attorney, Raoul Bleeder himself, calls on my cell and says Harriet's on board with this. Due to a mix-up she also met with this Charlotte Davison today. You know, Lainey, the young legal eagle who's trying to sell me on this mediation idea?. . . ."

"Mix-up, my ass. Yes, yes, go on, dear," regaining self-control she gently strokes the back of his flabby neck.

"Your ass? You know how I love it, sweet thing," as he grabs both of her lower cheeks. At least he's up for it tonight, she consoles herself. Elaine changed the velocity vector of the conversation and there's no going back – for now.

"Why Couldn't
We Say No?"

Raoul asks his partner Evan Roth after Charlotte leaves the conference room at the end of the day. The plan was supposed to be a dressing down where they'd tell Charlotte under no certain terms was she ever to suggest new strategies without consulting management. "I thought the idea was for us to give her a good talking to."

"She has some nerve recommending mediation to new clients. . . ."

"Without the founder's blessing. Me. Or you, of course, Evan."

". . . and man, were we lucky that the Toplers didn't get bent out of shape with both of them here."

"And just like that – off the top of her head. Instead, she convinces us that non-adversarial divorces are the new wave and we get both sides of the proceedings. Then why the hell not get our permission in advance? We're the senior partners here, right?" Raoul's voice begins to rise in anger.

"I have to tell you, Raoul, when this woman's eyes bored into mine, there wasn't any way I could say no to her. And don't kid me. You couldn't either."

Conceding nothing, as is his habit, Raoul ends the post-mortem, "As long as she makes us money, we'll let the sorceress have her way."

"Not There – Over Here,

Ronnie." Men need so much training. Just like mom always said, considers the soon-to-be-bride. I've got to ask mom how long it took to house-train dad. "Yes, that's right, dear," Coco says condescendingly. "Put the coffee table in front of the couch – not next to the front door." Romances can be like this one – sudden and definitive. When the electricity's there and each of the lovey-doveys meet all the numerous specifications on the other's what-I-want-in-a-spouse list, then it's wham bang and I do. The two of them can just swing the deal on the two point three mil love-bird starter co-op on Manhattan's Upper West Side.

They got lucky. A prior deal fell through on the unit just before closing and the owners had already moved out. Two of the board members – both attorneys – know Ronald's father, clearing the social admissibility hurdle. Her trust fund and last year's Universal Recycling W-2 form sealed an expedited approval on the mortgage despite the fact that Ronnie's just started his position at Viacom. It's early Thursday morning and there's some time before Ron has to get to work.

"Like this, honey pie?" Ronnie gazes adoringly at her. She's everything a man could want. Cute <u>and</u> efficient. I can consult with her about my work – she even has suggestions on the marketing plans I'm developing for some new programming. Not like other girls I've dated. She'll run the home and bring some bacon to it, too – maybe lots. "When do you think we can tell our parents, honeybunch? We can't keep this a secret very long without hurting their feelings, you know. Where should I put these linens?"

Nature created mothers with an excellent plan in mind. In this case, the plan provides for daughters to learn from their mothers. Consequently, the answer to where to store the long-nap bath-sized Bloomingdale's chocolate-dyed towels, "In your bathroom." . . . . *where I can't see them*, silently completes the thought. Coco wisely permits Ronnie to decorate his bathroom any way he chooses, ensuring his commitment to their home and blocking future gripes. Ronnie's home of origin prepared her for the worst – a brown room. But the damage has been contained.

"Well, how are we going to set a wedding date if the old folks don't know about us?"

"I told you. We'll tell them soon."

"What if I tell my mom and make her promise to keep it secret?" His backbone's not nearly as stiff as his beloved's. Coco gives him the female's how-dumb-can-you-be look until he comes to the same conclusion as his fiancée, "OK. All right. That's a stupid idea."

He's come to his senses, she thinks. Coco's certain that her parents' divorce could come at any time. She wants to avoid the backlash of taking sides that could hinder purchasing a spacious and more upscale nest in the next few years. Echoing a similar plaint she saw recently in a *Fiddler On The Roof* DVD, If they get divorced why should I suffer?, seems more than reasonable to the logical woman. The tightwad swallowed hard when she used her own trust money for the down payment and doesn't want to have to go through that agony again.

"Don't worry your pretty little head about it, Ronnie. Take that carton and put it in our bedroom, you big strong man," followed by her alluring invitation. "Worwhile," says she while blowing a kiss. Coco and Ronald's own private lexicon begins to take shape. It's their code for young couples' universal magic words, "I'll make it worth your while."

"He's All Yours,"

spoils the fun and doesn't make good reading, but Laura feels relieved just the same.

Trying to sound sporting and casual but nervous her friend might change her mind. "What happened, Charlie? Dan's not up to your level of competition?"

The light- and dark-haired women grab a quick lunch at the Grand Central Terminal lower dining concourse this Thursday afternoon so Charlotte can buy some groceries at the market upstairs when they're finished. Laura's always impressed that Charlie manages to look so down-to-earth while indifferently toting the latest Balenciaga motorcycle bag.

"I meant for now. I may not be through with him yet. And you? Are you still the chaste, albeit smutty writer after you dragged The Dandy Man from me?"

"No," followed by her confidante's delighted squeal. *For now* doesn't escape Laura.

"Start the shovel. I'm all ears for the dirt." Time spent with Laura fills a void keenly needed and felt more than ever since Charlotte's dad died.

"Well, it's kind of embarrassing. You know Dan as well as I do."

Laughing, "'Embarrassing' sounds strange coming from a nice Jewish girl who strips in front of druggies and drags a half-naked man out the door."

"We went to his . . . place," keeping the confidence of her father and Dan but not wanting to lie to her best friend either.

Unable to resist trying to shock her buddy, "Yes. Go on. Did he fuck you?"

"Charlie! How can you talk that way?"

"I talk the way you write, which is how I talk? Right?"

"If I can translate what you said, the answer is yes. But from now on I'm determined to compose stories with material from my own life – not yours anymore. Bruce called and invited me to keep coming to his pond extravaganzas as often as I like and I intend to do just that."

"Laura, I don't think that's a good idea. That crowd's into hard drugs, not just drinking."

"You party with them."

"Yes, but I can protect myself, and for some reason alcohol and dope don't bother me. They never have. Some of the lowlifes that show up there wouldn't think twice about screwing you if you were drunk or stoned. Or maybe line up to do it. Bruce invites them for atmosphere. It amuses him to keep guys like Pirot around, but they can be dangerous. The Dandy Man's just a harmless preppie by comparison."

"What makes you such an expert on Danny?" Laura blurts out, miffed at the unintentional slight of a man she craves. Laura can no longer restrain venting her envy at Charlie's success with men.

Charlotte's eyes flash briefly, then dim again. As a child her father read her the Norse tales of the bloodshed between the progenies of fire and ice that she overheard Professor Blackmun murmur about. Her essence from birth has been to battle every day – almost every hour. But the incarnated goddess of war doesn't want to be drawn into a fray with her college amiga. "I'm _not_ an expert on him, Laura."

But Laura's own competitive instinct hasn't subsided, "You can't stand it that a man would prefer me over you. This time, you lost big time and it's eating you up. You're jealous because he wanted me and not you," and storms off.

Laura challenged the wrong woman. Charlotte's bellicose streak overpowers her better nature. Flouting her logical mind and warm feelings for her friend, the specter deep within her must prove itself invincible to Laura and that handsome but weak frat boy, The Dandy Man.

What a Lame Excuse

to invite him over so soon, Charlie frets as she dresses in front of her mirror. "I just want to thank you for the wonderful lunch yesterday," couldn't have sounded more like a high-school crush. He must think I'm an overgrown teenager.

At the same time, a disheartened Barry primps in front of his own oversized antique looking glass dissecting his earlier words, "I would be delighted, my dear. I look forward to dining with you at nine this evening." I sounded so formal and old-fashioned. I'm such an ass, Barry says to a marble bust of Sophocles on the cabinet adjacent to his worn and furrowed desk. The temple men's meeting last night did nothing to take his mind off her. Just the opposite. The conversation dwelling on the mortality of his hometown friends only etched with more definition his diminishing time on earth contrasted with the infinite lives of the fictional immortal gods he's made his life study. I'm only too mortal and too alone, occupies his thoughts.

Barry glances down at the sealed university contract still sitting on his desk. Unusual for the efficient man. He had almost opened the envelope and signed his commitment to yet another year teaching classics at Columbia. It had arrived this morning in his office – only the day after his close friend Ganymede was buried. But it's not his friend he's thinking about. *Maybe my life will change. Start anew.* He had spent a sleepless night envisioning the straight-from-Olympus beauty and their lunch in the park. I'm some sort of elderly charity case for Zoë. An academic oddity, perfect for ridicule. If she even caught a whiff that I see her as a woman and not just the daughter of an old friend, I'll never see her again. I'm such a fool to become infatuated.

He surveys his small campus office where he's spent the last fifteen years. Dog-eared books in Latin, Greek, and ancient Norse lie tucked haphazardly in the large bookcase; on the wall hang framed Hubble Telescope images of galaxies and exploding stars; and on his desk sits a yellowing solitary picture. While at MIT as a joint astrophysics and classics literature major, he fell in love with a co-ed -- a geology major and near genius. She felt the same way about him, but their immature egos and powerful intellects never allowed them to speak of any subject deemed emotional. Naturally, since then he dated over the years and became "involved" a few times. And yes, Thomas guessed correctly, many years ago he even became briefly entangled with one of his students. But he sits now an ashamed bachelor fantasizing over a girl young enough to be his daughter.

When G.F. Davison died, Charlie decided to move into her father's penthouse co-op at the Hampshire House overlooking Central Park. It is there where she has invited the professor to a homemade dinner. After Laura abruptly left her at Grand Central, she bought truffles, caviar, and other delicacies in the marketplace upstairs to prepare for tonight and has for the time being forgotten the spat. Charlotte loves to cook but never finds the time. Always the wild parties. Doing drugs doesn't seem to bemuse her as it does the others. In her earlier phone call with Barry, she wasn't surprised to hear that he had been at the luxurious apartment many times to visit dad.

"Is William the doorman on tonight?" he wanted to know. "I wonder if his daughter got into NYU?. . . . You don't know him? A shame. Very delightful man who enjoys opera. He lent me a rare recording of Caruso. I'll find out about Sheila . . . Sheila, his daughter, my dear." William of course would let him pass and he'd come right up.

What planet is this man from?

A soft knock at the door. She first peeks through the peephole for a preview and then opens wide the door. "And who might this be?" Charlotte asks the transformed classics don. "I don't know, professor, but I might like you better in your comfortable teaching duds than the stylish tailored suit you have on."

Cheeks on fire like a boy, "I'd gladly wear anything that would please you, dear Zoë. This bottle is for you. But the first order of business is, are you old enough? Plato said, 'Shall we not pass a law that, in the first place, no children under eighteen may touch wine at all?'"

"I'm not a child," she laughs.

"Excellent news. I've been saving the wine for a special occasion. It's from a vineyard on Santorini Island in the Aegean Sea about 60 miles north of Crete. But the island's ancient name of Kalliste suits you better," he elaborates as he steps onto the terrace overlooking Central Park South and the park. It's getting dark, and despite the bright lights of the city one can see the stars.

"And why is that, Professor?"

"Barry. Please call me Barry. Because it means the fairest one." Panic. I've gone too far. What an aging buzzard. She'll politely ask me to leave, he thinks and unconsciously lowers his head in humiliation.

"You're so sweet, Barry."

Emboldened now. "Do you know how to use your father's telescope? I helped him select it." He pounces on the device. "It's a Meade 16-inch RCX400. Global positioning system. When the leaves fall this autumn, at night you can see exhibits in the Met across the park or the rings of Jupiter. With the filter on, dazzling sunspots during the day." He squints through the eyepiece now, getting more and more animated, "It has a precision front corrector lens. . . ."

"You know everything."

Ignoring her and still stargazing, "It's the MIT nerd in me. Don't pay any attention. But you see, with a lens like this there's virtually no distortion in the optics. . . . "

Putting a hand on his face, "Is there anything you don't know, Barry?"

Her electrifying touch gains his undivided attention. Now standing to his full towering measure, the two seem as if Zeus and Athena have reunited. "When I look at you, Zoë, I realize I don't really know anything at all."

He effortlessly lifts her off the ground to kiss her. Unlike other times when men have wooed her, Charlotte's as transported as her lover. The invitation for a homemade dinner becomes homemade breakfast instead.

"Some Fucking Friend

you are," Dan heatedly accuses Bruce in the mansion's library. After getting removed by two male nurses from Ally's room, he has spent the day in his cabaña on the internet, filling out forms and sending out emails. He bided his time until late this evening when he knew his Bexley Academy classmate would be back in the East Hampton hotbed of iniquity.

"I copulate to the best of my ability, old chum." flips out Brucie – forever unflappable.

"You've played some rotten tricks on me."

"Rotten is what I do best. What seems to be the problem?"

"Let's start with attempted murder when you tried to ply me with martinis in the haunted house upstairs last Saturday."

"They were for the twins – not you, Dandy Man," he lies. "Scrumptious *femmes* weren't they? How rude of Laura to snatch a potable for herself and waste the other dousing your penis." Now also chafed. "Why would I murder you when you're doing such a bonny good job doing it yourself?" Two can play a nasty verbal sport.

"You framed me, Bruce," dropping the familiar "ie" – the room grows hotter. "Charlie and Laura arriving in the room just as I'm set up as an object of ridicule for your druggie hangers-on. Laura wasn't supposed to be here."

"Not even you, my friend, can tell me who I can invite to my home. Anyway, Charlie invited her – not me. And what complaint do you have? That you didn't screw both of them that night? I'm sure you nailed Laura," now not-so-uninsultable, with malice, "who by the way lies upstairs now next to The

Chipster, with several lines in her nostrils. I wonder if he's drilled her yet?"

Brucie thought Danny was searching through the drawers of his father's desk for a cigarette. He's sorry now for the miscalculation. "Dan, don't do anything stupid," a newly-flappable Bruce calls with alarm to the enraged lover bounding upstairs.

"How's Tricks, Old Egg?"

the ever sociable Chipster inquires as Dan explodes in the door.

Upon entering the center "Chinese" bedroom, Dan looks out the window. Makes a quick calculation. Unlikely to kill him.

Chipster's terrified thoughts follow. The Dandy Man's one hell of a lot stronger than one might think, as Dan bodily lifts him out of bed and easily defenestrates him. Unfortunately for the wavy-potato chip heir, on more than one drunken occasion Dan has dived from the lotus-flower-designed-wallpapered bedchamber directly into the deep end of the heart-shaped pool below.

"What a marvelous host," the muddled crowd that can still see straight murmur to each other as they watch a naked Chipster sail out the second-story window, followed immediately by his clothes. "Brucie stops at nothing to amuse us."

Chip swims into the interior sunroom extension of the pool, with his trousers and underpants on his head, where his inebriation permits him to enjoy the applause and adulation of a job well done from the twos and threesomes groping on the cushions there.

"I guess that makes me Lois Lane, huh, Clark Kent?" Laura asks in a sultry voice Danny hasn't heard before. She's euphoric and more aroused than ever. The muscles from Dan's daily exercise have both of them pumped up.

"Get dressed." Dan takes note of her dilated pupils, blows jagged lines of white powder off the Qing dynasty dresser, seizes the silver vial on it, and dumps the contents into the handcrafted oriental hot tub in the middle of the room.

"Do I get to see the ice castle like in *Superman III*?"

"It was *Superman II*." Always the movie critic.

A bit tongue-tied from sniffing snow, "Why don't you come here next to me and take The Chipster's place?" She lies flat on her back and fondles her breasts seductively.

Daniel has never before considered a woman's prior love affairs his concern. He wears jealousy lightly. But not now. Danny's relieved to see she at least still has her panties on.

"When did you give up reading *The New Yorker* for *Hustler*? Put your dress on," he scolds and rolls her off the bed.

"Screw you, Dan. You're not my father. Where have you been all this time if you're so damn hot for me?"

Pulling his cell phone from his back pocket, "Let's ask Dr. Bernstein these questions right now, why don't we? See what he has to say about his daughter sniffing blow."

More sober, "Don't do that, Dan." Getting off the floor and throwing her dress on. "He's very sick. It would kill him. I'm going now. OK?"

Dan grabs her arm. "<u>We're</u> going." He reaches around her waist, kisses her neck, just as shirtless and barefoot Chipster bumbles in.

Eyes gaping open in fear and with arms up to defend a possible blow, "Don't hit me, Dandy. Not called for. Just getting my keys." Fumbling around the bed and covers, "Sorry to interrupt, fellows. Just carry on. As you were. You'd think keys had legs and walked away." Now crawling under the bed. "I try to always remember to put them in the same place so I won't misplace them. It can be so inconvenient, if you know what I mean. Of course, flying out the window without previously planning it can be disconcerting, don't you know. Ah! Here are these buggers. Now for my shoes." When The Chipster gets up, he realizes he's been talking to himself. Charles R. Siegel – the third– stands alone in the Chinese bedroom.

Maybe I'll Call Her

when it gets light out. It's Friday morning, 5 AM sharp. Harry Rosenthal hasn't slept all night thinking about his next call. Six thirty won't be too early. She's always up and around by then.

Harry lives in a one-bedroom Great Neck walkup only a short stroll from the temple. He oscillates in the oak rocking chair his wife Frances gave him for his sixtieth birthday nearly eight years ago. He's been marking time there since 3 AM when he finally gave up trying to get to sleep. Nothing on TV except reruns. He's watched *Father Knows Best* until he can't bear to see it again. Instead, all this time he's been staring at a picture – his son, Marc. That's his boy's best photo. You can see his intelligence and vitality, Harry reflects. What a great kid. The framed image of a smiling twenty-eight-year-old, long-maned blond man wearing a rented tuxedo sits on top of the television. There it's most easily seen from any vantage point in the combination living room slash dining room. Best man at his friend Bill's wedding. Marc looks so handsome in black. Nothing's happening this weekend until the Sunday night meeting. Frances could probably use some company, too.

The community service Harry's thrown himself into head-long kills most of the hours. Committee meetings to organize written campaigns protesting the new traffic light. And petitions for an additional stop sign on a neighborhood side street make him forget mostly that she wanted him to move out of their home a year ago. "Give Frances time," the guys at the temple meeting tell him. It takes time. Maybe I shouldn't have retired at sixty-five, but who knew what would happen only a week after I finally gave up my CPA practice? A damn good one, too. The younger guys couldn't wait to call my clients and take over.

Harry checks the time on the genuine Swiss cuckoo clock on the marble mantle. It's five after five. Only five minutes has passed since he last looked. Yes. Just another one hour and fifty-five minutes until I'll give her a buzz. Now that I think of it, it's still less since a few seconds just ticked off. He laughs at his little arithmetic drollery. The friendly, tired, and retired CPA now counts seconds instead of dollars. It helps him to fall asleep. And he finally does, in the rocking chair with the black-and-blood-red tessellated pillow his wife crocheted for him.

"Is This Our Relationship?"

demands Dan. "Market research for the great American novel?" Going to LFOD again was out of the question for them. He has to get back there before he's missed in the morning, so her quarters in the city got ruled out, too. He sits dejectedly on the basic motel chair of East Hampton House, a few minutes from Brucie's manse.

His parents' impending divorce flits in and out his mind. It's their life, but maybe his problems had something to do with the breakdown of their marriage. The whole family started going to hell when he turned on to junk. On the phone dad said maybe they'd try mediation. At least they won't become antagonists, with attorneys battling for money and the death of the opposing party. Maybe they'll have a happy life again – together or apart. Elaine's the open secret behind this – Dan's guess had been confirmed by his best possible LFOD source. The paramour has a key role here. A vivacious and sexy woman – and single. For sure she's not helping mom and dad's resolution.

It's not lights out yet, but he pulls the curtain apart just enough to see the moonlit lawn beyond the studio suite's small balcony. Dan's been watching Laura for over an hour now in the motel's standard-size unit.

Though the coke's high has receded into a low, Laura scribbles the night's events in her journal. "The armed and dangerous poverty-stricken boy couldn't wait to relieve his lust. He forced her into a nearby motel where he ravished the stunning, braless, and nearly unconscious author," she writes.

He cranes his neck to read her prose over her shoulder. "I'm unemployed to be sure, but I wouldn't exactly call myself destitute, Laura. And who's been trying to ravish who?"

"Ravish <u>whom</u>," corrects the Ph.D.-in-English candidate. Yanking the pad away from him. "Go find your own job if you can. This is none of your business. If you don't want to get laid, why don't you go back to the little girl? She's more your speed."

"You know I'm crazy for you, don't you, Laura?"

"You're crazy – period!"

"But not only in the bad way." She lets him kiss her neck.

"Were you really going to use that weapon in your pocket?"

"We've both used it before. I thought you liked it."

"Not that one, wise guy. The real one."

"I don't know what I was going to do. In movie scripts they say the writer should never show a gun unless someone's going to pull the trigger."

"Don't scare me, Dan. It's not funny."

"Let's take a swim, love," manages to change her mood.

Laura holds his face, "You're such a bad boy," and kisses him.

They walk, hands clasped together, outside to the pool beyond the dogwood trees, take off their clothes, and swim laps until they're both exhausted.

"Is this where I get violated?" she laughs, squeezing herself alongside him. The waterdrops on her wet blonde hair prism the rising rays of dawn into an arcing rainbow silhouette.

"Take me back to my dungeon before I do just that. We're in the deep end, Laura. Over our heads here."

"Here are some towels, Mr. and Mrs. Topler," the cheeky but tired-out receptionist/owner from last night surprises them with her sudden appearance. The matronly lady in a daffodil-patterned dress standing over their heads chirps, "The complimentary bed-and-breakfast coffee and muffins won't be ready for a few minutes." As the proprietor tramps back into the motel she recites a Hail Mary – to thank the lord for the wild parties at the Langfords nearby – and the motel's high occupancy rate.

"The Yellow Stickers

indicate where you need to sign. May I call you Charlotte?" Davian Corbeille ever so tentatively inquires in the polished Goldman Sachs conference room. She had refused a Friday lunch invitation and would meet only in the late afternoon when even hard-driving Wall Streeters normally head early for their country homes in Connecticut and the Hamptons. He spreads the closing documents for the Aramark/G.F. Davison Vending Machine Corporation merger on the table.

"Ms. Davison suits me fine."

The queasiness begins anew for him. "You're very kind to take the time to come see us. We wouldn't bother you so soon after your loss except the transaction could fall through unless we move forward. It's a pooling of assets – complicated finances. These are the final papers, but possibly you'd like your securities attorney to review them one more time to ensure nothing's changed. Your father worked so hard to complete this merger, so I'm sure you'll want to proceed." The department head starts to break the company admonition contra perspiring. When she focuses her gaze on him, he feels hot and cold flashes.

"Not necessarily. My father's dead. He'd want me to do as always – exactly as I please."

Fuck me. There goes my bonus and that canary GranTurismo Maserati, Malcolm Bennett internally whines.

Sitting next to the exotic target, Mason forges on. "What can we do to help make this a win-win wind-up for a beautiful woman?" He inches closer to her with just a hint of a warm smile. His charisma has closed more than one deal in this firm.

Good work, Rextal, keep pushing, thinks Davian.

Her eyes flash. "If you come any closer to me, I'll break your neck in half."

Mason urgently excuses himself to go to the men's room. He zips into the lavatory but zips down a few seconds too late – and doesn't return.

Bhadra gets to the point. "Are you seeking a higher price, Ms. Davison? We'll have to go back to our client. Our analyst Chung Fat can run the numbers again." The two women can get to the heart of the matter without interference from the heightened testosterone in the room.

"Let me get back to you, Bhadra. I have other matters on my mind just now. I need to review the papers and see what I want to do. And please, you can call me Charlotte."

"Whoa! Is she ever something out of the sci-fi channel," Malcolm gushes after Charlie leaves the room. But all eyes turn to the glowing Bhadra who's become the possible key to getting the job done.

"Maybe she's a dyke," Davian unthinkingly speaks his mind – another GS prohibition for department heads. Trying to save himself from the politically incorrect gaffe, "Did you all know Queen Christina of Sweden was a lesbian?" Despite the icicles darting from his subordinates' eyes, he adds, "She was only five years old when she was crowned queen in 1632."

Same year as you, thinks Bhadra.

"Professional Courtesy

notwithstanding, Dr. Bernstein, I'm happy to answer any of your questions and help any way I can," Dr. Henry Singleton tells Jacob. Henry takes a quick glance at his watch. He promised his wife that this one time he'd be home on time to beat the weekend traffic to their cottage in the Berkshires. "How is Mary, anyhow? Haven't seen in her in ages."

Jacob finally booked an appointment with the Columbia-Presbyterian Hospital psychiatrist recommended by his own therapist at Stony Brook. "Please call me Jack. Mary's fine. Lucky to have her as my surgery therapist. It was very nice of her to contact you for me. I'd like to get to know my surgical operating team. I would very much appreciate an introduction so that they can fully understand my case. The surgeon and anesthesiologist in particular, but also the nurses."

"She told me it scared you not to know them."

"The staff at my own hospital have been like a family to me. More so since my wife died. I'm frankly terrified to be cut open and perhaps die in the hands of strangers.

The operation's scheduled for next week." Jacob's agitation flares as his pain returns.

The lower aches from the tumors have grown much worse despite medication.

"Jack, you don't seem well. Has the pain increased? Jack? Jack?"

No Date for the Weekend

or maybe the last thirty weekends for that matter. Morty Mavis mopes around the kitchen he keeps clean himself in his contemporary home and plays this sad violin music in his mind. It's a two-hour drive from here on a Friday afternoon, but what the hell else should I do with myself? No community meetings have been scheduled – nobody to push around.

During a coffee break at the last temple meeting, Dan told Morty that a very hot single woman who likes older men, a redheaded tennis and swimming instructor at LFOD with a great figure, might like to meet him.

"I can ask her first," Dan said.

"Who needs an intro?" Morty replied. "Me, for crissakes? For forty years I made intros for others as a consultant. A babe who wants to glom a real man? – I'm the guy."

So now Morty heads for LFOD without calling to see if she's there. Maybe he hopes she isn't, to save himself possible embarrassment.

What am I doing here? Morty asks himself after the long drive.

He's panic-stricken and filled with remorse for wasting his time or, worse, risking rejection and ensuing mortification. Do I need the runaround from some dame I know zilch about? He parks in the lot. On the way to the reception area Morty gets assistance just before he enters.

"May I help you?" the doctor asks him.

"I'm looking for . . . uh . . . he's a young man. His name is Daniel."

"Oh yes. You must mean Daniel Topler."

"That's him."

"Sad case, poor boy."

"Yeah?"

"I may be talking out of turn. Are you a relative?"

"No. Just an acquaintance, kinda. We're in the same men's club."

"I see. I see. Well then perhaps you don't need to know the details of his homicidal inclinations. I'm his physician here."

"You mean he wants to kill people?"

"Sir. Please don't be concerned. To our knowledge he's never been successful – although we could be wrong. I have to watch my words. Litigation precaution, of course."

"Of course. You know, maybe I don't need to see him today."

"I can see I've alarmed you, Mr. . . . . ."

"Mavis. Morton Mavis. Morty."

"Morty, may I call you that?"

"Huh? Oh, yeah. Sure."

"Listen Morty, Why don't we sit over there by the pool?"

Morty follows him and sits down with some hesitation, "You know, I really can't stay that long so. . . ."

"I'd like to speak confidentially to you. May I, Morty?"

"Sure, Doctor."

"Why are you really here? Look at your elegant clothes. Your oily salt-and-pepper hair carefully combed. I can smell the freshly applied aftershave lotion. You're here to chase some woman, aren't you, you reprobate? It can't be one of the putrescent scags incarcerated in this hellhole so it must be some staff member." The physician puts his palm to his forehead to ridicule Morty. "Now let me think who the lucky lady might be."

I've been caught! The doctor can tell I have an ulterior motive. They're really sharp at this joint, Morty thinks. "Well it's true that I also want to see. . . . "

"Why am I here?!" the doctor violently interrupts. "Can it be that we're all here just to watch TV, play shuffleboard, and eat the crap they serve at this fucking joint?"

"Doctor, I'm not sure that I follow."

"You do know Live Free or Die is a rehabilitation clinic for all sorts of ailments?"

"Well, I've heard something to. . . . "

"We're required to sugarcoat it here. The staff that is," doc whispers in Morty's ear.

"What do you mean?"

"This is a nuthouse. Now I know I shouldn't call it that. Well, then, but there it is. And that Daniel Topler. . . . " now the doctor stands with his arms lifted as if in a priest's blessing. He looks out over Long Island Sound, " . . . Oh, Lord, he's the biggest nut here." The physician places his nose almost touching Morty's as he grasps the terrorized man's shoulders, "Is that the kind of friends you have, Morton Mavis?"

"I must be going." Morty starts to rise from his seat.

"Just stay where you are, Mr. Looney Tunes Friend of Daniel Topler's," the doctor commands. Morty plunks himself down again.

The man in white rises with arms uplifted to heaven. "See? Do you see what I mean, Jehovah?" Lars shouts at the top of his lungs. "The pernicious Topler conspirators like this pathetic sinner are off their rockers. And here am I, Dr. Jacob Q. Bernstein. . . ."

"By coincidence I know a Dr. Jacob Q. Bernstein. . . ."

"Will you please shut your yap! I'm the senior nutcracker here and have to put up with insane patients and their whacko visitors too." He pours a heaping bowl of cashews and almonds on Morty's head – luckily the kind of nuts he likes best. It's only now when Morty notices the bunny slippers on the doctor's feet that he flings himself from his chair, trips, then scrambles away at a breakneck speed that can only be deemed amazing for a veteran AARP member.

Recently, at this time of day, Elaine would be on her way to the Marriott to meet Albert and keep the amiable soon-to-be-bachelor on ice with her body heat. But today she's depressed and lingers at LFOD chatting with Helen at the front desk – alone for the weekend.

"Albert's taking the advice of some female attorney. He won't see his tootsie in person until the divorce papers have been signed. And I couldn't talk him out of mediation either. Evidently this gal at Al's law firm has some kind of magical hold over him," she confides to Helen – not a gossiper for some crazy reason. Maybe Helen's a Scientologist or Christian Scientist or something? Elaine always confuses the two.

Elaine's correct. Helen's not one to gossip. But giving the scoop to her dear Danny on what's happening to his parents' marriage doesn't count. Just now she sees a man fleeing into the lobby.

"May I help you, Sir?" Helen asks the nicely dressed, goateed man tearing up to her desk. He seems upset. Poor, stuffed Nipper staring at him adds to his dismay.

"Who the hell is that guy by the pool?" Morty puffs.

"The one sucking on the giant binky?"

"Yeah. That *mumser.*"

"Lars. One of the guests here. He's harmless."

"Uh, huh, harmless." Not wholly convinced he's out of danger but unwilling to give up on his former quest. "Well, I'm trying to find Dr. Bernstein's medical student who I understand helps out here," Morty continues to pant. Then he takes a gander at the shapely redhead dressed in a white halter top and short shorts, twirling a tennis racket. It doesn't take more than a glimpse for him to guess she's the able-bodied recreation head of this high-priced, human dry cleaning center. He has just the spoon to lick the cream off this yummy creature.

Elaine and Helen eyeball each other quizzically. Medical student? Lars, the self-degreed physician, comes to Elaine's mind. Helen catches on first, "I think you must want Daniel Topler."

"Yeah, that's the boy." Gaining courage, "Dan told me I might get tennis lessons from the athletic cheerleader here. He says she resembles a movie star – Kim Novak. Someone who probably resembles you, <u>Mrs.</u> . . . ."

Helen sees him nearly salivating while taking in Elaine, then notices his blue blazer and freshly pressed dress trousers. She puts it all together. A counterattack, she surmises.

"<u>Miss</u> Bushkin," Elaine announces demurely but without any chance of being misunderstood. "I'm the one Danny probably meant, the activities director here at Live Free Or Die. I have been told I resemble the star of *Vertigo*. . . ." she purrs. And now for the punch line, "but that was <u>years</u> ago," begging for compliments as a sexy, unmarried woman of her age might.

Morty comes through on cue, "It couldn't have been that long ago, Miss Bushkin. It's only been a few years since you were in grade school," he gallantly gurgles.

Hashing through the customary preliminaries, "Would your <u>wife</u> like lessons, too?" hoping for the best answer from this affluent-looking charmer. Elaine's no dummy – she gets the picture. Danny's trying to run interference in her fling with Albert. But she's also starting to feel she's being taken for granted by her boyfriend. Maybe a little competition would perk Al up a bit.

"Sadly, I've been divorced for years. My wife, whom I loved, ran off with my best friend," parroting a movie plot he'd seen not long ago – *Little Miss Sunshine* maybe, he can't remember. Not a complete fabrication. The wife did run off after all. What wife wouldn't when her clothes were thrown out the second-story window? And it always pays to tell a woman you're capable of love. They eat up sensitive men. A little sympathy doesn't hurt either. On balance, getting dumped by another woman works for a plus impression despite the possible inference, "if she didn't think much of him, why should I?"

"Poor man," Elaine says.

But Morty hasn't finished his sales pitch, "I live alone in my mansion – giant Sub-Zero fridge with icemaker I might add, Olympic-sized swimming pool, and grass tennis courts."

"Grass, huh? Expensive maintenance." Elaine's analysis: At least Danny didn't send some lame *schlepper* my way. "When would you like your lessons? I'm only free nights and weekends." Elaine can hint with the best of them.

Morty scores again with, "How about this weekend? Would you like to talk about it over a drink or dinner tonight? I can always get a table at The Palm nearby. Know the management well. Used to do some consulting for them," wishing for the best of all possible lessons from this knockout.

Helen decides to have some fun too, "I'll go ahead and call Dan for you now, Mr. . . . "

"Who? Nah, don't bother. Don't need the kid now. I've found what I wanted." His and Elaine's eyes light up like double-whammy pinball bonus bulbs. "Tennis lessons, that is. I'm Morton Mavis. But please, ladies, call me Morty."

The deal's signed, sealed and delivered for the evening as far as Elaine's concerned. He passed the last test with flying colors by suggesting a very expensive restaurant. I hate cheap men, which, judging from the shiny new gray Lexus convertible I'm sliding into now, Morton Mavis (is that what he said his name is?) isn't.

"You Can't Have the Keys, Honey,

until I have permission from Dr. Heine," Helen somberly tells her favorite "guest."

"Who the hell is he?" Dan wants to know.

"I know how you must feel, Danny. You want to see Dr. Bernstein, your doctor and I hope by now your friend – and Laura's father."

"I don't know who this Heine is, but tell him I want the keys to my car now or I'll put his lights out."

"Dr. Wolfgang Heine is your new therapist until Dr. Bernstein returns. Maybe a little sugar will work better than vinegar, dear. He's in his office."

"And Helen. That fruitcake Lars claims he's a real shrink."

"Former chief psychiatrist at Bellevue."

"What happened?"

"He was picked up one day sitting stark naked in Bergdorf's window with a sign on his neck that said:

SHMUCK! YOU CAN LOSE TWO DRESS SIZES LIKE ME

"Yeah?" Dan leaves trying to sort out the new info and catches a glimpse of Morty and Elaine driving off. One job well done, anyway. On the way to Wolfgang Heine. Oh. Ally's wolfman – something of a pushover. A knock on the door and please enter. Sitting down and sure of himself, "A very good afternoon to you, Dr. Heine. I'm. . . . "

Cool and stroking his beard, "I know who you are, young man."

Maybe not such a pushover. "Before you left for the weekend, I just wanted to get briefly acquainted and let you know the routine Dr. Bernstein and I formulated."

"Sad to hear of his illness. Probably von't make it, I imagchin."

Ally didn't mention the heavy German accent. Some gall, burying Jack so quickly. "Well, naturally, I'd like to pay him a visit and thought while I'm here to say hello I'd pick up the keys to my car."

"Out of the kvestchin. Zank you for coming, Daniel. Ve'll be seeing a great deal of each other. But you must leef now. Gut bye," and returns to paperwork on his desk. The furious Dan has almost slammed shut the door behind him when he hears, "I don't think this Jewish group you attend can help you. So you von't need the keys for zat, eizer. Haf a pleasant veekend."

While Dan's passing back through the lobby, Helen catches him by his sleeve. She sees blood in his eye. "Don't do anything foolish, Danny. You're not a voluntary guest here." Helen pulls a blue form out of a drawer. "Until this release is signed by a staff psychiatrist, by court order you're a prisoner here. Dr. Heine has control over your life now that Dr. Bernstein's ill. He can make it comfortable. He can make it hell."

"<u>He</u> can go to hell. That Nazi's not telling me what to do."

"He's a concentration camp survivor – Orthodox. He has to get to Shabbat services before sundown."

A somewhat disappointed, "Oh," follows the sudden deflation of that self-righteous train of thought.

"I know what you're thinking now, sweetie. Don't do it."

"From now on, Helen, I'll only do what will make you proud of me. I promise." Seeing the skepticism etched over her wrinkles, "Sooner or later you will be anyhow," and he saunters off toward the pool.

To his back, "I'll hold you to it, honey. Don't forget you made a pledge to <u>me</u>. Not just anyone." She knows no strings bind him more tightly than those of her apron.

Even if I get lucky, hitch a ride from the road to the East Hampton train station and catch the 6:03, I won't get to Columbia-Presbyterian Hospital for hours. I've got to see Ally at Stony Brook Hospital, too.

Eating Crow's the Only Way,

Dan concludes.

Thirty minutes later, "My oh my. See what bird the cat dragged in from the funny farm next door! Still feeling huffy, Dandy Man, or are you coming to the bash early?"

Dan's caught the infamous Georgica Pond host in the midst of making preparations for Monday night's infamous Devils-Take-All costume ball.

"Look Brucie. . . ."

"So it's <u>Brucie</u> again, is it? Are you going to throw me out the window, too? Toss Bertrand instead. He does that kind of errand for me. Any more of those shenanigans, old man, and I'll be forced to cross you off my invitation list."

Speaking frankly and ignoring Pirot standing a few feet away from them in the ballroom, "I'm sorry for the other night. What happens to me is my fault, not yours."

"*Exactement, mon ami.*"

"Give my apology to The Chipster. The poor guy couldn't force a life-sized plastic doll to have sex with him."

"And he's tried, I assure you," Langford the second jests. "Enough of that. We've know each other forever. Everyone but me flies off the handle sometimes. So. You're here to carouse nicely this time?"

"Brucie, do you ever sniff the pixie dust you serve at the parties?"

"Me? I never touch that junk. Never have."

"Never have? Don't you remember the very first time the four of us bought snow together at Times Square during Christmas vacation? We all got ripped."

"How can I not remember? Have you forgotten? That's where we met Pirot. He sold it to us. You got so stoned we had to carry you to the parking garage. You begged us not to tell anybody, otherwise you might not get the award for head student again. You were the school star. It was funny to see you so spaced out."

"But you took some, too. We all did."

"No, Dandy Man. Only you. Ronnie, Chipster, and I faked it. We were too scared to try the stuff. None of the four of us has ever dusted our noses with coke but you."

Dan stares at his smirking friend for a few moments. "I need a favor. But first - "

He knocks Bruce to the floor with a hard punch to the jaw. Pirot draws out a switchblade and advances toward Dan.

"That won't be necessary, Pirot." Rubbing his chin. "What the hell was that for?"

"The drugs I've taken have always come from you. You know I'm an addict. You could have been a better friend to me, Brucie."

"You were always the brilliant, successful one in school, Dan. Everything always came so easily to you. I never thought it, I swear, but maybe it was to level the playing field. Was this slug to my chin the favor you wanted?"

"No."

From the French doors to the patio, the junior Langford thoughtfully watches Danny pull out the gates of the driveway in his green Aston Martin. He'll have to drive his stepmother's Silver Cloud Rolls – ordinarily a bit ostentatious even for Brucie. Uh oh. I forgot to get back that certain item. Dad will be livid if he finds it missing when he gets back from Holland with his new wife next week. Still rubbing the sore spot on his cheek, "That reminds me, Pirot. Invite those twins again from Amsterdam. They were a big hit. And can we find a sequined mask for that rubber, life-sized Barbie Doll?"

We Have Unfinished Business, Danny,

an irresistible voice tells him.

Dozens of images and thoughts whirl through his mind as he enters the Midtown Tunnel to Manhattan this Friday evening from Long Island. When he hears his cell phone ringing, he thinks it must be Laura. "Come to the Hampshire House. 150 Central Park South. Charlotte's waiting for you here. Now."

"Yes, now," he says and hangs up. Maybe it's because she referred to herself in the third person like a queen, or the imperial "now," but it doesn't occur to him to say no to her though he urgently wants to see if Dr. Bernstein's all right. And then on to Ally. I'll stop and just say hello to Charlie. This is a good thing. I need to make amends anyhow for ruining her dress. I'll say, "Can I pay for the dry cleaning? Or buy you a new outfit if that would make you happy?" The Toplers aren't cheap. Just shake hands, tell her that Laura's my girl now and be on my way. No hard feelings. Very sophisticated. She'll understand.

The doorman waves him to the elevator as though he's expected. On the way up Dan's not so sure of the outcome.

Inside her penthouse haunt, though unsuitably dressed for it, an incensed Charlotte practices deadly karate kicks and punches on a male dummy in the master bedroom. When Charlotte succumbed to Barry as would an ordinary woman, her emotions began to nag at her with a fury. Her emotional vocabulary can't yet handle the challenge of having a true lover and not just a sex partner. Now the flesh-and-blood reincarnation of a warrior goddess finds herself unable to quiet the combative Athena within her. Laura challenged her in winning Danny. The sting of the conquest lost to Laura hasn't subsided.

Dan raps at the door. It opens to a divinely transparent, black lace negligee and the white-skinned deity underneath. Her piercing violet eyes blind him for an instant. Giving her the once-over. "You didn't tell me we were going to the park to play baseball, Charlie. I would've brought my mitt," he creaks, doing his best to keep his resolutions intact. "Nice digs. Love the view," he says, trying to make a getaway to the terrace overlooking the park.

But the fuming Charlotte takes his hand and silently leads the mesmerized boy to the Indonesian-style, sparely decorated bedroom that was her father's. She slowly undoes his belt, unbuttons his shirt, sits him on the four-poster wicker-aproned bed, then pulls off his chinos. A Ravi Shankar album plays in the background. In a slow undulating motion to the sound of the musicians' sitar and tabla, she slips off the translucent fabric. Reversing roles, she's a snake charming the shaman. The warrior wraith inside her must prove itself invincible. It's only later, when with surprising strength Charlotte pushes him out her front door – tossing his clothes out in the hallway after him – that Danny feels the extent to which he's been devoured and then regurgitated. The episode somehow feels like déjà vu.

He knocks on her door. Flying out come his jockey shorts followed by a loud slam. "Nice to see you again. Let's have lunch," the ejected, naked sex object shouts with mock appreciation. "Just visiting," he smiles weakly at the peeved co-occupants of the floor waiting next to him by the elevator with their German Shepherd.

The huge pooch licks his behind as he scrambles to put his pants and shirt on. Simultaneously, he answers his ringing cell. Still dazed, he hears, "Dan, where are you. I'm worried. Helen said you left LFOD hours ago."

The film buff recalls the singular, magic movie moment in *Man, Woman and Child* when Blythe Danner sweetly inveigles Martin Sheen to confess his infidelity to her – and the dummy does, to his regret. "Stuck in heavy traffic, Laura, but I'll be at the hospital soon." The aggravatingly slow elevator door finally opens and he's off to Columbia-Presbyterian Hospital.

The Glare Burning in Her Eyes

tells Dan immediately who Laura's speaking to on her father's hospital room phone. On the other end, a lonelier-than-ever woman hangs up and sobs over her bitter victory.

"Did I ever tell you the one about the traveling salesman with a broken-down car who knocks on a farmhouse door?"

"Just leave," Laura says. Bernstein lies sedated on the bed.

"The door opens and the salesman says to the farmer, 'I sell insurance and I need to sleep here tonight.'"

"Get out now. I'm calling security," she picks up the phone and does just that.

The sick doctor tries to sit up and talk but can't.

"So the farmer says, 'Would you like to sleep with my daughter or my magic pig?'"

"Please arrest this lunatic who forced his way in here," Laura says angrily to two orderlies in white who burst into the room.

Dan – talking more rapidly as they manhandle him. "'Well, it depends,' says the salesman. 'Which one can sign the premium checks?'" Dan's holding on to the doorjamb, but losing his grip as he gets dragged out. Dan screeches to her, "Laura! I'd rather sleep with the doctor's daughter than with her enchantress friend," and out of the patient's room he's flung. "Just sign the check," he shouts from the hallway – the last words she hears from Dan until she decides to try to post bail for him the next day.

Maybe This Info
Can Be Sold Twice?

Norman Butterworth, or Mr. Norman – as he refers to himself in the third person – kicks around in his thoughts. This private investigator *par excellence*, or at least that's what his calling card claims, regularly works both sides of a dispute. It got him fired by Harriet Topler, but that goes with the territory for investigative double agents. Mr. Norman's planted himself across the way from the Hampshire House in Central Park where he's spying on Charlotte. He nearly knocks over his telescopic camera when he spots the Topler son standing on that loaded gal's apartment terrace.

I'll bet that boy's breaking court orders by tooling around in the city. Won't that Bhadra gal from Goldman Sachs be impressed with my work. Maybe a bonus. Then he follows Danny. That kid kinda looks out of it, with his hair standing on end and his shirt inside out, Mr. Norman thinks an hour later when Dan stumbles out of the apartment building. Dan leads him to a very familiar-looking two-seater, green Aston Martin DB9 Volante with the license plate BL-II. The pieces fit together. I've followed Davison to the Bruce Langford pond house a half-a-dozen times in the past month – close to the nuthouse for the rich nearby where the Topler kid's supposed to be under wraps. Woowhee! Dirt turned to gold before my very eyes.

Still Angry,

but more with herself than with Laura, Charlotte orders her Ferrari to be pulled around to the front of her building. It's late Friday night, and Brucie's bash must be in full swing. She's not done flouting her prowess over one half of the human species. Shifting her car into gear she questions, Why not go to Barry first? I lost control last night. What's wrong with me? Her fury's not yet spent. She wheels to SoHo where he lives in a contemporary-decorated loft bequeathed to him by his late parents, both keen commercial developers in the late 70s. She's determined to prove herself unconquerable to him, too.

To the intercom, "Let me in, Barry. Now."

"Certainly, Zoë. What a pleasant surprise even at this late hour," slows her down a bit.

Buzzed in, she races up the stairs of the three-story un-elevatored former meatpacking plant, now prime property. Door opens. Her eyes flashing. Body and mind prepared for battle. "We're going to screw."

"What's the matter, Zoë dear? You seem distressed." Barry stands there huge as a sleepy mountain – an Atlas in pj's.

"I said get in the bedroom. We're going to fuck. Now."

Barry puts his Herculean arms around her and hugs her so tight she winces and then plants a big wet kiss on her forehead. "You're going to bed – alone." He picks her up as though she were weightless and carries her into his bedroom. She bounces on the oversized bed. "And don't come out until morning. I need some rest, sweet girl." He gently closes the bedroom door behind him and stretches out in the two-story-high living room on the extra-long double-spring couch constructed especially for him. "Women," he says to himself as he dozes off – the complaint and loving compliment given by all men to their lovers.

"Am I Ever Glad to See You,

Officer Franklin." With a gleaming smile, Dan vigorously shakes the dubious cop's hand. The two beefy interns holding Dan in custody downstairs let him loose as the policeman arrives in his patrol car.

"What're you doin' here at the hospital making trouble, Mr. Topler? I thought we turned you over to some crackers holding pen."

Ever the smoothie, "Please call me Dan. We're like old friends now . . ." Dan reads the man's ID, ". . . Ben. My dear physician's not well and I'm here to see him. I have permission from Live Free Or Die to come here." To the men in white, "Sorry for the inconvenience, gentlemen. I was overcome at the sight of seeing Dr. Bernstein so ill. Feeling just hunky-dory and back to normal now. Thanks for the hospital-tality. I'll be going," but he's blocked at the door.

"Just a second. Let's call the nuthouse. I want to be sure you're not lying to me." Franklin knows Dan's full of tricks.

To Dan's relief, just the right woman answers. Please don't tell them I'm in Africa, he prays.

"Yes, of course he has permission to be in New York to see his doctor," the wary policeman hears. "May I speak with him, please?" Dan picks up to Helen Clausen's gruff, "You get your stupid butt back here before Dr. Heine comes in tomorrow at sundown or your ass is grass." Then after a pause, "And try not to get in any more trouble, honey," she ends sweetly as she must when talking to Dan.

"I'm still not so sure I should let you go on your own. Tell you what, fella. Call some responsible person to come and fetch you here or I'll have to take you in." Franklin's taking no chances with this troublemaker at midnight on a Friday.

"You Have Only Yourself to Blame.

I'm not leaving here – ever," the previous night's intruder tells Barry Saturday morning while watching him shave. The shadow of her gladiator spirit has evanesced – maybe permanently.

"Suit yourself, Zoë. You're committing yourself to a boring professor's life of lectures on the lives of dead Greek poets, trips to mountain observatories in far away places, and season tickets to the Yankees."

"That's it. You're a goner now, for sure." She goes up to him from behind and almost can reach around him as they gaze at each other in the bathroom sink mirror. "This is your last chance to bolt, professor. I'm going to call Thomas and have him bring my things here."

Paying no attention to her embrace – he's not done shaving. "Ask him to be careful with the telescope," ends Charlotte-Charlie-Zoë's search for tranquility.

"I Didn't Know I Was in the Phone Directory,"

Glen Sobel tells Dan at the Red Flame Coffee Shop in midtown Manhattan at 1 AM, Saturday. Ordinarily, the workaholic tax lawyer would have blown off a request to go bail out some guy from a police altercation he didn't know from Adam. But he was stood up tonight by a hot waitress he propositioned yesterday at La Grenouille – big tip notwithstanding – and the boy's been attending the men's meetings, so. . . .

"You aren't. Officer Franklin got it for me. I also tried Barry Blackmun, but his phone was off the hook," he lies. "Thanks for coming to vouch for me."

"I'm really sad to hear Jack collapsed. He'll probably need his operation sooner than expected. What was the commotion about anyhow at the hospital?"

"A misunderstanding. I was mistaken for a baby snatcher by the night nurse."

This kid has me mistaken for one of his dumb friends. Changing the subject, "How's it going, working for Jack? I understand you've got a summer job with him or something."

"Yes, at Live Free Or Die on Long Island. Ever hear of it?" Dan never called Barry. Glen was also on his hit list for the outing to the Big Apple.

Glen's antennae start to vibrate, "Yes. A clinic in the Hamptons somewhere."

"You should pay it a visit. There's this wonderful teenage girl undergoing treatment I met. Suicidal."

"Just a moment, young man." This sophisticated international consultant's not putting up with impertinence from some boy.

"She tried it again the other day and almost succeeded."

"She what? What is this? Some kind of setup arranged by her mother? I'm outraged by Jack's breach of confidentiality!"

"Ally's in Stony Brook Hospital now begging to see her father who's never visited her once."

"No one called me. When you talk to Jack, if he wakes up, tell him to call me directly instead of having some kid wet behind the ears do his dirty work for him."

"No one had your number, Mr. Father-of-the-Year. It's not listed. Jack had nothing to do with this. Ally told me herself. Patient-to-patient, you know."

"Patient?"

"I'm one of the crackpots there. Not a medical student."

Hell Warmed Over

Dan assesses himself in the bathroom mirror of his apartment. Less than an hour ago, Glen Sobel stomped out of the coffee shop without a word to Dan's "Catch you later." Stuck me for the tab, too. But what the hay. The Toplers aren't cheap. What a night. No one told me my shirt's inside out, either. My old school headmaster would choke if he knew, he laughs. No time to waste. Can't stop to see Ally. Helen said to be back by noon or else. After a bit of grooming and a quick shave, he grabs some papers from his desk and makes tracks for his home-away-from-home.

Swooping into the LFOD parking lot just before noon, Dan nearly collides with a gray Lexus convertible entering at the same time. "Hello. Good to see you both," Dan happily greets the couple.

Elaine's frankly not thrilled to see Al's son right now. She didn't bring her makeup to dinner with Morty last night – or a change of clothes. "Hello, Danny. I hope you enjoyed your tennis lessons this morning, Mr. Mavis," giving her new beau a wink.

"You bet, Ms. Bushkin," he says to his last evening's companion as she hurries off to her car. "I can't wait to improve my overhand shot," Morty calls to her. She climbs into her vehicle. The men watch her with appreciation as her still firm backside shimmies onto the driver's seat.

"Thanks for the suggestion, Dan," Morty warmly tells him.
"You heard, Morty? About Jack?"

"Yes. Nothing but disaster for some of us. Did you hear about David's wife? He thought she had disappeared, but the police found her hiding in their closet. A panic attack. The poor woman's had agoraphobia for the past two years. Hasn't left the house since then. Won't see Jack for help, who's a dear friend of hers, too."

"Agoraphobia? I have an idea for this Sunday's meeting, Morty. Will you help out?"

"Vat are you doink in your automobile, Daniel?" Dr. Heine wants to know. Even though it's the Sabbath, he came early to LFOD. He's been suspecting Dan has been leaving the premises against his express orders. He saw Danny in the driveway and insisted Helen join him outside for an explanation.

"Maybe we should talk later, sport. Give me a call," Morty says to Dan and drives off.

"I told you, Helen, not to gif him ze keys."

"This isn't my car and she didn't give me my keys, Doctor Hiney," as he parks Bruce's chariot.

"It's pronounced 'hein-uh'."

"Yes, hiney."

"You were forbidden to leef this clinic, my impolite young man."

"I was driving around the lot. Practicing for when you grant me a warden's pardon."

To Dan, but glaring at Helen, "If you leef again, Daniel my boy, without my permission, it vil be in a straitjacket to Bellevue Hospital. The food is not nearly so gut zer as here, I am told. Do you both understand?"

"No Need for Fisticuffs,

was there?" The Chipster asks Frederick Saturday morning. While The Dandy Man didn't exactly strike him a blow the other night, unexpectedly landing in Brucie's pool from the second-story terrace constituted a decided breach of gentlemanly etiquette as far as this congenial young man is concerned.

"You're absolutely correct, Charles," Frederick continues. "Daniel needed only to say that the young lady was spoken for and that would have been that, I'm sure." It's not his place to ask – not at all proper – and anyhow Frederick's much too polite to inquire as to the exact circumstance of the disagreement between the two friends. But he wonders, That same woman again is on his mind. Was Charles trying to screw her? I certainly hope so. He doesn't generally seem to get on with the young ladies. Frederick's a confirmed bachelor, and since he won't have any drooling tax deductions of his own, he thinks it a shame for the male line of Siegels to end with the agreeable though a trifle empty-headed Charles. Surprisingly for a man in his career and circumstances, Frederick likes children. Even babies. Although infants aren't on Chip's mind, a certain woman is.

"Oh, well. Got to dash off. I need to pick up my laundry."

"I'll get it for you, Sir. While I'm on the East Side I can take the Bentley out of the garage for a bit of a spin as well. The tires need to be rotated, and it's good to run the engine occasionally."

The Chipster's nearly forgotten that he owns the limousine. Living in Manhattan he had always simply rented a car when he needed one – whether to go to Brucie's house or horseback riding at a friend's spread in New Jersey. Chip would rather pick up his shirts himself. Frederick's presence has forced him to let the butler do some of his odd jobs and it's creating more leisure time than he's used to. He can't stop fantasizing about Karen – cute – smart. A real dignified lady, too. Crapola. I know she won't call.

"I'll go with you, Frederick," he says to the horror of the gentleman's gentleman. He needs to get out of the apartment to take his mind off her.

"I don't know how that would look, Sir."

"You must at least call me Charles, if not Chip."

"Well, <u>Charles</u>, Sir, it's really not done for the master of the house to do the chores with the . . . uh . . . household manager."

"Tell you what. We'll just pretend we're friends."

"I don't know if I could be your friend, Sir. Charles, that is." Not just in pretense. Frederick's also not sure that he wants to pretend to be a confrere what with the mischief young people get mixed up in these days.

"Oh, come on. We'll take the crosstown bus and go to the Chinese laundry first."

"A bus, Sir?"

They compromise on a taxi and arrive at the Eastern Chinese Hand Laundry at 39th and Lex. "Do you have a twenty you can lend me, Fred?" The manager doesn't take plastic.

Fred? This familiarity has gotten out of hand. "Of course . . . Charles." Pretty cheeky of the lad.

When they later arrive at the parking garage at 60th and Third to pick up the limo, to Frederick's dismay Chip insists that he wants to drive. With no small difficulty, he maneuvers the stretch vehicle out of the garage without a dent and parks in the driveway. "Hey, take a look at this!" Chip opens the back door of the Bentley and puts on Frederick's chauffeur cap.

* * *

"I am looking, Mr. Siegel," Karen says to him. It's the last day of the handbag sale at Bloomie's, down the block. Although she really can't afford it, Karen has sprung for a second designer purse and it dangles gaily from her shoulder as she passes the Kinney Parking Garage. "I'm insulted that you thought you had to make up some cockamamie story about working as an expert witness. A professional driver is a perfectly respectable job."

Chip's stunned and thrilled to see her again.

"I quite agree, Miss," the dignified Frederick tells her.

"Oh my gosh. I'm sorry, Chip. I didn't realize you were at work. Please excuse me, Sir," she says to the tall man in a black suit.

"It's quite all right, Ma'am. You see. . . ." Frederick begins.

"You see, I'm just getting off duty, Karen." He can't let her go again. He's turned on big-time for this busty cherub. "Would you like to go for a spin?"

"What? I'm sure your employer, Mr. . . ." the concerned woman tells The Chipster.

"Smithfield, Madam. Smithfield," Frederick offers.

"That Mr. Smithfield wouldn't approve. I don't want you to lose your job over me."

"There's been some misunderstanding, I'm afraid," Frederick says.

"Fred's a regular guy. This is my new friend, Karen, Fred."

"Charmed, I'm sure."

"He lets me drive his car all the time, don't you, Freddie?"

It's Freddie now? "Of course, Sir . . . uh . . . Charles. Be my guest."

"Hop in the back, Karen, and I'll take you wherever you want to go. Do we have gas, Fred?"

How peculiar he asks his boss that, muses Karen.

"Yes. Quite enough to get you where you want to go, I should imagine." Frederick supposes it's to her place to get shagged – or so he hopes, for Charles' sake. Nice bum on the bird, he thinks.

"I Never Want to Talk to You Again.

Is that clear? Stop calling me."

"How's your father?" Dan's called thirty times and she's finally picked up. Got to keep the conversation going, if possible. In his mind, she's the lifeline that might pull away forever if he can't redeem himself.

"He's awake now and asking about you."

"Me? He'll be fine, Laura. I'm sure of it."

"He wants to make sure you'll carry on with the meetings. I didn't tell him what a louse you are. They're going to operate Monday. And why aren't you in jail? I called the police to see if I could file a complaint."

"No you didn't, dreamboat. You were sorry you made me leave and wanted to bail me out. I'm at the booby hatch, but without wheels now. Come see me so we can make up. That's when couples have the most fun." But the current of his sad mood flowed through the telephone wires. The pretense of gaiety and charm failed.

"You think you know everything. Well, you don't. We're no couple and never will be. You should be put away where you can't do harm to anyone, including yourself."

End of conversation. Dan has no chance to say "Catch you later" this time. After he calls Morty, Dan gets back to work on his project, ashamed that his lying almost cost Helen her job. A few minutes later the phone interrupts him.

"Guess what?" the deliriously happy caller asks him. "My daddy came to see me at the hospital and brought me a gigantic teddy bear. It's kind of babyish, I know. But I love it."

Dan and Ally continue to catch up. "Daddy's coming again tomorrow to bring me back."

"I almost went to jail."

"I wouldn't feed the lousy food they serve me here to Finster."

"I'm sorry I can't come to see you. The wolfman says he'll put me in an insane asylum."

"If I had drowned, would I see you again someday in heaven?"

"Laura says she's mad as hell at me."

Silence on the other end for several seconds. Then, "That makes two of us," Ally says giggling.

When they hang up, both feel warmed by the long talk. Dan resumes where he left off.

"Me, a Blackmailer?"

Norman Butterworth, private investigator, asks Albert Topler at the Northeastern Shore Country Club this fine Saturday morning. The club visitor's perspiring. It's a mistake to beard a lion in his own den, he thinks, as the two sit over coffee in the nineteenth hole lounge. "Al, here I am doing you a favor by telling you your son's gallivanting all over Manhattan, when by court order he's supposed to be at that medical facility in the Hamptons. Is it a crime to think you'd want to thank me?"

"Uh huh," says Albert, staring the man down. Topler may be aging, fat, and sociable, but he holds firm. I didn't become a junkyard magnate by rolling over for every *nudnik* with his hand out. There's a flinty guy wound tightly underneath his gregarious skein.

"Here. Here. Take the pictures. OK? They're yours. See? We're friends again," Norman nervously hands the manila envelope with the pictures of Danny on Charlie's terrace to Albert. It only took a few words from Al and seeing the man's expression for Norman to realize he's misjudged the intended mark – he tried to shake down the wrong man.

"The negatives?"

"Oh," pretending to forget he had them. He reaches inside his breast pocket and hands a second packet to Albert.

All's well, and Al's back to his normal friendly self. "You're OK, Norm."

It's Mr. Norman, the P.I. wants to say to him, but doesn't. Mr. Norman hates to be called Norm. Al scans the pictures,

"Who's the broad? She's some dish my boy's chasing. Don't kids put on some clothes when they're outdoors? She could catch a cold at night even in this weather." As a father he wouldn't want his Coco to do such a thing, God forbid. Now that he takes another look at the half-naked woman, he knows he's seen her somewhere but can't put his finger on it somehow.

"Just one of the girls that hang out at the Langford place near Georgica Pond." Butterworth's pix came from his Goldman Sachs assignment, so he has to watch his words.

"I see." Albert has long suspected that Dan gets his drugs at the infamous parties there. He likes Brucie, whom Al's known from the boy's childhood.. But that's a fast crowd, and in his opinion Bruce has never been a good influence on his son. "Tell you what I'm going to do, Norm. I'll pay you double your normal rate if you can catch Harriet. . . ." Al hesitates. Telling this stranger that she might be sleeping with another man – some wimpy art professor at that – hurts his pride. Not once has he suggested to Harriet's face what he suspects.

He stops before continuing his conversation and goes over it in his mind. Truth be told, I still love my wife. I never would have started with Elaine if Harriet hadn't kept going on long trips with that Castillia character. He got depressed in the middle of one of her artistic travel thingies and checked himself in at LFOD. "Tennis anyone?" the rah-rah activities maven-ette called out and knocked on his cabaña door. "Come in," Albert said to the statuesque, radiant redhead. While admiring her curves he took on a smoldering glow of his own and their hanky-panky started then and there.

" . . . in the company of somebody else. You know what I mean," he finally tells Mr. Norman. Both Al and Harriet have agreed to start mediation sessions soon, but Albert still wants to know the truth. What's her exact relationship with Castillia? Are they lovers? Besides, if the talks break down and war breaks out, it'll be smart to have some of his own ammo for the mud slinging sure to follow.

Butterworth's been in the investigative biz a long time. Jealous husbands go with the territory. A little delicacy on the subject's often called for. "I know exactly what you mean."

Pacing the One Room

after her insufficiently spiteful hang-up on Dan, Laura doesn't know what to do with herself. Alone in her studio apartment on the Lower East Side, she's anxious for her dad, grieving over the loss of her best friend, and furious at the man she thought was "the one." Giving that cheating rat a piece of my mind felt good. Maybe when I go to LFOD I'll slap his face for him. Laura laughs at the thought. He wouldn't dare hit me back would he, the brute? Getting worked up again. If he dared, I really would file a warrant for his arrest. Put the lout in prison. Imagine! Hitting a woman. Cooling down once more. He'd look kind of cute in one of those striped jailhouse outfits you see in movies. I should have known better than to tempt Charlie. She's so proud. And fierce. She sounded terrible on the phone. She didn't know I really liked him or she'd never have done that to me. It's all just war games to her. Her cell phone rings five times before it breaks her reverie.

"Can you forgive me, Laura? It was so shitty."

"Daddy's in the hospital. He's very sick, Charlie. I'm at home but going back there before I go to LFOD later this afternoon to pick up some things for him."

"I'm coming over right now. We'll go together," relieving the two women of their very worst fear – losing their friendship. When Charlie arrives, the two hug but say nothing. As they leave, the phone rings. Dan's put down the papers he's working on in his room. He tries again. He has to.

"It's him. Pick up for me, Charlie. I won't ever talk to him again. Maybe he'll listen to you."

"You forgave me."

"We're friends. I shouldn't have challenged you. That was my fault. But he can't be trusted. Tell him to forget me and stop calling. I'll wait for you downstairs," Laura says as she leaves.

"Please pick up, Laura. You know I love you," the answering machine says.

"She'll be at LFOD about four."

"Thanks, Charlie," Dan says to the dial tone.

"I Told You Not to Talk to Me,"

Laura scolds Dan, who's tapped her on the back from behind, then jumped in front of her. She's not trying very hard to get past him to get into her car parked in the LFOD lot.

"Then why have you been waiting here for five minutes for me to show up? I was hiding behind the bushes watching you."

"You are such a bastard," and pulls her hand back to slap him.

Dan sticks out his chin and closes his eyes, "Go ahead if it will make you happy, angel puss." But Laura switches from an open hand to a fist and delivers a solid right jab from her shoulder to his jaw.

"Charlotte taught me how to do that," the proud girl says cloyingly to the man lying flat on his back.

Rubbing his jaw. "Thank her for me, would you?" and closing his eyes in a faint. Dan suddenly grabs Laura and pulls her to him on the pavement when she leans over to see if he's really hurt. "Also kiss her like this," he pulls Laura close and delivers a winning smooch. "And tell her we're all even now. World War Three is over."

"This doesn't change anything between us, Danny. You're a self-centered, unfocused, unemployed drug abuser."

"Nobody's perfect."

"Everything's fun and games with you. I can't disobey my father's wishes concerning our seeing each other. Other than taking you to the meetings to make my father happy. We're through." She hesitates. "After tonight."

When they both get off the ground and brush themselves off, the two glide off hand-in-hand – but to his room this time, not to a swimming pool.

"Just Anywhere,"

Karen tells Chip. She's never been in a limo, let alone a real Bentley, and doesn't care where he takes her. What fun, and a chauffeur, too. "I'll bet on anyplace you take me."

"You're a gambling woman?"

"Yep."

"OK. Off we go." Through the Lincoln Tunnel and down the New Jersey Turnpike he takes her.

"Hey, where're we going, driver?" she asks.

"You said you like to gamble."

"So?"

"Harrah's in Atlantic City is my fav," he tells her. "I always win." He's telling the truth. He may not be lucky at love, but money flows to Chip like magnets stick to his restaurant-sized cast-iron oven. Though he's a conservative man, gambling's his passion and, lucky for him, he's good at it.

"You're such a bullshitter, Chip – pardon my language. But first you're a professional witness. Now you're a pro gambler. Gimme me a break. Where are we really going?"

"We could go to Caesar's Palace if you like it better." Chip's excitement at both hitting the tables and hitting on Karen at the same time has given him a rise. When he turns off the Garden State Parkway onto the Atlantic City Expressway, she's knows he's not bluffing.

Soon he pulls in front of Harrah's.

"Listen, Chip. This seems like fun, but I can't let you lose your money on a chauffeur's salary. Why don't we just have lunch and take a walk along the boardwalk? I like you. OK? You don't need to go without eating for a week to impress me."

"What a darling. So considerate, but you weren't going to call me, were you?" he asks her as he hands the key to the parking lot attendant.

"Yes, I was." Chip looks down at her rear. "And my pants aren't on fire either."

"When?"

"Today."

"Really?" he asks hopefully.

She pinches his cheek, "Really."

"Then let the games begin." Chip dashes inside to the cashier, with Karen hurrying to catch up. He takes out his money clip and pays for the casino's twenty-five coin from the cashier and puts one in one of the few one-armed bandits left in the gambling town that's not electronic. "Put out your hands," he tells her, indicating the payoff slot.

"Oh broth-ther," she says. "What are you, a magician?"

He pulls the arm. Three cherries pop up. And three hundred dollars plops into her hands.

"Wow, Chip. You _are_ a lucky guy."

"I am now," he replies, flashing her a wide grin.

"Nice ass on your girlfriend, for a wimp like you." A hefty, drunk passerby in jeans and a gold Hard Rock Café T-shirt puts a hand on Chip's shoulder. He turns around to face a twenty-five-plus-or-minus, rooster-mulleted, muscular brute with a tattoo of a snake on his left arm. "How'd you like a big kiss, honey?" he slobbers and lurches toward Karen.

Chip steps between them. "I ought to punch you in the nose," The Chipster threatens him. Normally a wee timid, he's not going to give up this woman as easily as at Brucie's.

Some people you don't threaten.

"Chip! Chip! Are you OK?" Karen asks him. She bends down and delivers a tender kiss on the lips to her prostrate defender with a bloody schnoz. Security has already dragged the inebriated assailant away.

"Where I am?" he says her. "Who are you?" he asks, leaning his head forward closer to hers. "Kiss me again so I can remember."

"OK. But no more until later, my hero," and kisses him passionately.

"At precisely what time will that be, Miss? I need to set my watch." He gently touches his sore nose. "Nothing broken I think."

"You big faker," and she plants another.

Three hours later and two thousand dollars richer from practically every form of gambling, they leave the casino. She has to be at the Kit Kat Club by 10 PM. "They even work you on Saturday nights?" Chip asks. "I didn't know research could be so strenuous," her gullible date says.

Despite his protests, he agrees to let her off at Washington Square, near her workplace she tells him. I sure have her fooled about my line of work, he thinks with a self-satisfied grin. This time he wheedled her phone number from her. She's the one, echoes in his thoughts.

Did He Score

one for the old home team? Frederick wonders Sunday morning as he serves Chip garden-variety English Breakfast Tea (thank God for small favors – no more impossible-to-find leaf imports) with a dash of cream. "Would you care for some scones, Sir?"

"Huh?" The Chipster's disconcerted. He can't stop going over yesterday's events, *We did kiss, and I got her number. But neither of us mentioned a future meeting. What a dopus I am.*

"Karen seems a lovely lass. How went the spin in the Bentley?" Did they or didn't they? the professional organizer wants to know, but of course can't ask.

"All right, I guess."

They didn't, thinks Frederick. A pity.

Chip's cell rings. "Fiftieth floor of the Time Warner Tower at Columbus Circle," he tells the caller. "Yes. It is quite a nice address for a chauffeur. It's . . . uh . . . Mr. Smithfield's. What's that? Well. . . . "

"What is it, Sir?"

"It's Karen. She had to hang up. She's on her way here."

"Splendid."

"Put on your pajamas, Frederick."

"Pardon me, Sir. How silly of me. I thought you told me to put on my pajamas."

"Yes. I'm going to serve you breakfast. And call me Chip."

"Your family has such a keen sense of humor," Frederick replies, then sees the concern in Chip's eyes. "Really, Sir?"

"It's Chip."

"Yes, of course. Chip, Sir."

"And I work for you. OK? Can you do it?"

"I'll certainly try. Why don't I fix a welcoming drink for us before she comes?"

Ten minutes later the doorbell rings. Reception permitted Karen entrance after calling first. Chip answers the door, "Come in, Madam," and lets her in.

Frederick, seated in his robe and pjs at the table on the Mexican-tiled terrace, calls to her, "Please join me for a mimosa and scones, Miss. I'm already on my third. I try to combine both sides of the Atlantic on Sundays." He's into it now.

"Chip, you didn't tell me you were on duty. I wouldn't have intruded."

"Not a problem, Karen. You've met my employer. We'll just be going," Chip tells her, trying to push her out the door. He sees Frederick has already imbibed a bit too much of the sparkling orange libation.

"I won't hear of it, young man. Please join me. Karen, is it? I insist."

"Well, if you insist," she says, enjoying the opportunity to take in the impressive view of the city. Today's her only day off of the week, and she doesn't want to spend it by herself like she usually does.

"A mimosa for the lady, please," Frederick tells Chip in a haughty tone. This will teach the lad a lesson. Perhaps this will put an end to tearing down the sacred wall between a gentleman and his gentleman, the butler thinks, but not all that clearly. Karen giggles and takes a seat.

"Where can I find it?" Chip asks Frederick to Karen's puzzlement. Frederick recently arranged to move both of them to the Time Warner Tower and won't let him get near the kitchen.

"In the refrigerator." A blank expression from Chip. "To your right behind the dining room. And step on it, my barefoot boy with cheek." Frederick winks at Karen, "Whittier, you know," he says in an undertone.

"Of course," she whispers back.

"I'm on it, Sir," calls Dan as he hurries to fetch the potables before the conversation goes too far.

"Dear, dear. The kind of help one gets these days. Nice boy, but not all that bright," Frederick says a might too loudly.

"Does he really think I'm a dunce?" Chip wonders, hustling to the kitchen.

"What brings you to my humble domicile, Karen?"

"Well, at college I played squash, but I don't know where they're any good public courts in the city, so I thought maybe Chip and I would take a walk."

"You play squash? One can't play a set in public courts, can one? You're welcome to play at my club, my dear woman. The University Club. I'll call to reserve a court for you. You'll have to wear whites, of course. Club rules, you know."

"You're a member of the University Club? I can't accept your generosity."

"Tut, tut." Then he calls loudly, "Chip, you worthless servant. I'm going to arrange some squash court time for you and your friend. Get the load out and bring drinks and scones," the sloshed household manager castigates his supposed servant.

Chip finally wends his way to the kitchen and back. Maybe this charade wasn't such a famous idea.

"Do you play, Chip? I played varsity at Brown."

"He plays a little, Miss," Frederick says, waiting for her response.

"Only a little? Well I could teach you. What do you say? Are you chicken?"

She's not familiar with the term "a little squash" on the private club circuit, I see, thinks Frederick.

"I don't think. . . ," says Chip, not wanting to be recognized there by friends.

Frederick crocodile smiles, "Tut, tut, lad. You must. As my employee, you cannot refuse my generosity."

"Thank you, Freddy, Sir," Chip says with a note of irony on his way out with Karen.

Did I a detect a certain tone from young Mr. Siegel? Better pour myself another mimosa to be sure, the lubricated manservant concludes. The normally sedate butler takes the one-liter carafe of mostly champagne with a dash of orange juice and quaffs it down in a single gulp. But the tipsy man's still thirsty. What the deuce, he exclaims. The fridge has been emptied of OJ. "I'm going to have to let him go, I suppose," he mutters in a bit of a haze. For the moment he's completely forgotten that he's only pretending to be Chip's employer.

A knock at the front door. Miriam Gutfreund from down the hall is lonesome and waits outside the apartment to pretend that she needs to borrow a cup of sugar. The unfortunately widowed, albeit rich and still handsome London-bred woman was just informed that her grown son Kent can't make his customary Sunday call. A little conversation with anyone would cheer her up. Anyway, she's curious to see who purchased the cavernous co-op on the floor – the one with the just fabulous view of Columbus Circle and beyond.

Though the fashionable Mayfair-district transplant has on a delicate organdy robe – and she didn't forget to put on a little lipstick and the four-carat brilliant-cut diamond pendant her late betrothed gave her – she looks downs and decides that it won't do to go calling next door with her long black negligee on display. She turns to go back.

"Ah, an adjoining inhabitant," the gentleman's gentleman opens the co-op portal and welcomes her before she can decamp. He tries not to ogle the surprised lady but noticeably fails in the attempt. He does manage to stand nearly upright.

"Would you be so kind as to lend a cup of sugar to a neighbor? We're just down the way," and points to her own door down the hall.

"Won't you join this bachelor in his modest home for some refreshment, dear lady? I'm home alone, and my servant has left me for the day. Freddy Smithfield's the name," forgetting again he's not the master of this big-bucks bungalow.

"Well. . . ."

"Please do. It's the least I can do for a fellow countryman. From Gloucestershire, myself. My guess from your fetching smile is that you're a Cheshire-born woman."

Perhaps it was his familiar refined English accent, or that she'd seen the distinguished-looking man on the floor before, but she accepts his invitation. First she offers, "I have some pastry baking in the oven. Why don't we share it?"

"How generous. But before you go, Mrs. . . . . "

"Please call me Mimi."

"Mimi, it is. Could you spare some orange juice for our refreshment, Mimi? My worthless manservant finished off the entire lot."

"Of course. It's so hard to find good help these days," and leaves to retrieve the delicacies. Frederick couldn't agree more.

When she arrives back, they lounge on the terrace enjoying the late morning sun. Freddy makes yet another carafe of mimosas. An hour later they're both dazed and warmed to each other. "How do you like my hot cross buns, Freddy?"

"My dear, Mimi," he says with a leer. She had volunteered her nickname what seems years ago to the man. He feels inflamed from the drink and his brief encounter with that athletic girl, Karen, on the terrace and drops his blue-striped bottoms to the ceramic floor, "You're buns may be hot and delicious, but I certainly hope I won't find them cross."

The lonely Mimi bares witness to his aroused condition and succumbs right then and there to his charms. Thereon begins the infamous Time Warner Tower heiress-and-chauffeur romance which will be gossiped about for months by fellow residents.

"Whadja Do That For,

you big fat idiot?" Ally's mad as a wet Long Island pullet at Terrence O'Connor, a brand new 14-year-old guest who just performed a perfect cannonball inches from her at the LFOD pool, drenching her desert-dry swimsuit. "You must weigh a thousand tons. Just watch it, stupidhead!"

"Who you calling fat, four-eyes? I have endocrime problems. If you don't like it, call your mommy. Or go inside like some mama's girl." In all, a typical way for early teens of the opposite sex to get acquainted. Terry couldn't think of a better way to talk to her – no mustard or ketchup bottles to squirt on her were handy – just yet. He sits down on her chaise lounge, tipping it a bit, and purposefully flops his shaggy bear-brown hair over the teen to make her wetter, if humanly possible.

"Hey, you're going to break the chair. Who said you could sit there?" She takes off her lenses and affects a womanly tone. "Well, now that my glasses are off I'm not a four-eyes, but you're still gross."

He surveys the nearby, much older guests. "I'm Terry. You're not that cute, but at least you're not going to croak on me."

"I know what you mean. I'm Alicia, but you can call me Ally." She looks around at the other guests, "It's creepy being around these people all the time." Remembering he scored the last insult, "And what's so handsome about you, squirrel face?" but she's still glad to have some company. It's late Saturday afternoon and Daniel's nowhere to be found.

"You mean because I have some whiskers here?" pointing to the half dozen short black hairs just above his lip. "I'm nearly an adult. I'm almost fifteen. How old are you?" he asks, wanting to establish their pecking order.

"I just turned thirteen."

"A kid, huh? Well, don't sweat it. I can still remember being only thirteen."

Ally's impressed – he's almost fifteen. "You can? What's it like to grow old?"

"Lotta responsibilities. Got to take out the trash to get my allowance, and my grades count for college now that I'm a freshman. If I get even one 'C,' dad says I can kiss getting a convertible goodbye when I'm sixteen. I'm here to get help with my medical problem so I won't eat so much. Why are you here?"

"I keep trying to kill myself."

"Yeah? Cool! How are ya going to do it? With an axe, or shoot yourself in the head? Maybe hang yourself or something neat like that?"

"No. I just try to drown myself in the tub," Ally offers half-apologetically.

"Oh. That's too bad. You never see that in a video game. Sounds like a kinda boring way to do it. No blood or nothin'."

"You really think I'm not cute?"

"You're OK for a girl," he carefully considers.

"So your endocrimes make you eat too much?"

"I also have an eating disorder, the psychologist says."

"In other words you're a pig!"

"Hey! I also get nervous a lot. When I do I could eat a whole loaf of rye bread with butter and cream cheese. Yum. Mom says Dr. Heine can talk me out of doing that if they put me in this dump. He says I've got an oppressive-combustive disorder. Very rare. Not just anybody can get it, you know."

"Yeah?" Terry succeeded in making Ally a little jealous. "Maybe I'll catch that, too."

"Say, when do we eat around here? I could eat a cow."

"Oink oink," Ally laughs, followed by another tidal wave, courtesy of her plump new friend.

"Good to See You

again, Mr. Siegel," the University Club's gold-epauletted doorman greets Chip when the now tennis-whites-clad couple enters. "We haven't seen much of you lately."

"Very nice treatment you get here, Chip," Karen says suspiciously to her date.

"Professional courtesy. From one doorman to another doorman slash chauffeur. If we're not cordial to each other then the whole system of service personnel checks and balances breaks down. What next then?" queries Chip, now carried away by his own made-up nonsense. "Will we slam the door in the face of the wine and spirits delivery man? Should we tell our employer not to give a Christmas gift to the poor garage attendant for the stretch limousine? Will we deny little crippled LaMaze, who washes the floor and cleans our luxury cooperative, a new broom? I say no. A thousand times no!" He almost believes himself at this point.

"The maid's handicapped?"

Down to Earth. "Don't know who cleans the place to tell the truth. I never seem to be around when it's done. But it's the principle of the thing."

"Uh huh," she says, signifying that now they both know he's full of it.

The two arrive at the squash courts. "Hey, The Chipster's here," a panting young man says to his sweaty friend as the two exit the nearest court. They take a seat in the gallery.

"They know you?" Karen asks Chip.

"I bring Mr. Smithfield here frequently. Let's go in," he nervously replies as he escorts her through the door to the court.

"Do you play?"

"A little," he says.

"Do you want me to show you how to hold the racquet?"

"Do I hold it like this?"

"No. That's the beginner one-grip system. But you'll never improve that way. Let me show you." She moves close to him and then rotates the handle. "The plane of the racquet must be the same as the palm of the hand."

Chip moves even closer to her. "That feels much better," he says, snuggling up. The men in the gallery – some with smirks on their faces – intently watch the two as she gives Chip a lesson.

"This is the forehand, not the foreplay grip," she laughs. "Why don't we just volley? "

"It's a bit like tennis, I recall."

"This line's called the T," she says and serves the ball, which travels right past him. "Have to hustle more, Chip. Make it hurt. The most important thing is don't hit me with the racquet. It's considered very rude if you do. If I'm in the way, just call 'let'."

"Okey-dokey." He feebly returns the next serve. Karen wants to prove her superiority in the sport. She rushes to the ball and slams him in the face with her racquet when he fails to timely give way. The growing crowd stands and cheers the blow with great enjoyment.

"Oh my gosh. I'm soooo sorry, Chip."

"You'll have to kiss it and make it better," he says, offering his cheek. Chip sees she senses the gathered men enjoying the show. "It's all right – a tradition here, I'm told, to kiss your opponent if you strike him . . . if you're the opposite sex, of course." She obliges to huzzahs and wolf whistles from the onlookers.

After a few more volleys Karen announces to her apparently befuddled opponent, "OK. Let's play a game."

"Ladies first," Chip says, gives her the ball, and takes a defensive stance. "What do we play to? Twenty-one like in ping pong?"

"No, silly. Nine points."

He returns her serve, but she slams an attacking boast, a drive along the side wall to the front wall that drops before Chip can reach it. The twenty or so men who have gathered in the gallery applaud her shot. Relentlessly, she presses on with point after point until she beats him nine to one.

"Well, I guess that's it. Shall we call it a match?" he asks.

"No way, hombre. We're just getting started." Her competitive spirit's ignited. She wants blood. He, on the other hand, only wants her.

They play another game with a similar result. Nine to two. "Can we quit now?"

Karen catches on that her white blouse has turned nearly transparent with perspiration and that Chip can't keep his eyes off her. "I tell you what, Chip. Since you're a gambling man and I'm sweaty, if you can win this game we'll shower together at my place," she laughs.

"I forgot to bring my swimsuit," the dummy tells her. She gives him a look until he says with a red face, "Oh."

She fails to notice that they now have the company of almost three-dozen male witnesses who howl at the proposal. And they start placing wagers among themselves as to the winner.

"What's going on?" she asks Chip.

"They're betting men, too, it seems."

Karen serves the ball in a lob that almost dies on the back wall. Chip races to the corner and yells, "Coming around," as he makes a 180-degree turn and slams the ball into a nick, the juncture between the floor and the wall, at the front.

The crowd roars, "Way to go, Chipster."

"My serve," Chip announces.

"Coming around? Where did you learn that?"

"I told you. I watch Mr. Smithfield play." He serves again, but she doesn't get out of his way and interferes with an easy return. "Stroke to me," he says, gaining another point.

"Stroke?" She looks at him suspiciously. "I know you <u>watch</u> other people play. You listen, too, I gather."

On the next serve he runs Karen from pillar to post all around the court before driving the ball into the opposite corner. Chip continues to run her ragged with a mix of cross-court volleys, lobs, and drop shots. He whips her nine to zero. The men rise and applaud at the fun.

One pushes forward and shakes the winner's hand while staring at Karen. "Good going, Chipster." Offers his hand to her, "Have we met? You look familiar. I'm Malcolm Bennett. Much better in bed than our friend The Chipster and I stand to earn a million-dollar bonus at Goldman Sachs. One thousand bucks to each of you if I can take the winner's prize, miz."

"No thanks. But I'll take your word for it."

"My word for what?" ask Malcolm.

"That except for my date, you know how most of the men here are in bed," she meows.

"Oooh. Clever girl we have here," Malcolm says to Chip. "Saw it in the papers, Chipster. Congrats! Old Aunt Lizzie finally bought the farm. I've got some great investments for you. Insider stuff for buddies like Siegel family members," he whispers.

"Have we met?" Chip asks him and hustles Karen out of the club and hails a taxi before Malcolm can inflict further damage.

"They seem to know you pretty well here."

"Very gentlemanly of them to remember servants' names, I do say," says Chip.

"Uh huh."

When they reach her apartment Chip takes a deep breath. "Karen, it was great fun playing. You don't have to go through with the bet."

"I want to," she insists and pulls off his white shirt and shorts. "Your turn." He does the same, but more slowly.

Once in the shower Chip asks in a humorous tone, "Pardon me, Miss, but I've been wondering," and from behind takes a breast in each hand.

"Yes, you're correct. They're not the same size." Before they're finished drying off, she leads him to her bedroom. "Let's check your symmetry now, shall we? And by the way, what year did you win the world's junior squash championship?"

"Won it twice, don't you know." Young buck-in-headlights looks at her, realizing he's caught again in a lie.

"On the way out I saw your plaques on the wall near the squash court. So. In the member clubs, 'I play a little squash' means. . . . "

"Nationally rated. Otherwise, you're a gentleman just saying, 'Not really, but I'll give it the old college try.' Unless you're low enough to hustle for money."

"Or sex. Who are you anyhow, Mr. Siegel?" and yanks him under the covers.

"I Guess We're All Here,"

Dan tells the temple group Sunday evening at 7 PM sharp. Laura dropped him off when he was sure the wolfman had left for the day. He's surprised to see Glen Sobel here after their blowout the other night. No hard feelings maybe. They're sitting under two green umbrellas around a large, wrought-iron, glass-surfaced table on David Ansterman's patio next to the Jacuzzi and oval pool. With Morty's help, the men were convened to this location instead of their usual meeting place.

David's wife pleaded with him not to invite them to their home. But they're friends. We're taking turns, and now it's mine. You don't have to do anything. Yes, I'll get some food and drinks. You don't have to even greet them if you don't want to. Eventually David wins Diane's reluctant approval despite her violent apprehension. She wants to flee to her bedroom, but nevertheless, with her stomach in knots, she does greet them. Tentatively at first. It's only polite. The way her mother taught her to be a *baleboosteh*, a proper homemaker, decades earlier.

"You're Harriet's son?" Diane asks Dan. "I haven't seen her in ages. We've played golf together at the Northeastern Shore Country Club many times." She even gives Morty a kiss on the cheek after his, "Long time no see, babe." When the men go outside to the patio, she retreats upstairs.

"David, ask them if they want something," Diane calls from her bedroom window.

An almost unnoticeable shaking of the head, no, from Daniel.

"I can't hear you, dear," David replies, pointing at his ear. The men all wait in silence.

"Oh, for goodness sake," Diane says and disappears from the ledge. Two minutes later. Nervously standing just inside the sliding glass door to the patio. Shaking slightly and with a soft voice, "I said, would anyone like something to eat or drink?"

"Nothing for me," the men all reply nearly in unison. Except for Danny.

"A coke. Any soda is fine. Or even ice water. Thank you, Mrs. Ansterman," Dan responds, ignoring the disapproving expressions of the others.

Five long minutes elapse and Diane appears again at the door. She wants to walk onto the patio but can't quite gain the courage. David gets up, takes the glass of cola from her hands, and kisses her cheek.

"Thanks again, Mrs. Ansterman. This will hit the spot," Daniel Topler, Harriet and Albert Topler's polite young son from Long Island, tells her.

Diane searches the seats at the table, "Where's Jack, Dave?"

"His operation's tomorrow. We're all going to visit him when they let us," Harry says.

"Such a nice man, and his daughter Laura is so sweet and beautiful. Wish him well for me. Please tell Jack to come and visit me when he's better, so we can talk. David, ask them if they want something to eat. Don't starve our guests. Barry must be famished. He's still a growing boy," Diane jests to snickers from the men. Exhausted by her efforts, she returns upstairs for the evening.

"Yeah, Barry. You must have trimmed down to three hundred pounds," Morty cracks to his unusually well-groomed friend. "Getting some exercise you'd like to share with us?" he jests. "Since when is your shirt pressed, and what's with the shit-eating grin?" makes Barry blush.

"You've got a smile pasted all over your *punim* too, Morty," taunts Rob. "What's going on? Is everybody here getting laid but me?"

Lightening up, Sam breaks his silence with, "No one here's supposed to be getting any except Barry, Morty, and Dan – they're single." The men break into uproarious gurgling, choking the men so that tears come to their eyes.

When the laughter subsides, "Men, I need to confess something. I hope you'll let me continue to come to meetings. I'm not a medical school student. I'm a patient of Jack's trying to recuperate at a rehab clinic, Live Free or Die, in East Hampton."

"So what else is new?" says Morty.

"Did you think Jack wouldn't tell his friends that he wants to bring some nutcase to our meetings?" asks Sam.

"You're doing a great job as our new leader. Fuhgeddaboudit," says Harry with a mob cadence.

"No one told me," Glen protests.

"Who can reach you, Mr. Big Shot? No one has your private number except Dan, I guess," Rob responds.

Dan realizes that Jack always keeps one step ahead of him. Live and learn. "I thought we might discuss our children – that is, your children. I don't have any yet, I hope."

"I finally saw my daughter, Alicia, guys. She's beautiful but not too well. I picked her up at the hospital today where she's recovering from bronchitis. Then I took her to the same place where Dan's at to finish her recovery."

"I'm so sorry, Glen," Barry sympathizes. "You introduced me to her once. Marvelous girl. She has quite a mind of her own, if I remember correctly."

"Thanks. You couldn't be more on the mark," Glen agrees.

"How's your daughter Jennifer, Harry?" The men don't ask about his wife, Frances, who has never stopped grieving for their son, who was killed in an automobile pileup. She separated from Harry shortly after the accident. It's still his fault. He had asked his son to go out and buy a six-pack for him that night.

"She's great. Just great. Hasn't found a boy yet. But she will," Harry tentatively answers.

"I thought she was engaged," says Glen.

"She was. But you know how these things go for kids these days."

"A kid? She's over thirty, for crying out loud," says Morty.

"Where does she live now?" asks Rob.

"She bought this house in San Francisco. A condominium, really. You can't believe how expensive it is there."

The men have often discussed their personal finances, so David's not too timid to ask, "I thought she was a school teacher. She can afford it?"

"No. She quit her job. Wants to be a writer or something. I send her a little money now and then."

"Who're you kidding?" says Morty, not letting go. "You bought her an apartment and now you support her. Right? "

"She hasn't found her way yet," Harry protests. "But she will. She will. What am I supposed to do? I'm her father."

"What are parents supposed to do?" asks Dan.

The men reflect on how to relate to their grown children. None of them has an easy time communicating. Their sons and daughters will talk pleasantries with them but slam the door shut on personal problems.

"Last week, my son, the successful litigation attorney, tells me he's in Boston heading for D.C. on Amtrak." Sam's slight head-shaking palsy becomes more pronounced as he continues. 'I'll fly up and meet you at the station and we'll go together,' I tell him. Anything to try to open the door a little bit. He's reluctant, but agrees. So I meet him and we sit opposite each other in the café coach. At a table you know, so we can talk. After an hour we're through. He won't talk about anything – only brag about winning his cases. Not a word on his children or wife. I get off at Penn Station even though I had a ticket to go all the way to D.C.. So when I get home, my wife's still not up, of course. It's the middle of the day. And I say to the motionless frame, 'Did you know they're going up to Maine to spend a week with his mother-in-law? She's so wonderful?' So Margaret turns over. She looks at me and says, 'Yeah. She's perfect. She didn't have to raise him.'"

"There's no competition there. No history. It's easy to be friends with in-laws. Although I don't know that from experience," the three-time-marriage-loser says laughing. Then a heated discussion on the role of parents. When to watch. When to intervene. Mostly how to listen.

"Our kids don't want to hear from us about our ailments or that some day we won't be there," Rob says.

"When I called my son and told him I was taking Coumadin and couldn't take aspirin also because it would make my blood too thin, he said good-bye in thirty seconds," Morty complains.

"We're part of the furniture. They don't want to talk to us. They just like to know we're around. They think we'll be here forever," sighs Harry.

"I went to Turkey last summer for a tax treaty meeting with firms we do business with there. I called my two older daughters and asked them if there was some kind of special present I could buy for them in Istanbul. I haven't spent any time with them in some time and thought I'd make the gesture. No, they all say. We don't want anything. Kids are so hard to relate to."

The men move on to Turkey's history. I can't believe how knowledgeable these men are, Dan thinks, as they discuss Mustafa Ataturk's role in creating the modern secular nation. Barry talks about its historical military importance in keeping Russia from a warm water port. Bob describes how the U.S. keeps submarines in the Bosporus to monitor submarine traffic into the Sea of Marmara past the Dardanelles and into the Mediterranean. Then the discussion segues to the expulsion of Jews from Spain and their migration to Greece and then to Turkey where they were welcomed centuries ago.

The conversation drifts to the Middle East and Gertrude Bell's drawing the map of modern Iraq in 1921 and her peculiar role as an anti-suffragette. Dan, the forever critic of everyman's foibles, listens with esteem at the temple men's vast knowledge on such diverse topics. And not just one or two of the group.

Harry asks Glen if he visited any synagogues in Turkey while he was there. "Yes. But I had to email photocopies of my passport to the rabbi. Security's very tight at temples. Almost all of them are Orthodox synagogues in that Moslem country, regardless of the official stance of neutrality toward Israel. They have central chambers with one-way mirrors to inspect visitors before entering. I was warned to take off my yarmulke when I forgot I had it on and walked outside after the services."

"Are you taking more political science courses this term?" David asks Rob. After weeks of mostly listening to their conversations, only now does Dan discover they almost all regularly take college courses in economics, literature, art, or music. It's so easy to look at aging men and only see their lost hair, wrinkles, and liver spots.

At 9 PM, Dan breaks up the meeting. "That's it for tonight, guys. Dr. Bernstein's daughter's picking me up and taking me to that LFOD as a favor to her dad.

"Bullshit," says Morty. "I know Jack's daughter, Laura. When you said goodbye to her in the car, the two of you coulda charged tickets to watch the fireworks. She almost got pregnant French-kissing you. What's the real dope? Don't just come here like some voyeur. Come clean with us for a change," he demands.

He doesn't embarrass easily, but Dan turns a bright red. "OK. All right. She's my girlfriend. Maybe a lot more than that."

"You love her. Is that it?" Rob says, sharing a grin with the other guys.

"I met her in the parking lot outside after the first men's group meeting I came to. We're still making up over a fight we had." Dan opens up to revealing more about his life to his new friends, "So this fantastic woman. . . ."

"Yeah. Yeah. You mean Laura," Morty urges him on.

"No. Some other woman named Charlotte – practically a hypnotist. She's a divorce attorney and close to Laura. Screwed my brains out Friday night, then threw me out of her pent-house apartment on Central Park South. Then she blabbed to Laura and got me into deep doodoo."

"<u>Your</u> brains out?" asks Glen.

"You're laying your girlfriend's friend?" from Sam.

"I guess it's a modern thing," says Harry.

"What kind of kids are these nowadays?" Rob wants to know.

"They're all young. They'll figure it out," David good-naturedly tells them.

"Friday night, Dan?" asks Barry quietly. The story fully sinks in.

"Yes. Why?" Dan senses after keeping secrets from the group maybe he's said too much now in his zeal to become one of them.

"No reason. I'm just getting old, but slow to realize it," and stands up.

"I'll give you a lift to the train station, Barry. You can still catch the nine fifteen to Penn Station," says Harry.

"I'll walk. Thanks Harry. It will do me good," he says in an undisguised lonely voice and almost seems to limp like a colos-sal wounded bear from the patio into the house, out the front door and into the neighborhood he's known so well since he grew up there over fifty years ago.

"What was that all about, Dan?"

"I have no idea," he tells the men.

"Aw. He's one of those intellectuals. Your story probably made him think of Hamlet or something," says Morty.

Or maybe his very own Jezebel, Danny guesses without saying it to the others. Laura mentioned to Dan that Charlie has an interest in an older man – a college classics professor. Could it be?

"Do You Know
a Friendly Giant,

Professor Barry Blackmun?" Danny asks Laura in his cabaña later that evening. "He's one of your dad's friends from the group." Daniel had snuck into LFOD from the beach side when they both returned from David Ansterman's house. They're not finished making up.

"That's why he looked so familiar there."

"Where?"

"At Charlie's dad's funeral. I wasn't used to seeing him in a coat and tie. I didn't recognize him. He's the man I told you about last night. Charlie's first true love. That's where they met, at the cemetery. She's moving into his place in SoHo as we speak. Maybe she's crazy for him because he's the first man in her life who could say no to her besides her father."

Dan glances at his watch. It's almost midnight. "He might be saying no to her again right about now. Don't be angry with me. Tonight I told the men maybe a little too much about us and the reason for our spat on Friday. Barry was there."

"I'm Not a Modern Man,

Zoë. I told you at the park. . . ." Barry sadly starts to explain when he arrives back at his loft that night.

She's setting up the telescope on the open-walled top floor where the stars can be seen through the skylight. Thomas brought it there from her co-op.

She hears his heavy footsteps. "How was the ancient order of grumpy men?" The fever of never letting her guard down has gone. She turns to greet him, but he stops her from kissing him. "Hello, darling. What's the matter? I know you're an old fuddy-duddy. That's why I love you," she says trying to tease him from whatever's bothering him.

"Daniel Topler, I think you know him, a patient of Dr. Bernstein's, runs the club meetings while Jack's sick. One of the men decided to prod Dan about his own private life." The clouds begin to gather over SoHo. A storm begins to brew inside and out the loft. "Without giving her last name, he talked about a strange experience last Friday night not long before you rang my buzzer. A deliriously magical woman named Charlotte, a divorce lawyer, commanded him to get in her bedroom and fu. . . . "

"Barry. Don't think about anybody but us. We're all that counts. Listen to me. I've been thinking. I'm selling my father's business . . . changing my law practice just to become a woman you can be proud of. I'm not the same person now. I know. . . . "

"Please don't explain. You're a young and beautiful woman. It's not for me to judge you. But I can't take part in the kind of life you're enmeshed in. You'll never know how much you meant to me."

"Hear me out, Barry. Won't you?"

"Please extend to Thomas my *mea culpa* for moving your things once again.

This was entirely my fault, sweet girl." Then Barry lumbers out of what he thought had been his sanctuary from the foul grasp of contemporary culture. He doesn't return until late the next day when he plans to ensure modern life won't intrude on him ever again.

She'll Die Soon,

he tells himself. The KGB spy carefully sneaks up on his prey. A nitwit to expose herself – so easy to kill. She's asleep. Completely unaware.

"Bang, you're dead," Terrence O'Connor shouts into Ally's ear as he squirts yellow Dijon from his water gun all over her swimsuit. He blows the invisible smoke away from the barrel – video-game-style. With a staccato Russian inflection, "A pity to die so young," he tells the motionless body. He's not sure if the PlayStation World War II commando said it just that way, but Terry does know his Commie accent stinks. He also knows he likes his new girlfriend.

She knows how to play dead and waits for him to lean closer. "Wham, so are you," and returns the favor by pumping out a half-pint of ketchup from the plastic squeeze bottle hiding underneath her directly atop his long curly hair. Ally likes him, too.

"Whatcha wanna do now?" Terry asks her as they both rinse off in the outdoor shower by the pool. Neither of them expects any visitors this Monday afternoon.

"Dunno."

"Hey, there's a giant empty TV box at the back of the building. Let's take it to the beach 'n have a pretend funeral. It'll be a coffin. You wanna die, don't you? I'll be Reverend Pilatus, the principal back at Riverhead Episcopal where I go to school. He loves to bury people."

Not quite sure if that sounds like fun. Ally agrees. "OK. I guess." Lately death doesn't sound so inviting.

"Hi, Ally. It's great to see you," Dan waves to her as he approaches.

This sucks, thinks Terry, "Who's he?" he wants to know.

With a silly fake woman's voice, "He was my boyfriend. I'm still very fond of him."

"What's going on, guys?" the intruder asks. "I'm Dan. What's your name?" and sticks out his hand to Terry, who declines the offer. The teen treats the greeting as if he had just been offered cholera.

"We were just going, Mister," Terry tells Dan. He's not interested in sharing his only possible playmate at this detention center.

"Yeah? Where?" Dan asks.

Ally – still with the tone. "Just somewhere, Daniel. Older people probably wouldn't be interested." She didn't want their affair to end this way. As Ally and Terry whisper to each other on the way to retrieving the TV carton, Alicia Sobel very considerately hopes that she didn't let Daniel down too hard – poor boy.

"What a Lovely Bathroom.

My favorite shades of brown," Harriet Topler lies to her future son-in-law. She and Dolores have finally been invited to Coco and Ronnie's co-op by the secretly engaged couple to hear the news they both suspected some time ago. The three women exchange knowing looks. Every happy home must bow down to one room – preferably a small, rarely used one – to be decorated by the male of the species. The apartment tour continues.

They enter the microscopically decorated purple-hued master bedroom – Harriet's favorite color and therefore, by genetic design, so too her daughter's. Dolores takes in the fluffy, gray valance over the aubergine shades and the monstrous mauve silk pillows. She can only manage to choke out, "Very original, my dear," to Coco.

Now Harriet knows a backhanded compliment when she hears one – especially from a woman she knows so well. "What's the matter with it?" She won't let the insult go by.

Nothing if one wishes to live in a bordello, Dolores thinks but says, "It's marvelous, Harriet. I wish Coco had helped me when I redid my bedroom." White lies were invented for this occasion.

"Next time you redecorate, I'd be happy to help out, Mrs. Schwartz," Coco happily volunteers to unwelcoming ears. Neither the Toplers nor the Schwartzes ever approved of the now modern vogue – children addressing adults on a first-name basis.

"Please, Coco, call me Mother now," Dolores says sweetly, hoping for the décor subject to die a natural death.

Coco waits for her mother's forthcoming approving nod. "OK. <u>Mom</u>."

Now for lunch. Dolores prays for carry-out. She's heard many times from Harriet about Coco's financial acumen – big deal B-School credentials – but she knows for a fact that the daughter wouldn't know how to find the Topler kitchen if it weren't for late-night snacks rummaged cold from the fridge.

The four sit down at the oval Lucite dining room table. Each mother feels confident it's not her child that bears the responsibility for this furniture abomination.

"How charming," Harriet says. "We can all see each other's feet."

The two invited ladies hold their noses and manage to politely swallow a few sips of Coco's homemade cold rhubarb soup – a palette cleanser, they're told. They're very reasonably terrified of what might come next.

"Turnips béchamel, anyone?" Coco asks, ladling heaping mounds of white-atop-white mush into blue-porcelain Japanese bento bowls.

"Did you make this yourself, sweetie?" the future mother-in-law not-so-innocently inquires. She wants to know the answer before exposing herself to any further possibility of botulism.

"<u>I</u> made it, Mom," Ronald proudly announces to the alarm of both mothers. "Coco and I take cooking classes together at night now. It's the main course. French."

"Why of course it's French, Ronald. Béchamel just wouldn't be béchamel without it being française," Harriet says, hoping Dolores catches her drift.

Dolores does.

"What I think Harriet means is that you know how women are, Ronald," his mother says, knowing full well her ignoramus son knows nothing of the kind whatsoever. "We're always dieting. French foods are so fattening."

"Not a problem. I substituted canola oil for butter and soy milk for cream, so there's nothing to worry about, ladies. Dig in." Ronnie evokes a response from the matrons that nearly allows the engaged couple to see what palette cleansers look like when not fully digested.

The two captives take tiny tastes and then must be going. Their very lives at stake, the women make a common social-ite's excuse for rushing off so soon – a spa appointment. By this time, Harriet and Dolores have each privately come to the same agreeable conclusion. Her child deserves better, but at least he/she's marrying into a respectable, solvent family.

Diversity Is Not Optional,

it is what we must be, reflects Bhadra Raj in the Goldman Sachs conference room Monday evening. The firm's business principle #13 sounds great, but not many Indian women before me have chaired such an important meeting for a Midas-sized merger.

GS wined and dined her on two continents as only it can to leave her HITEC City engineering consultancy job in Hyderabad and join the world's capital of capitalism. But until now she feels her talents have been grossly underused. Despite recent feminist gains there, she left her homeland mostly to renounce the sexism prevalent in Indian employment. Lately she's begun to wonder if it's all that different here in the States. But this meeting's her chance. If this conference proves successful, Ms. Raj knows there's no limit to how high her star can rise at GS. She wasn't born a *dalit* – an untouchable – at the very bottom of the Hindu social barrel. Still, not bad for a thirty-two-year-old, lower-caste chick from New Delhi to run with the big dogs at the world's financial summit.

To Mason Rextal's dismay, after the last such meeting Davian Corbeille instructed that the lead on the G.S. Davison deal switch from his hands to Bhadra's. This time Rextal couldn't charm his way to success by hosting the client with a few rounds of golf at the site of many a PGA tournament – the exclusive Westchester Country Club. After the previous debacle, the GS worldwide head of structured finance told him flat out, "You can't cut the mustard." Davian restrained himself from pointing out that Mason did however loudly cut the cheese in the last meeting with the heiress on his post-haste exit to the men's room.

The receptionist announces over the speakerphone that Charlotte Davison's on her way in. Bhadra watches with amusement as the male investment bankers brace themselves for the onslaught.

"Hi, Charlotte. Beautiful bag," Bhadra notes, complimenting the new Givenchy, wrinkled-leather Nightingale on the client's shoulder.

"Thanks, Bhadra. Later I'll tell you where I got it on sale," Charlie cordially replies.

It's all Bhadra can do to keep from laughing, seeing the other investment bankers turn leprechaun-green-with-envy from the men-not-invited encounter. Davian keeps his counsel. Any comment from him on the female topic could kill the merger and possibly land him in the hospital with this black-belt hellion.

"Fat Chung ran the numbers, and we have Aramark's approval for bumping the price one hundred million," Bhadra tells Charlie.

"I suppose I should take it," Charlie says nonchalantly in her best negotiating stance.

Sighs of relief all around. Sugarplum Maseratis dance in Malcolm Bennett's noodle. At last I'll get my wife off my neck about that Mediterranean island, thinks Davian.

"But. . . . " says Charlotte. Panic sets in again. ". . . I have one more condition that I think the buyer will agree to."

"Looks Like Pornography

to me," Dolores tells her best friend. Since the two women were already in the city to visit the children, she had her arm twisted to accompany Harriet to one of those evening Gallery Talks at the Metropolitan Museum of Art – a tony soirée carrot for President's Circle patrons. As far as Dolores is concerned, a twenty-thousand-dollar contribution seems like a lot of dough for a special tour of naked statues. The one being described by the guide, a sculpture of an Indian couple dressed in those funny costumes, does exhibit a new way to copulate, Dolores considers. I hope Coco doesn't bring Ronnie here, she thinks fleetingly and then shoos the disgusting thought away. At least guests attend free. And I'm finally going to meet the mysterious art professor tonight.

"How can you say that, Dolores? This is art!" Harriet replies in alarm. She hopes the guide didn't overhear the remark. He did but pretends he didn't. By tacit custom, after talks at the Met, Harriet visits Florenz at his apartment downtown. Now that she's proceeding with a divorce, something might just happen between them. Perhaps the sparks will finally start to fly. She wants to introduce Dolly and get her estimation of the man. A second opinion never hurts.

"Aren't we supposed to be at Professor Castillia's place soon?" Dolores asks. She's had enough of the tantric art displays. Now, if it had been a Broadway musical – that's another matter. Harriet couldn't drag her away.

"I suppose so," Harriet replies, and they slip away from the resplendent group – mostly wives of investment bankers and Manhattan real estate developers. She's excited anyway to show off Florenz's exquisitely-decorated residence to Dolores. He won't care if I'm a tad early. Perhaps I should have mentioned I'm bringing a friend?

"What a Damned Bother,"

Florenz mumbles to Billy. "For the umpteenth time I have to pack my gorgeous original paintings in the closet and hide my statue. Screw it! Let her see my little faun and lovely pictures. It's too heavy to drag around, and she won't notice it anyway with a girl in my lap. Where the hell's this thespian anyway? She's late and we need to practice our lines."

Florenz begins, "Oh my goodness gracious, Harriet! Is tonight Monday? You've caught me in the arms of my lover." Ugh. A few moments of silence, then Florenz nudges Billy.

"Huh? Oh yeah. Oh my darling Florenz," Billy says in falsetto. "Who is this woman? Please don't ever leave me."

"Mary . . . . Florenz interrupts himself. "It never hurts to toss in some religious connotations, Billy," then continues, "is having our baby, Harriet. I hope this won't diminish your contribution to the Columbia University's Art Department Fund-Raising Campaign." Florenz pushes Billy off the couch.

Billy stands and delivers Harriet's hoped-for lines in a deeper falsetto, "I understand, Florenz. I only pray that you'll both be happy together. I'm going to give an extra one million dollars to the art department chair if you'll name the baby after me. Harriet, if a girl. Harry, if a boy." Now himself, "How was that, Prof?"

"Just great. You could be another Theda Bara in drag."

"Who's he?"

Professor Castillia stands still for a moment after this fantasy and congratulates himself on a job well done. "Brilliant, even if I say so myself. This actress should be here any time. Better get going, handsome."

But when the art grad leaves, Florenz has second thoughts. What if Harriet feels slighted that I'm with some pubescent young chickie? She could get insulted that she's not attractive enough for me. Not young enough. Not young enough? Oh dear lord! That's the ultimate insult for these women. Not young anymore. That'll be the end of the Topler Chair For the Arts, that's for Goddamned sure. Man oh Man Ray, what the hell was I thinking?

Florenz has only started to replace his erotic paintings with Daumier political cartoon reproductions when he stops dead in his tracks. Got to call Pirot and cancel this fiasco. Before he reaches the phone, the doorbell rings.

"Tonight's the Night,"

Butterworth told him earlier in the day. "Whenever Harriet goes to the special tours at the Met, she always goes to his apartment afterward." Against Mr. Norman's strong warnings, Albert's on his way with the private investigator to see for himself. Butterworth will jimmy open the door. Then take pictures. They'll both be gone in a flash.

Albert begins to regret his decision as he parks his car in a lot and they get out. It will hurt like the devil to see my bride in someone else's arms. At least I'm getting an evening rate for the parking. As they approach the address from a block away, neither of the men notices the two women entering the building ahead of them.

Maybe She'll Go Away

if I don't answer the door, Florenz hopes.

Tapping her foot impatiently, Carrie Blade waits outside Castillia's apartment. She's arrived with all the necessary equipment for the assignment. If I can get out of here in about an hour-and-a-half, I might still make it to Bloomie's before they close. They gave her a rain check in the SoHo store for the sale on that cute Coach Hobo handbag she stole for only a hundred and fourteen bucks. It's in.

Florenz squints through the peephole. Damn. Maybe I'll pretend I'm not home. Several thunderous knocks later and he opens the door a smidgen. "Are you trying to raise the dead, for Christ's sake? I've got neighbors. . . ." he starts to complain as Ms. Blade pushes her way in and starts the festivities in motion. She craves that bag. And she's getting it tonight. even if she has to whip him unconscious to do it.

"Just relax," she tells him and pushes flustered Florenz onto the sofa. Lots of S&M customers like to pretend that they're victims of assault. A real turn-on for some.

"Pardon me, Madam, but there's been a mistake." His eyes gape open at her leather accoutrements. His gender predilections notwithstanding, the art professor's an altogether conservative man. "You don't understand. I vote Republican. You see, I was just in the process of calling Mr. Pirot when. . . ." But that's all Florenz will say for some time tonight – muffled bleating withstanding.

The athletic Carrie Blade quickly ball-gags the chairman of the art department and handcuffs his arms to his legs. As she slowly cuts his clothes off the way Pirot taught her, Karen considers that he's wearing some nice duds. Most customers buy cheap suits or sometimes a kangaroo costume. Now that he's naked and bent over, she sprays him with a couple of shots of cheap perfume. It's for both of them.

"You've been a bad boy, haven't you, Florence?" the lissome gentleman's club dancer asks as she removes her dress to reveal a black lace bodice. He's not the first john to use a woman's name for one of these gigs. She slips on a ruby-red mask and menacing stiletto heels – purchased very reasonably at La La Lingerie dot com. Carrie turns up the '70s disco music volume on the CD player she unpacked – some neighbors get upset to hear a solid hour of moaning next door. Then takes out the soft velveteen cat o' nine tails that hurts, but not so much that the man won't tip generously. And she gets to work.

"I had no idea that Florenz likes that sort of music," cringes Harriet. Her best friend grimaces with a condescending, uplifted brow. They stand outside Dr. Castillia's door and can hear the obnoxious beat inside – certainly not Stephen Sondheim tunes, Dolores thinks with disdain. Harriet's been knocking on the door for two minutes. She's impatient to finally show off her traveling cohort to Dolores. Mrs. Topler turns the doorknob. Unfortunately for Florenz, he didn't lock the door behind him when Ms. Blade shoved her way in. The ladies enter.

"I'm going to break him in two," Albert shouts and, amazingly to Butterworth at his side, breaks into a fast trot down the hall leading to Florenz's ornate apartment. The jealous husband recognizes his wife's voice and she's shrieking, "Oh my God, no!"

Mr. Norman tries to catch up with his portly client. He's seen Albert's surprisingly tough-guy side and considers the possibility that the art professor could end up with a broken nose or worse. But there's another woman's loud voice, too. And she's laughing deliriously, both men note just as they push their way inside the professor's magnificently appointed co-op, thereby accidentally breaking into smithereens a nude goat boy statue.

"Zealous Advocacy

can't be all bad," senior partner Evan Roth whispers to the firm's founder, Raoul Bleeder. "It made us rich," making them both chuckle.

"Yeah, warring divorce litigation might burn down our clients' houses, but it sure as hell built ours," Raoul answers.

"Shush," Charlotte tells the guffawing bad boys.

The two men create a small stir in the mediation proceedings Charlotte Davison conducts this Tuesday afternoon. They have decided to sit in on the discussion between Albert and Harriet Topler to see if they were wrong to permit their firm's foray into reasonable, mature discussions between husband and wife. To the litigious warriors, peaceful negotiations instinctively seem like a rotten idea – not nearly as much fun, and worse – possibly a hit to the law firm's bottom line. Still, the parties today agreed to waive the right to get their retainers back if there's an immediate settlement.

Charlotte officially starts the meeting. "Mrs. Topler, your husband cooperated fully and gave what appears to be a full reporting of his assets not in joint accounts with you. He also supplied us with his full beneficial interest in Universal Recycling, excluding what the two of you have already carved out for your children."

Charlotte and the two partners notice Albert and Harriet smiling at each other – nothing less than an extraordinary encounter, considering that there's another woman involved in the break-up. Extramarital dalliances almost always cause inconsolable anger for one party or the other.

"How about his funds in the Cayman Islands?" Harriet asks.

How the hell did she know about them? Albert wonders, withering under Harriet's self-satisfied smile.

Hiding assets from wives in tax havens always proves irritating if discovered, Raoul thinks. But disclosing them can cause the IRS to come down on both parties with leaden feet. He repeats the LLC's private motto to himself: It's good to be the attorney – not the litigant.

"They're right here on paper," Charlie says to everybody's surprise but Al's.

He wants to stick his tongue out at his wife but doesn't.

"Was there any ownership of any kind indicated in the company holdings or other of Albert's assets belonging to a Miss Elaine Bushkin?"

"Harriet, I thought we weren't going to bring her up?" Albert says defensively to his wife.

So much for this mediation baloney, thinks Evan.

Not bring up the other woman? Raoul says under his breath. Who does he think he's kidding?

"There is no evidence whatsoever of any such ownership," Charlotte replies to Albert's I-told-you-so look and a non-committal expression from Harriet. "And no evidence of cash transfers, either. Albert's prepared to give you fifty percent of everything he owns and not ask for half of any of your individually-owned assets, Mrs. Topler. He told me he owes it to his lifelong wife and companion and the mother of his children."

Raoul's take on the offer: Uh oh! Here come the malpractice lawsuits. He jumps up from his seat. "Now, Ms. Davison. . . . " but stops in mid-sentence.

Albert and Harriet also stand up. The Hereford-calf-sized husband almost canters around the mammoth conference table to his wife. The two kiss in a long, amorous embrace that embarrasses the three attorneys. Then – to mystified gawking from the attorneys – the couple says thanks to all and walks out of the room, hubby's arm around his bride's waist.

"God almighty, Charlotte. You sure did one heck of a job," Raoul tells her with amazement.

"Since we keep the retainers, on an hourly basis the firm comes out status quo, I suppose," says Evan.

Charlotte just smiles knowingly. She's frankly dumbfounded herself by her clients' behavior. But she's savvy enough to take credit for what-the-hell-happened she couldn't say.

Two blocks away from the Raoul Bleeder & Associates offices, Harriet slips into Al's Mercedes close beside her husband. He pulls away toward the Midtown Tunnel and their home on Long Island. They made sure that the lawyers wouldn't see that they came together to the meeting.

"Poor Ms. Davison. It seems so important she show her bosses that mediation works," Harriet told Al before the conference. "We must go to the meeting." Not mentioned to Albert was that she also fully intended to find out about his previous financial intentions for her and if that hussy had weaseled any money out of him.

After seeing his supposed rival's rear lashed by a dominatrix, Albert moved back home last night. He had to buy Harriet's explanation that her relationship with Castillia could only be platonic. And the pictures on the walls. "Holy moly! Did you get a load of them?" Albert asked his wife on their hurried way out of the professor's apartment.

She forgave him when he told her he had never loved anyone but her. He only began his monkeyshines with Elaine because of his LFOD-diagnosed depression. They spent the night making up – frolic usually reserved for younger couples. "How is Daniel doing?" she also asked Albert. "Did he ever find a job?" understandably forgetting her son's predicament due to her pressing daily routine of women's luncheons and rounds at the golf club.

"Tonight's the Grand Finale

for the summer," Langford junior tells Pirot, who's not happy to hear the bad news. Bruce's merger and acquisition business at Morgan Stanley has picked up, and dad must pop up here sooner or later with his latest wife. "And it must be smashing," Bruce continues. "We have some VIP guests this evening."

Brucie sent out special invitations for the costume ball tonight to the LA-LA movie studio and record company executives who have their own palatial digs nearby. He hopes to generate some film financing deals on the investment banking side by schmoozing with the execs. They'll show up, he feels sure. He's turned down dozens of pleading requests for an invite to the number-one sublimely-low event in the Hamptons. Only the devil himself can drag it further down.

As for Pirot, he's piled up some real dough-ray-me from this customer by arranging all the details for the parties. He's going to miss garnering more. Pirot final-checks to see that the three bands have set up – hard rock in the ballroom, jazz on the pool patio deck, and new wave Asian in the upstairs theater. He hired four additional bouncers, oversaw the catered food with hot Latin overtones and personally interviewed each waiter. And the female talent. Due to overwhelming popular demand, he brought the Dutch platinum blondes back, a spicy new routine he discovered at the Kit Kat Club, and of course many models (they call themselves) to mingle with the crowd. Finally, the booze and drugs set back his client Brucie one hundred Gs alone. Understandably, Pirot's damned proud of this devil's bash.

Pirot checks to see that the front gate security is covered. No one gets in without either an invitation or his personal imprimatur. By now he knows most of the regulars by sight. A limo pulls up with the third sister of the trapeze act from Holland. Surprise. He was told she couldn't make it. He waves her in with what must be some sugar daddy of hers. Then three Hollywood types show up in a rat-pack white-stretch caddie. Pirot climbs in to give them a personal tour.

"Nice duds, man," Thom Tremont, a young and yet powerful Warner Brothers production chief, says to Pirot. Thom takes in his guide's very cool, faded tuxedo and stained blood-red cummerbund. He looks down at his all-too-yesterday's Armani hung over a blue-black T-shirt. My wardrobe assistant has her head up her ass, he thinks. She's got to get with it. "What's your handle, dude?"

"Pirot."

"Just Pirot?"

"Yes," the offbeat cicerone nods.

"One name? Like Sting or Gandhi, huh? Cool." Then Thom sees the partially clad dolls, the costumes, the klieg lights. "Who put this gig together?"

"I did," says Pirot.

On the jaunt through the mansion, Arnie Bratsworth ("He's a *macher* from the Bertelsmann Music Group," Thom whispers to Pirot) instantly grasps the diverse musical talent of groups he's never heard of before. He takes a sip of the raw goat's milk with paprika and vodka from one of the wandering servers. "What a kick, guy. Who arranged the food and the music?"

"Me," says Pirot simply.

The three execs look at each other. They each know what the other two guys are thinking.

Shitskies. Why did I come here with these putzes? This is going to jack up the bidding, computes Yamada Takahishi, U.S. Head of Sony Pictures Entertainment. I'll have to offer him a two-picture deal, at least. But if I don't hire this *pisher* first, I'll lose face and it'll be my *toochis*. Yamada's a native-born Japanese, but *Daily Variety* and lunches at Spago in Beverly Hills have taught the Stanford Business School grad to become well-versed in Hollywood lingo.

"Excuse me," Pirot says to the tour. He spots a guest – one of Bruce's dodo sidekicks putting his hands on Carrie. "I can't let the talent be disturbed," he tells the Hollywood honchos to their considerable approbation and hurries to stop the intrusion. Nobody puts his claws on his girls unless they – and he – get paid for it – in advance.

Just as well, they all consider silently. Each in his own way and own jargon has the same plan: I'll sign up this dude privately later tonight before these bozos know who they're messing with.

"I Can't Just Call

to give the guys the news, can I?" Ronnie begs his sweet betrothed.

"That's right. They can just wait until they get the wedding announcement like everybody else," Coco tells him in no uncertain terms on that fateful Friday evening. On her fiancé's desk she saw the Devil-Takes-All masquerade ball announcement from Ronnie's lowlife Bexley Academy friend, Bruce Langford. There'll be alcohol, women, drugs – followed by drunk women, more alcohol, and drunk naked women. No way in hell will she permit her Ronnie to go to the Hamptons' most notorious bacchanal.

"But, darling. . . ."

"OK. If it's so important to you, we'll go together."

"What a horrible idea! I can't let my fiancée go to one of Brucie's parties."

"Neither can I."

"You don't trust me. Is that it?" demands Ronnie, raising his voice for the first time to Coco.

"I don't trust your idiot friends," pitching to a rage herself.

"I'm going alone and that's that," Ronnie replies and stomps out of their – mostly – purple palace on the Upper West Side. It's their first fight. Had to come sometime, the future groom gloomily decides. Someone has to be the boss of this family . . . and it can't always be her, he fumes.

As Ronnie pulls slowly though the crowded Midtown Tunnel toward the Long Island Expressway, he tries to convince himself that he has no interest in one final debauched party. I'll just stop in and say, "Hi guys. I'm getting married to Coco," to his pals, collect the good wishes from all around, and leave. He has no intention – he tells himself – of one last time to ever put his hands on a little grass, a little booze, and a little flirtatious hottie all at the same time. I'll show Coco she can trust me, he repeats to himself over and over.

Until he nearly believes it.

His chance to prove his good intentions will come later tonight. An hour after her beloved leaves, Coco decides to go to Brucie's party, too. She knows all of Ronnie's dumb friends – they're the same nincompoops as her jerk brother's – and will garner her own congrats from them. She can't wait to see their faces. Who'd have guessed? – she and Ronnie together. She has the invite in hand – not that the Marines could conceivably stop the determined woman – and takes off for the Langford East Hampton house in her new silver BMW Series 3 convertible. Daddy made good on his promise.

"Brucie Will Be So Surprised

to see us, Gisela," says Skipper Langford, Brucie's father, as he cuddles with his young platinum-blonde Dutch wife. The long flight from Holland exhausted them both. He couldn't reach Bertrand to fetch them in the new custom-pink Rolls he bought for his new bride – the line's been tied up the whole day – so they're taking a limo service from JFK. "I still think it's a pity I didn't get to meet your two sisters, Tiffin and Adelle, while we were in Amsterdam. I've never met triplets."

The senior Bruce Langford got his nickname from his number-one hobby. As Commodore of the prestigious New York Yacht Club, Skipper had thought it his duty to attend the annual Watersportvereniging – the Amsterdam boating club – party celebrating its auspicious beginning in 1918. Of course they're johnny-come-latelys compared to the grand year of 1844 when we started, he sniffed as he read the invitation. He met Gisela, his fourth wife, at the shindig. Skipper named his 150-foot schooner The Velis, after his club's motto: *Nos agimur tumidis velis* – We go with swelling sails. It was Gisela's own voluminous sails that first caught his monocled eye at the celebration and which, she took note, immediately rigged his mast below. That she spoke of the champagne they drank together that night in terms of its aromatic intensity, crisp acidity, and well-delineated woven texture only added to his intoxication over her silvery aura. Oenology is his second and only other hobby. They married six days and two-dozen magnums of Dom Perignon later – 1996, his favorite vintage, of course.

As for Gisela, it's just as well that Skipper didn't meet her sisters. It could slip out she's not truly the curator for the Netherlands' cultural center, the Amsterdam Public Library. During a rare sober moment they had together before tying the knot, the Skipper dragged her into a massive edifice on the Oosterdokskade – she had no idea that it even was the library. He wanted to invite her boss in person to their private wedding ceremony that night at the InterContinental Amstel hotel. She ended the emergency by asking the receptionist in her native language if her father could take a leak on the floor. Absent Skipper's knowledge of Dutch, the universally understood vigorous-head-swiveling-left-and-right sign for no assured him that Gisela's employer, a Mr. Rembrandt van Rijn she told him, wasn't in that day.

Also, her siblings live only for today. They're still into parties, weed, and making Euros – and they do make sizable dough for pretty Dutch girls from the hinterlands. Gisela, on the other hand, thinks long-term and very big money. Bruce Sr. seems an all-right Jozef, and not bad looking for an *alte mann*, but still he might not have tied the knot with a woman who the night before they met was balancing upside-down on a single dance pole with her triplet sisters at the Blue Bell Nightclub on the Thorbeckeplein.

"You'll like Brucie, Gisela. He's at the country house. Haven't been there for months myself. Very conservative and serious young man. I don't know where he got those genes," the elder Langford chuckles. "Probably in bed hours ago. We'll have to tiptoe in quietly so we don't wake him. I hope you two meet in the morning before he goes off to work in the city."

The summer traffic to the Hamptons moves haltingly even on weekdays, and it takes hours for them to reach the pond house. Rave-loud music blares from the mansion and dozens of luxury cars fill the driveway, spilling onto the grass. The jet-lagged Skipper has fallen asleep in the arms of his newlywed when the driver is stopped at the gate. Skipper wakes up enough to see a peculiar-looking mustachioed man in a tuxedo peer inside the limo.

"I thought you couldn't make it, Gisela. You can change in the Chinese bedroom upstairs. Who's the john?"

Langford senior hears the stranger ask Gisela in an unidentifiable accent.

"We're not staying," says Gisela, trying not to panic.

"Of course we're staying, my dear," pipes up Langford, wondering who the odd fellow is. "Let us in, my good man."

Pirot allows the car onto the grounds.

Partially clad couples lying on the flagstone pavers litter the patio just ahead of the limo. Suddenly, Gisela hears several men shouting. Then loud tinkling of breaking glass. A young man wearing a black-devil-rhinestoned shirt and headband horns of red-velvet – but missing his pants and jockey shorts – hurtles headfirst out the front door. Skipper now completely awakens just before Gisela can ask the driver to turn around and go back to Manhattan. She knows trouble's brewing right here in River City.

"Time to Say Goodbye

to Brucie's raucous parties," The Chipster tells Frederick, finally dragging himself home after thirty-six hours straight with Karen. He wants to stay true to his new sweetheart and not get involved with some trollop he might come across at one of the pond house carousals – though despite his best efforts it's never happened before. She had to work tonight and booted him out of her apartment at last. He thought it peculiar that a limousine waited for her outside when he left. Must remember to give Freddy a tidy Christmas bonus this year, he thought. Good help sure must be hard to find.

"Sorry to hear of it. I know you find them amusing. Can't blame you after your fall from grace – and the second-story window there. But how did it go with Karen, Sir?" Freddy asks with a hint of an upward curve to his lips. He stifles a smile. If the lad didn't get some this time, I'm going to seek other employment, he resolves. I can't bear a wallflower.

"Beat her pants."

"Oh did you, Sir?" Frederick perks up upon hearing about his employer's frivolity – a House of Lords practice, both in giving and receiving – so thoroughly covered in the London tabloids.

"In squash."

"Oh."

"I can't say more. We're gentlemen, aren't we?"

"So glad to hear it, Chip, Sir." Thank God he finally screwed her, Frederick surmises. Maybe he'll stop interfering with my duties now.

"About the ball tonight . . . I can't just not show up after accepting the invitation, can I?"

"Of course not, Sir. That would be rude."

Chip's too exhausted after last night's amorous workout to drive and asks Frederick to take him to East Hampton in the Bentley. He'll only stay a few minutes to say farewells. Frederick's happy for the occasion. He's always wanted to see the goings-on at the pond house. Bertrand Jenkins, co-chairman with Frederick of the International Guild of Professional Butlers, serves as the Langford's major domo there. Bertie often spoke of the amusing hijinks that went on at the mansion when the senior Langford left for vacation or one of his frequent extended honeymoons. This might be his last chance to witness the satyr gaiety himself. Besides, Frederick's been in deep contemplation. Perhaps now's the time to change the association's name. Something more up-to-date and fashionable might be in order. Maybe something like The American Live-In Professional Household Organizers – ALIPHO – has a bit more zip to it for these modern times. I'll run it up the flagpole with Bertie while I'm at the pond house, he decides.

When they arrive at the gate, an odd-tuxedoed man recognizes Chip and hands Frederick feathered burgundy masks for them to wear. "Keep the hat on, Jack. It's wicked," the bizarre gent tells him. Frederick has never really thought about his chauffeur's cap in just that light before. As the two men enter the house, they're warmly greeted by Bertie, who offers his colleague a grand tour of the premises.

"They Sail Through the Air

with the greatest of ease, the braless young girls on the flying trapeze," boisterously sings the drunken costumed crowd. They wildly applaud Tiffin and Adelle's obscene antics on the bar swinging above them, just below the tall ballroom ceiling. During her intermission, a masked, stunning, nude, auburn-haired woman climbs down from an elevated, glass-floored, red-lit Amsterdam room situated in front of the long mirrored wall. Carrie Blade demonstrates what an exercise pole can do for an audience's libido. Pirot finagled to get her out of the Kit Kat Club for tonight's assignment that's paying her five thousand smackers in cash – enough to quit her summer job and focus on her new relationship with Chip.

During her gyrations she fantasizes that her performance is for him alone and consequently nearly literally brings down the house. Men start howling and throwing full wine glasses until the bouncers step in. The bruisers have trouble safely escorting Carrie on her way upstairs when an inebriated Ronnie Schwartz steps up and throws his arms around her to ask for a spin around the crowded floor. When he pulls off his mask for a kiss, he's stopped by another guest.

"Just a minute, my dear Ronnie. What crust. Very ungentlemanly to accost one of the performers," says an indignant Chipster to him. He comes between Carrie Blade and the would-be ballroom dancer. The masked Chipster's also been dazzled by the disguised cage dancer – particularly her familiar-looking asymmetrical bouncing bosoms.

Chivalry's not dead, thinks Carrie. I think my own Chip would do the same.

Coco has by now caught up with her future hubby. She grabs Ronnie's shirt collar and tugs him away from Karen just in time for him to miss a roundhouse punch from Pirot who won't stand for anybody molesting his talent. The shot almost lands on poor Ronnie but instead connects with the dazed elderly john Pirot saw earlier with Gisela. Down to the floor poor Langford Sr. drops, alarming the guests in the packed ballroom. The startled mob starts to stampede and fight among themselves to reach the nearest exit. No milquetoast himself, Skipper manages to stand to defend himself and mistakenly pokes a nearby bouncer in the eye, missing Pirot – the intended target. A panic-stricken Brucie spots his father in the melee and rushes to his side.

"Brucie, is that you? This won't do. What if the admissions committee to the Knight's Templar were to hear of these goings-on? You know how much entrance to the order means to me." They're both about to be pulverized by the enraged bouncer when guests fleeing the house trample all three. At this point, an alerted police enforcement enters the mêlée.

The foregoing's the best account of how the ensuing brawl started and nearly demolished the pond house ballroom and foyer, according to the East Hampton Village Police Blotter that night. After he's bailed out with the others in the early AM, Yamada Takahishi feels he has no choice but to pony up 500 thou on the spot to Pirot for the rights to a Devil-Takes-All Sony Entertainment TV special. And a three-picture deal.

In the confusion, no doubt Frederick's stature, uniform, and his chauffeur cap must have made the real cops think him a policeman. The misconception allows the dutiful servant to pull his master to the kitchen as the cops pile in. His polite nature also causes him to include a partially dressed performer. "Would you like a lift home, Miss?" and

"Please borrow my coat." In the din of the donnybrook, the confused contortionist knows these disguised gentlemen from somewhere. But where? Bertie shows them a path down the basement, then up the back steps through a Bilco steel door to the backyard. From there the three depart posthaste to the Bentley. They've left without her belongings, and now, in the quiet of the night, chilly, skimpily dressed, kitten-masked Karen Bladner realizes the men's identities.

Frederick at the helm floors it out the gate. "Where to Ma'am?"

"Home, Frederick," she says to the surprised driver and takes off her mask. Frederick has the decency to raise the window separator, but not enough it seems to turn off the intercom. "Your home, I hope," she says to the amazed Chipster as she takes off Frederick's coat and climbs onto the lad's lap. And The Chipster drives home as well.

"You've Won Our Baseball Concession Lottery,

Mr. Blotkin," a woman with a dignified English-Indian accent, excitedly informs Sam Tuesday afternoon when he drowsily picks up the phone. He's fallen asleep once more in front of *General Hospital* and can't be sure if he heard the announcement on the phone or the TV. Since his retirement, he's seen every rerun of the serial, broadcast since 1963.

"What's that?" the bare-chested, unshaven man dispiritedly asks the caller.

"Goldman Sachs has conducted a lottery drawn from Long Island telephone books to determine the winner of a lifetime, non-transferable food concession stand at Yankee Stadium compliments of the Aramark Corporation. You're the winner! All you have to do is. . . ."

"Very funny," Sam interrupts her. "Who put you up to this? Morty Mavis, that son-of-a-bitch? Tell him to go screw himself." He's depressed enough without that prankster making fun of his lifelong fantasy. Sam hangs up with a crashing bang that sends the wireless device flying under the plastic-covered living room couch – the wife Margaret takes off the polyethylene only for company.

An impatient car horn honks outside.

The phone rings again. "I'll beat his brains out with my cane," Sam cries out to no one in particular.

The wife's still sound asleep in the bedroom. His anger supplies the adrenaline required for the lame man to crawl on his knees to fetch the unrelenting noisemaker. Now rising and with his oak walking stick in his left hand to steady him, he stands to deliver a stern warning into the receiver. "If you call again, on my mother's grave I swear I'll torch Mavis's house, Goddamn it."

Maniacal knocking at the front door. "Sam! For crissakes, I've been waiting for you to come outside for ten minutes," Morty shouts from the front porch. "Did you forget we're having lunch?" He loudly raps again.

"Aren't you funny, you bastard?" Sam roars back.

"Hurry the hell up. I'm famished," Morty yells.

That's when Sam's boxer shorts fall down – the elastic has finally given out.

"You made my underpants fall down. Are you satisfied?" he demands of the telephone caller.

"What? Please, Mr. Blotkin. This call is real. Let me give you my number and you can call me back to confirm," the alarmed woman says.

Meanwhile, Morty pummels away at the portico, "What're you doing in there? Putting on makeup? Open the damn door, putzface!"

"Keep your pants on," the naked man screams to Morty, although he hasn't done the same.

Sam calls Bhadra Raj back. "You really <u>are</u> from Goldman Sachs. Say again what you told me," says Sam.

She repeats her message. "Just come to my office at 85 Broadway to sign the papers, and please, please come right away," she almost begs.

Still more pounding at the door. "Hey in there! I said I'm dying from hunger. Let's go, you lame, dumb Nazi!" bellows the convulsed consultant.

Sam finally opens the door.

Morty looks at the smiling nude man. "Happy now? I've lost my appetite."

"Hot Dogs Hot Dogs,

get em' while they're hot!" the cheerful vendor shouts at Yankee Stadium. He stands with the traditional, insulated metal box slung around his neck in front of the dozen Sloane & Sobel Attorneys-At-Law box seats along the first base line. Though the firm has gone through numerous name changes since the park opened to a triple-run homer by the Babe himself in 1923, it's always kept its catbird seats on one of the best views in sports anywhere. Glen Sobel managed to convince his law partners to let him have all the LLC's tickets for this one game and takes pride in treating the men's club to an evening on him. Jack's here, too – his surgeon let him out of his recovery hospital bed to let him attend. Only Barry's missing. He left the country for an indefinitely long sabbatical a few weeks before.

It's a tie score with the Cleveland Indians in a mid-July double header. Two strikes at the bottom of the ninth inning, and the bases are loaded. A hit's a run and could bring an end to a sensational game. But all eyes in this section focus on the beaming foot-long salesman whose health has improved enough to walk without his cane.

"I'll have two more dogs and a Brooklyn Lager. And make it snappy, young man," Morty kids the pitchman – Sam Blotkin.

The men all look at Danny. "Now's the time," Rob tells Morty.

Three Weeks Earlier,

at the conclusion of the temple meeting, Sam gleefully unfolds his story. As he spins his wondrous tale, the other men notice that Dan, their interim leader, not only congratulates Sam but seems completely blown over by the news. After the congrats, Dan rushes first to his sweetheart Laura, waiting for him outside.

But the other men stay behind.

"You're not in any of the Long Island telephone books. Your number's unlisted, Sam," David points out.

"You're right. I didn't think about that," the recipient of good tidings replies.

"We're all thrilled for you, but don't you think Dan went a little overboard?" Morty asks.

"Like it was an act or something," Rob joins in.

Now, these mostly-retired guys still consider themselves businessmen and religiously read *The New York Times* and *The Wall Street Journal* as avidly as kids watch rock music channels.

"Didn't Aramark recently sign a merger with the G.F. Davison Vending Machine Corporation?" Glen, the still active corporate attorney, remarks.

"Yeah. Davison up and died not long ago and left the whole shebang to his gorgeous daughter, Charlotte, a divorce attorney with a society-page reputation for turning men into dead cockroaches." says Rob.

"Didn't we hear a story about a gal like that?" Harry adds.

The clues could lead to only one man. Before they leave, they all agree that when the time is right, Morty will baldly put the question to Dan in the straight-talking man's own inimitable way.

Back at the Baseball Game,

Morty plows ahead as planned. "OK, Danny Boy. So tell us, oh wise seer, why did this Davison dame who was fucking your brains out arrange for Sam to get this concession?"

Dan sees there's no point in pretending he doesn't know. "Well. . . . "

"Yeah, yeah, go on," Morty urges. The men all eagerly lean forward to hear the gossip.

"I told Laura Bernstein to tell her best friend Charlotte Davison. . . ."

"Yeah?"

". . . that it might help to arrange the concession as a sign of atonement and peace offering to Charlie's real lover. You know, to make up for the fight she had with him."

"Who the hell is he?" Morty asks for all of the guys.

"Barry Blackmun."

"Barry?!!" they all screech at once, knocking Sam's steaming dogs and mustard all over Morty's lap.

"Put Him in a Straitjacket,"

Dr. Heine says to two burly CA's who take hold of Dan as he climbs out of Laura's Chevrolet. The couple's just arrived from the latest temple meeting a week later. Not enough caution tonight. "Zis iss enough of your nonsenz, Daniel. I told you not to leef here. You're going straight to Bellevue zis time. And you, Laura. Your fazher vill findt out you helped him geht zhere." Although the CAs have a firm grasp on him, Danny's in the best shape of his life. He shakes the men loose and scrambles back into the car.

"Head for the hospital, Laura."

"The police vill be waiting for you zhere, sonny boy," Heine shouts to Dan as Laura pulls away.

After an hour of driving in nervous stony silence, Laura fills the vacuum, "At least knowing you has gotten me published. *The New Yorker*'s bought my short story about a trust-funded, directionless cokehead from Long Island. They think it's fiction," she informs him with an ironic smile.

"Congratulations, lover! I knew my self-abuse would do somebody good. Does he win the girl in the end?"

"No. He's too far gone. A complete loser. It's called *A Snowball's Chance In Hell.*"

"You're going to have to change the title when you find out why we're seeing your father."

"Why's that?"

"I'm going to ask his permission to marry you."

"In a pig's eye. I wouldn't marry you in a million years. You're a selfish, suicidal, ne'er-do-well addict without any possibility of a job."

"Flatterer," he says and kisses her neck.

"You might be some rich kid, but you're impossible. And take your hand off my breast. We could crash."

"You love me."

"Your chances are zilch that my father will say yes to you."

"And if he does?"

"You mean if you can make the Earth spin backwards like in *Superman II*?"

"It was in *Superman*, not *Superman II*. 1978."

"OK, Mr. Know-It-All, then I'll say yes – I'll marry you. Fat chance you have."

"You can move your things to my place later tonight. You haven't seen it yet."

"What a big head you've got."

"Yes, I do. And you'll see that tonight, too."

When the two arrive at Columbia-Presbyterian, they discover Heine meant what he said. He called the police. An officer stands in front of Jacob's hospital room. Dan shakes his hand.

"Ben, thank God you're here. Don't let any policemen into this room," Dan says.

"I am a policeman, Mr. Daniel," Officer Benjamin Franklin tells him. "You know we have better things to do than to chase your behind all over this island."

"Just give me five minutes, Ben. And then I'll go peacefully." Officer Franklin considers the offer and greenlights the two inside.

Jacob's propped up somewhat in the mechanized bed and looks reasonably comfortable despite the oxygen being pumped into his nostrils from two tiny tubes. "How're the meetings going, Daniel?" First things first with Dr. Bernstein.

"Great . . . Dr. Bernstein, I want to ask you for your daughter's hand."

"Don't say yes. Tell him how selfish and irresponsible he is, daddy."

"You've done a marvelous job with the men's group, Dan. I'm very proud of you," the doctor says slowly, trying to conserve his energy. "They've all been to visit me. David can't say enough about how you helped his wife, and you found a girlfriend for Morty. Glen didn't like your ambush at the coffee shop, but he's finally seeing his daughter. And Sam? What can I say? Just brilliant. No, Laura. Dan's not selfish or irresponsible. Quite the contrary."

"He's a druggie."

"Except for the first night at LFOD, he's been clean. Not a trace of any substance in his blood or urine in his lab reports."

"He's an idler. No job and no prospects, even if he does have a trust fund."

"I've got something to say about that," Dan interjects.

"Have you sent in your acceptance for readmission to Cornell Medical School? I heard from a longtime friend of mine who's the head of the admissions committee there. He noticed you're from my neck of the woods and asked if I knew you."

The policeman pops his head into the room, "Time's up, Mr. Topler. We need to go now."

"That won't be necessary, officer," Jacob says and asks Laura to hand him a blue form and a pen from the drawer next to his bed. "Dan's no longer under the court's jurisdiction." He signs the physician release and hands it to Dan. "I've been waiting for this day. Congratulations."

"Jesus. Can't I ever get a step ahead of you, Jack?" Dan asks.

Jack smiles – Dan has never called him *Jack* before. "You will when it's necessary, my boy. As Rabbi Meier said, 'My life was blessed, because I never needed anything until I had it,'" he tells him.

"Actually, it was Rabbi Michal, a Chasid in the 18th century," Dan says. The father and daughter look at each other in surprise. "Sometimes during coffee breaks at the meetings I read the Meditations in the temple library prayer book."

"Well, then, Laura. Any other objections to marrying this nice young man?"

Jacob asks.

"No, father, I don't. I never needed Dan until now that I have him."

"Please Give a Final Feces Specimen,

Daniel Topler," announces Nurse Linda over the LFOD loud-speakers. "Daniel Topler, report to the nurse and give a final specimen for our records."

"These people need to see the movie *Network,* because I'm mad as hell and I'm not gonna take it anymore!" Dan bellows for all to hear. Danny's cleared out his belongings from his cabaña and shoved them helter-skelter into a duffel bag. Now, to the onlookers' horror, he reaches into it pulls out a gun. Armed and dangerous, he starts to march into the speaker booth to scare the crap out of his tormentor.

Lars stops him. "Look, Danny. Don't do anything fool-ish. You're getting out of here. Marrying a fabulous woman, I understand," the real-life shrink prudently advises. "Don't do anything to jeopardize your freedom." The white-coated man gently requests, "Just give me the gun." Dan stares at the sane-sounding man for a moment, then hands it over. "And if I'm not at the wedding, don't forget to give that big-boobed blonde a kiss from me," he screams at the top of his lungs as he sallies headlong into the booth himself.

Two gunshots resound, echoing throughout the LFOD compound. Lars blows the smoke from the barrel of the 45-caliber revolver as Nurse Linda runs out screaming for help. The amplifying system smolders. The rounds of ammo have left gaping holes in the now dead loudspeaker system. Too bad, because minutes later Harriet Topler finally gets around to calling her son to see how he's doing, and the receptionist can't page him before he leaves LFOD for good. His failure to return her call confirms his egocentricity, in his mother's opinion.

As for Dan's father, Albert Topler couldn't have been happier when Dr. Bernstein calls him to say that his son's cured. But dad's not so sure about the recovery when he later gets the LFOD twenty-five-thousand-dollar-loudspeaker damages bill – twenty thou of it for Nurse Linda's psychological stress and not reporting the gun to the cops.

What a Beauty,

Barry Blackmun marvels.

Even from the distance across this wide expanse of the temple's east façade he can spot his favorite telescope – a 16-inch Meade with all the latest gizmos. On this blindingly sunny day in July, the device is pointed at Athens below, from where the Parthenon still dominates the ancient city. Barry wanders aimlessly here on his beloved architectural site. He returned here only yesterday after a decade's absence to do research on Alcaeus of Mytilene, a 6th-century BCE lyric poet; take up on an invitation from a fellow astronomer to visit The Institute of Astronomy and Astrophysics research center; and brush up on contemporary Greek jargon.

Anything to forget her.

He didn't sign the university contract renewal. Instead, when he left Zoë behind in his loft to pack up her things, the long-tenured professor went directly to his office to type a request for an indefinite leave of absence. Not a man to lightly make a commitment, the Parthenon has been relegated to second-favorite place on his architectural triumph list. The New York Life Insurance Building retains its primary position because it reminds him of that special day in Madison Square Park.

Her back to Barry, a woman in a wide-brimmed Panama hat aims the telescope up at an overhead view of the temple. He taps the observer on the shoulder. "Don't miss a close-up of the friezes, Miss."

"They're ninety-two of them," she says. "My favorites are the metopes on the west end. If you don't know, metopes are the rectangular architectural elements between two triglyphs."

"I know."

"The west end has the Amazonomachy, the combat between the Amazons and the Athenians. That's why it's my favorite. It reminds me of you," and she turns to face Barry.

"Zoë. I. . . . "

"Please don't interrupt me this time. I'm not finished." Pointing at the temple as if to give instructions to a tour group, "The base of the Parthenon is 69.5 meters by 30.9 point meters."

"I'd forgotten."

"It was erected with marble carved from Mount Pentelicus starting in 447 of the Common Era and mostly completed by 432 – more than twenty-four centuries ago."

"It was so good of you to help Sam. I heard."

"The internal colonnades were constructed in two tiers, which were needed to support the roof."

"Forgive me, my love."

"Outside, the Doric columns are 10.4 meters high and 1.9 meters in diameter."

"I'm sorry. I was a fool to leave you."

"Yes . . . you were. Did you know that my father married my mother right where we're standing?"

"I was here, then. Ganymede looked proud and handsome. He married the most beautiful woman I had ever seen . . . until I met their daughter. I was the best man."

"You still are the best man. Who will be yours for our wedding? Laura will be my maid of honor. At this temple. Right where we're standing."

Bluer Waters

flow this time beneath the men.

"Let the fuck go of me," Dan says.

"Can't do that, sonny boy," says Officer Franklin as he gives Danny a big kiss on the cheek before unbinding his thick arms from around Dan's morning coat.

On this late July, early Sunday morning, Daniel gazes up at a bright sky dotted with just a few wisps of cirrus clouds. He peers down to overlook the sparse West End Avenue traffic and then into the decidedly uninviting muddy Hudson River. "Coming here again wouldn't be the same without you, Ben." Dan smiles at the man in blue and shakes his hand.

The entire temple men's group, including Barry back from Greece with Charlotte, surround Daniel Topler on the George Washington Bridge. Jacob doesn't look well so soon after his operation, but nothing could stop him from coming to walk his daughter down the dividing barrier on the upper-level of the highway to her marriage vows.

"New beginnings for you, Danny," says David, as all but Dan raise plastic goblets of Champagne in a toast.

"I don't know, guys. Maybe this isn't romantic enough for my angel."

"Hey! It was Laura's cuckoo idea to marry here, for God's sake," Morty says.

"You're starting over, Daniel. It's appropriate. Not everyone gets this chance," Dr. Bernstein tells his former patient.

"We could have had a more traditional wedding for my beautiful bride."

"Oh, so the fast-and-loose big city playboy has gone senti-
mental on us!" laughs Rob.

"Think of this as your own Bifröst, Dan," Barry says. "The
rainbow bridge in Norse mythology leading from the realm of
mortals to the realm of the gods."

"Daniel, quit the lollygagging. Even a hundred-thou contribution to the mayor's campaign fund won't shut down traffic
for more than thirty minutes," Al Topler yells to his son.

The groom's mother stands patiently next to her husband
in the bridge's eastbound traffic lane. There's no time to set
up chairs. Notwithstanding slamming Ronnie, her soon-to-
be son-in-law, onto a marble foyer floor, the still Mrs. Albert
Topler remains a lady of dignity. Despite the unconventional
surroundings, she bravely holds her head high, talking with
her best friend, Dolores Schwartz. Harriet's sense of noblesse
oblige has forced her to agree to Elaine Bushkin's invitation to
the wedding. Anyway, the tart seems safely engaged to another
guest – one Morton Mavis. *Satan will personally serve my*
chicken *soup with kreplach to sinners in hell before I attend*
that *ceremony*, she swears to herself. Turning her thoughts to
the blessed event at hand, "Why," she asks Dolores, "do these
two Jewish children have to be married by a justice of the
peace?"

Dolores nods sympathetically, "Only God knows," she
says, agreeing with the sentiment.

"I left a hand-written message at the LFOD reception desk
for Helen Clausen, their receptionist who's standing behind
you next to Daniel, to please find one for me."

"I'm glad they saved you the trouble, Harriet. You have so
many other things on your mind. They owe your family a few
favors after all, don't they? With the fees you've paid, you and
Albert could have started your own clinic."

The wedding couple holds hands. Dan gives his sister and
bridesmaid, Coco, a kiss. "Thanks for untying me from the
family crypt," he jests. "You're next in line for the gallows,

Ronnie," he says with a laugh to the best man. Charlotte, maid of honor, flanks her best friend.

"Make this quick, your honor," Albert whispers to the full-bearded justice of the peace dressed in a splendid court's robe. "We've only got ten minutes before they open to traffic again."

"Do you, Daniel Topler, before this group of your friends and relatives swear to take this beautiful, sexy woman to have and to hold in sickness and in health?"

Danny looks into Laura's eyes. "I do," says he, feeling uncomfortable for some reason. *Sexy?*

"And do you, Laura Bernstein, before this august assemblage swear to obey this unemployed man and to have and to hold him in sickness and in health?"

Laura's peeved. Dan obviously forgot. She explicitly told him to exclude the obsolescent "obey" from the ceremony. And to remind the justice, in case he's brain-dead, it's "husband and wife" nowadays. But after two beats she decides what the hell and says, "I do." *Did he say unemployed?*

"Then under the laws of the State of New York and by the powers of great Jehovah above, I declare you man and wife."

Man and wife, did that bastard say? thinks Laura.

It's only now, when the justice of the peace pushes Dan aside, pulls off his beard, grabs Laura, and gives her a wet kiss on the chops, that Dan looks down and sees the man's feet underneath the robe. Bunnies smile up at him.

And now Lars feels a terror in his heart he's never known before. But it's not Zoë who's scaring the bejesus out of him. At a rapid clip, eyes narrowed, and with brows tightly knitted, Helen Clausen is headed his way.